Russell Helms

Fade

Fade

One

Michael had wanted to ask Anna out, had somehow known in his bones that it was necessary, but he had lost his opportunity. Talking to her mother after it happened, he could only think *What if? What if?*

Anna's mother, Mandy, was hosting an informal faculty meeting. It was the first time Michael had seen her since the news, and he was nervous, determined to share his sympathy. She and her husband Tom lived in a convoluted part of town, curvy roads, alleys, and it was hard to find the house. He used his cell phone to navigate, as usual.

He walked in clutching a bottle of Italian red, and Mandy was at the table arranging little rounds of spinach quiche, a bowl of hummus, and bacon-wrapped figs. She was short with faded blond hair swept back. He saw her and gravitated toward her. She looked peaceful, dressed in soft jeans and a light blue sweater. He found himself at the table, the words just there.

"I'm so sorry, Mandy."

Mandy winced.

"I just wanted to say that I'm so sorry. She was a great person."

Mandy brightened and moved closer. "Thank you. It's been so . . . hard. Thank you for saying so."

Michael felt breathless and drained, his throat dry. He nodded and turned to the group, six gathered in the living room around a high coffee table. There was wine, wine glasses, and a plate of crackers with a soft cheese. A visiting writer from Corsica sat like a bird on the couch, her hair brushed out like a broom. She had visited Michael's creative writing class earlier that day, and he was grateful.

Mandy's husband, Tom, a writer who translated Corsican works, eyed the bottle Michael had brought. "From Montepulciano. Good choice." He raised his eyebrows. "We love our wine."

A graduated student of the program. The visiting writer. Tom. Two neighbors. A local novelist. And then Michael. Mandy joined them, sitting behind Tom, her hand on his shoulder. Michael felt small, thinking. He had wanted to ask Anna out for coffee, but there had been the age difference. The conversation drifted, soughed, stopped, resumed. The visiting writer spoke good English. The annual writing workshop was coming up soon, and Michael was in charge of the poster and flyers.

He left the social that evening, having had three glasses of wine. Truly, he had only met Anna on two occasions, in that same house. The first had been just a glimpse. The second, he had brought a crockpot of spinach-artichoke dip. There had been some trouble finding a plug. Having rearranged an extension cord, moving with grace, Anna had plugged it in and disappeared. That was it, but he had been impressed with her attention.

The next day, a Thursday, he thought about Anna. He imagined she was twenty-eight, and she had been. There had been something troubled about her, a creasing in the forehead, a deep-seated worry, a battle being fought. She was slender, her long brown hair shimmery and bouncy, girly it seemed, with a smile that came and went. He thought she had sighed over the crockpot, had taken a deep breath, as if to make sure her lungs still worked. *What if?*

Four months had passed since he had last seen Anna, summer leading into fall, from heat to less heat and leaves falling, crumbling on the streets, clogging the gutters. The news had come in a group email. A tragedy. A great sadness. He had been looking forward to running into her perhaps at the next social. He had imagined them talking, her opening up, them standing on the front porch in the twilight, perhaps smoking. He would learn more about her, possibly a battle with drugs, probably a history of sadness, clinical depression, an explanation, a big reveal, and he would return the favor, highlighting his own personal darkness, the struggles, the years lost to sleep and thoughts of death. *What if?*

Michael had to do something. He had to find out, had to show Anna that he cared even though she was gone. He thought himself foolish and prying but determined. He first approached Anna's dad, Tom. Surely he would understand, but Tom was astonished, wary, and jealous of his wife's fragile state. But perhaps being a writer opened him to the idea, and he gave him Mandy's email. What would Mandy say?

Michael worried over the email and deleted it., paused, and let it fall to another day. A week passed, and he couldn't sleep, the undone invading his dreams. Anna was no longer living. Or was she? He had to find out. At midnight, sitting on his small patio, he wrote the email again. He read it over and over. He changed "misery" to "sorrow." He made it clear that he was only trying to be helpful, to give to Anna, to honor her life. What did Mandy think? And he added his phone number. He stared at the email.

It took a full twenty-four hours. It was midnight and he stared at the reply, hesitant to open it. What if she was angry? He clicked on the email, and it was quite long. She said that at first she had been shocked, but that she had thought about it and what harm could it do? When did he want to start? And she ended by saying that he must be careful and slow, that Anna was special, is special, and not to be trifled with. He sighed in relief, immediately thinking about how to prepare, and replied that Friday would work, that he would start with lunch, just casual, at the coffee shop where they served soup and sandwiches. He had two days to prepare, and his heart raced with the possibilities.

The next day he got a haircut and shaved. He figured a day's stubble would work well, give him a more human appearance, less formal. He examined his pitiful collection of shirts and pants and decided that jeans would be best, but he would need a new shirt. It was early November and chilly. He drove the ten miles to Kohl's and found it right away, a dark green, long-sleeve pullover with three buttons. Perfect.

He barely slept that night, working out what he would say, his mannerisms, what he might indicate to the wait staff. That morning he drank too much coffee and felt jittery as he drove to the house. He had a single yellow daisy. And then he was at the door and knocking, as if at the gates of heaven asking for a glass of water.

Mandy answered, a worried look on her face. "Come in."

He entered the warm foyer that opened left into the living room. "Is she ready?"

Mandy stumbled on the edge of a rug. "I don't know. I think so. Tell me what to do."

"Nothing. I'll just wait here until she's ready. There she is." He held the daisy like a divining rod, seeking a well deep beneath the house.

Mandy looked around, confused. "She's here? Oh my God."

He held out the daisy and placed it on the coffee table. "Ready?" He stood back to let Anna pass to the open door. "I'll take good care of her. I promise," and he was on the porch. He looked back, and Mandy was there, wringing her hands.

"Be careful," she said.

"We will," he said.

He opened the passenger door for Anna and closed it.

"What kind of music do you like?" He changed the station to easy listening, soft rock. Neil Young.

He drove, glancing at her, noticing she hadn't buckled up. He reached and buckled her in. Nearing the coffee shop, he scanned for a space and drove around the block, before having to park on the bridge. "We'll have to walk a bit," he said.

He opened her door, closed it, and then with her at his side walked at a slow pace, soon reaching the busy coffee shop. He held the door for her, met with delicious smells of coffee and soup. The line was long, and he apologized, but she didn't mind. As they waited, he made small talk, the weather, his classes. He asked about her life, what she liked most, and she said that she liked cats, that she liked a nice glass of wine.

At the register, he ordered. "We'll have the lunch special, two cups of tomato bisque, one turkey on rye, and," he glanced at Anna, "one tuna salad on white. And two cups of the dark roast." The cashier looked unsure. Michael paid and took the metal number to place on the table, along with the coffees.

"Would you like to sit inside or outside?" He glanced around the bustling room and spotted a table, empty with one chair. "How about there?" He maneuvered between the tight tables. "Excuse me. Do you mind if we borrow a chair?" The woman dressed in purple shook her head, and he took it. He waited for Anna to sit, placed the number and coffees on the table, and sat.

"How about the fires?" All around the city there were forest fires, smoke hanging in the air. The fall had been so dry. At least one of the fires had been arson. "Yeah, right?" He glanced around and no one seemed to be watching. "I went jogging yesterday, wondered if I should be doing that with the smoke, but I have to get my run in at least twice a week."

Anna was quiet.

"I like your sweater. Matches the daisy I brought." He noticed crumbs on the table and brushed them away.

She nodded, looking at her sweater as if it had just appeared. She wore a delicate gold necklace and rings on three fingers, one on her thumb. He could see the piercings in her ears and the tattoo of a small star on her left hand.

Behind him, two young men sat eating croissants and drinking tea. One was espousing the joy of the full love of God in a relationship. The other seemed to be listening, as if receiving a sermon, perhaps from his mentor. "God is just so awesome. He wants the best for us."

Michael nudged Anna's knee with his own. "Agape love."

Anna nodded. She kept her hands in her lap, gazing through the window and then glancing at him.

The waiter arrived. "Two specials?" He placed one in front of him. "Still waiting?"

"No. We're here. Just put it here," and he pointed.

"Sure," said the waiter. He had poufy, curly hair.

"The soup is to die for," he said, watching her reach for her spoon.

"It looks yummy," she said. She couldn't lift the spoon.

"Yeah, it's not cold yet, but cooling off. It just feels right. Soup and a sandwich. Mind if I dip?"

"No, not at all." She touched the corner of her mouth. She wore no makeup,.

He dipped the corner of his turkey on rye in the soup and took a soggy bite followed by more soup. He watched her. His cell phone vibrated in his pocket, and he took it out, laid it on the table, and it was his youngest daughter. He worried and answered.

"Excuse me, it's my daughter. Hello? Now? How long have you been nauseated? You can't make it the rest of the day? Okay, okay, I'll come. What class are you in? Listen for them to call you over the loudspeakers if it's lunch when I get there. Okay, but give me about fifteen minutes. I need to finish lunch, and I, uh, have a friend with me." He smiled at Anna. "You'll like her . . . Okay, I'll hurry. Bye."

"Oh brother. I'm sorry. It's my daughter, and she's on a new medication, for depression and anxiety. I'll have to take you with me, if that's okay."

She smiled. "Sure. I used to call my mom from school."

He took big bites of his sandwich. "I guess I have the more flexible schedule so I'm usually the one. I mean Suzanne and I are divorced, but we still act like we're together sometimes. Do you want to take your sandwich with you?"

"No. I'm not really hungry."

"Sure?"

"Yes."

He finished the sandwich and two more spoons of soup. "Ready?"

A woman across the way was watching, whispering to her friend. He waved as if he knew her and smiled. Anna stood, and he opened the door then followed her outside into the haze. The unseen sun above, churning and churning, unable to penetrate the smoke with its rays.

In the car, she was silent, looking out the window. "This a new car?"

"Yeah, my Honda was totaled a few weeks ago. Got hit by a student, a football player, engineering major. I like this one better, though. Still has that new-car smell." He turned and then crossed the bridge spanning the river. The school was at the top of a very long hill and it was lunchtime traffic.

"Are you sure you want your daughter to meet me? Will she understand?"

"Of course. She may think we're crazy, but that's okay." He reached and patted her knee.

She drew away but smiled.

Soon they were at the school and parked.

"I'll wait here," she said.

"No, come on. You get to experience the rush of lunch hour and all the kids." He jogged around to open her door and helped her out. "God, this smoke is something."

They walked past students sitting on the grass, others on the steps eating their lunches. He pushed the buzzer on the main door, but it opened, kids coming outside. The two slipped into the vast open room filled with round tables, teeming with life. Inside the front office he asked for his daughter and signed her out. There was only one chair, and he insisted that Anna take it. The office was quiet, and he could see the principal back in her private office, talking on the phone, eating what looked to be a honey bun.

It took a few minutes, but Yancy knocked on the glass, motioning him to come out. He held the door for Anna.

"Gosh, what took you so long?" said Yancy.

"I was having lunch with my friend Anna." He winked at Anna and passed through the main door.

"Who the heck is Anna? Does mom know?"

"We're divorced in case you forgot. Plus, this is special. You should at least say hello." He paused at the bottom of the stairs.

"Say what? I need to go home and lie down."

Anna looked embarrassed.

"Anna, this is Yancy."

"Nice to meet you," said Anna. She held her stretched sweater sleeves in her hands.

"Yeah, nice to meet you. Anna? Get real, Dad." She bounded ahead to the car, hefting her bulging backpack.

"She's a pistol, that one," he said.

He unlocked the car. "Let Anna sit up front, okay? She's our guest."

"Pop the trunk, Pops." She dumped her backpack into the trunk. "What are you doing?"

"Take the back seat. Trust me, okay?"

Yancy scowled and looked around. "Have you lost your mind?"

He laughed. "Maybe I have. In the back seat for you if you want to go home."

Yancy crawled into the back still scowling. He opened the front door for Anna.

Yancy watched him buckle the seat belt. "What?"

"She's just not there yet," and he drove.

Yancy pulled out her iPhone and played show tunes, or what sounded like show tunes. Panic! at the Disco. She sang along.

"Gosh, you don't seem sick," he said. He glanced at Anna.

"Well I am. This new medicine."

"She's on new medicine," he said. "Nauseates her. I should know. I take the same drug, but quadruple the dose."

Anna nodded. She was experienced with antidepressants. "It can be hard. I quit taking mine because of the side effects." She gazed out the window.

"Yeah, so you know. Her mom finds it a little baffling."

"Dad, quit talking to yourself. You're creeping me out."

"Hey, have some respect. She's our special guest." He turned down the alley, gravel crunching, taking it slow through the ruts. "I wonder how old Craig is doing on the deck."

"God, he's been here for weeks. Mom wants him to finish, but he keeps finding other things to do. I think he has the hots for her."

"He's just an old friend with some time to kill. Seems to be doing a good job."

"Yeah, but I can't walk around the house naked, Dad. You ever think of that?"

"Okay, okay. I get it. And there he is." He pulled into the cramped driveway.

Craig was shirtless, wearing safety goggles with a pencil behind his ear. He was stodgy with a huge, toned belly and a shaved head. He waved at them, smiling.

"Okay, I'm just letting you out, okay? I have to get Anna back home. Her mom will be worried." He waved at Craig.

"Yeah, just leave me here with Craig." Yancy hopped out and waited for the trunk to open and then was gone.

"I'm not sure she likes me," said Anna.

"She's just a teenager. She'll come around. So, should we head back? Want to walk by the river?"

"It's been fun, but since it's the first time, maybe we should go back."

"Yeah, sounds good. I'm glad you were able to make it out today."

"Yeah, me too."

"I have to punch your address into my phone," and he did.

They rode mostly in silence, the heat on low, Steely Dan on the radio. He followed the computer voice to Anna's house and parked. "Your mom will be curious."

"That's a given," said Anna. "I bet she's peeking through the curtains." She laughed.

"Maybe," and he opened the door for her and walked her to the porch.

The door opened, and it was Mandy. "Is everything okay?"

"Hey," said Anna. She flipped back her long brown hair.

"Yeah, it went fine," said Michael. "We had lunch at Cosimos, the coffee shop. Had a little detour. My daughter called from school and had to take her home, but all is well."

Anna stood there like a little girl.

"Did you talk? What did she say?"

"Oh just small talk. She likes cats. I have two cats. Maybe she could come by and see them sometime." He looked at Anna.

"Sure, I'd like that," said Anna.

"I guess we need your mom's okay. Would that be okay, Mandy?"

"Anna?" Mandy looked small, like a leaf on the highway.

"She's here. She wants to go inside I think."

Mandy stumbled backward. "You're sure? Anna?" She began to cry.

"Mom, don't cry. It's okay. Everything's fine." She followed her inside.

Michael hugged Mandy. "It's a happy thing. But gosh, I'll go now. Let you two talk, okay? Can I call?"

Mandy mumbled through her tears. "Oh sure, but I just don't know. I just don't know. This is all so strange. What good can come of it?"

"All the good in the world. Bye, Anna. Bye, Mandy. I'll call. Feel free to call or email." He turned and left, wishing that he could have kissed her.

Two

He told his two cats about Anna. He'd adopted them soon after he'd moved out but before the divorce. Living alone had created a void, even though he still dropped and picked up his daughters from school. The cats had been kittens, just weeks old. They still play tumbled, shrieking at one another, bounding through the apartment, stalking moths on the wall.

Mandy had emailed him. "Can you come again, to see Anna? I think she would like to have dinner with you, maybe go for a walk. Let me know."

He was ecstatic to hear that and made plans. Their first dinner would need to be special, not necessarily romantic, but comfortable with good food and wine. He wasn't sure if Anna drank and asked Mandy. Mandy said that maybe she liked to drink too much and to be careful with her. He made the reservation for Tuesday night at The Market downtown.

This time he brought a yellow rose, thinking that yellow was Anna's favorite color. He'd forgotten to ask and just made the leap. At the door he knocked and Mandy was there, peering at him, examining his slacks and pullover.

"Come in." She took his hand in hers and squeezed it. "Have a seat. Can I get you a glass of wine?"

He sensed that Anna was not quite ready. "Sure." He sat in a soft highback chair and Tom entered with his own glass of wine. He sat in a similar chair next to him, wearing a baseball cap and flip-flops.

"So, you're here," said Tom. "To see Anna. You have a yellow rose."

"Yes, I hope so. We have a dinner date, at The Market. Mandy suggested it." He sat on his hands.

"Here you go," said Mandy. She handed him a glass of red.

"You'll like that. Cline. An old-vine Zinfandel. Very reasonable too," said Tom.

Michael swirled, sniffed, and sipped. "Nice."

"I'll check on Anna," said Mandy.

Tom looked at him. "See, she's buying into it. I really don't think this is a good idea. I mean, how can she grieve properly? It's only been four months. But, her mood has picked up."

Michael sighed. "Somehow, this is Anna's doing. She wants to do this, and I'm honored to be a part of it. I suppose you know that I found Anna attractive, but felt I was too old, that you guys would object."

Tom waved him off. "So, does Anna speak to you? Do you see her?"

"It seems that way. I want to see and hear her. What if we had actually dated? How would things be different? I've spent most of my life wondering about such things, but this time I had to see for myself."

"Wow," said Tom. "This is really heavy. I mean I loved Anna, even though she was my stepdaughter, but nothing compared to Mandy. She lost a part of her soul. They were best friends. Mandy went through detox with Anna, twice. She was clean as far as we knew. And then, *bam,* it happened." Tom leaned forward and frowned.

Mandy was back. "I guess she'll be out in a minute. You know, girl things." She looked small in her worn jeans and lavender sweater and paced into the dining room, arranging the salt and pepper shakers.

"Hello," and Michael stood.

Anna wore a cream sweater over an aqua top with latticed straps and a pleated skirt.

Tom looked around. "She's here?"

"Wow," said Mandy. "I can just see her, so . . . alive." She had to sit down before she fell.

"Yeah, you look fantastic," said Michael. He held out the yellow rose.

Anna blushed. "Thank you."

He finished his wine in a gulp and placed the rose on the coffee table. "We'll be off. Give us a couple of hours."

"Should I take my purse?"

Michael laughed. "She needs her purse, I think."

Tom sighed.

"It's on her dresser." Mandy hurried and returned with a small black purse, something you might wear to a concert.

"I'll carry it," he said. He took the purse. "Ready? Okay, off we go," and he opened the door.

"Have fun!" said Mandy, and she watched him open the car door for Anna. She watched them drive off.

Tom came up behind her. "You okay? I mean is this really okay?"

Mandy turned and gazed at him. "It has to be this way. Anna wants it to be this way. I'm so happy for her."

Tom hugged her and kissed her forehead. "For you then."

Anna watched the houses pass, smiling, wondering what the people inside were doing. "The Market is expensive. Are you sure? We could just get a burger."

"No expense shall be spared," he said. "You have the best smile."

Anna blushed. "They have really good desserts."

"I love the bread pudding. What about you?" He emerged from the tangled neighborhood and bore left, driving with one hand. The evening was cool and calm, the smoke from the fires on the tops of nearby mountains lifting as if they had been extinguished.

"Crème brûlée." She smiled.

"That too."

He passed the liquor store and pulled into the restaurant parking lot. Together they walked, but he didn't take her hand just yet, waiting for her to make the move. He carried her purse.

"We have a reservation," he said to the hostess. She had long curly hair and wore a pushup bra. The restaurant was half-full, a Tuesday night crowd of older couples and a few families.

"Last name?"

He pointed to the guest log.

"Okay, just follow me. Will she be joining you soon? I see you have her purse."

"No, she's here," he said. "I'm just holding it for her."

Anna glanced at him for reassurance.

The hostess said, "Hmm," and seated them, placing two menus of the day on the table. She explained that the special was swordfish grilled over binchotan coals and that the soup was artichoke-persimmon. "The waitress will be right with you for drinks."

He scooted his chair in a bit. "You look, uh, pensive. Everything okay?"

"I just worry about what people think. That's all. You can put my purse on the table. You don't have to hold it." She laughed.

"Right." He placed it on the other side of the table that was covered with a linen cloth.

"Hi, I'm Jackie, and I'll be your server tonight. Would you like to start with a drink, a cocktail perhaps? She lay a drink menu in front of him.

"Sure." He perused the drinks and then held the menu for Anna. She pointed to the lemon drop.

He cleared his throat. "I'll have a double Knob Creek on the rocks, and she'll have the lemon drop." He handed back the menu.

"Sounds good," said Jackie. "Your, um, date, will be joining you soon? Should I wait to bring her drink?"

He looked at Anna. "No, you can bring them both now."

"Okay, great," said Jackie. She wore brown corduroy pants with a white, men's button-up.

"We're giving them something to think about," he said.

"I hope they don't mind," said Anna.

"I'm sure they'll get used to it. So, how have you been, since Friday? Do you go to church?"

"Not since I was a girl. Mom and Tom never go. We just hang out. Mom makes brunch with grapefruit mimosas."

"Wow, that sounds nice. I love grapefruit. My parents dragged me to church for seventeen years, but that ended when I moved out. I've had my fill of religion."

"Maybe, though, I should go. Considering . . ."

Jackie was back with the drinks. She placed the bourbon and lemon drop on the table with two glasses of water. "Do you need some time to order?"

"We haven't looked at the menu. Yes, just a few minutes." He sipped his bourbon.

"It's always so hard to decide."

"The winter vegetables look good. I usually get the vegetable entrée."

Anna read the menu. "The Springer Mountain chicken looks good, and so does the porkchop. I've had that before, though."

"Appetizer? How about the cheese plate? Comes with homemade pimiento cheese. We could get a glass of wine with it."

"Hmm, I'll have to drink this first. But, sounds good." She reached for the glass and it lifted. "Jesus, I did it." She took a sip. "Yum."

Michael marveled. "Wow. Yeah, I should have just gotten a single. I'd hate to have you drive us home."

Anna laughed. "You're funny."

They talked and sipped. She wanted to know about his classes, what he taught, what he liked about teaching. He taught an introduction to creative writing, but his favorite classes were fiction workshops. He loved discussing stories with his students, searching for the images, the meaning, the bigger picture—character-driven stories with beautiful language.

"Ready to order?" said Jackie. She looked at the empty chair, the purse, the lemon drop where she had left it or had it moved?

"I think we want the cheese plate to start and then we'll order entrées after that. Taking it slow. And could we get two glasses of the Caymus 2000?" He reached and placed his hand over Anna's. "Mind if I order the wine for you?"

Anna looked at his hand on hers. "No, not at all. You couldn't do that, though, if my dad was here, order the wine I mean."

"Well, I'm no expert," he said.

"So, two glasses of the Caymus?" said Jackie.

"Yes, two," he said.

"Should I hold off a bit, let you finish your drink?"

"Sure, that would be perfect."

"You're so good," said Anna. "Thanks for taking care of me. I hate to say it, but you remind me of Tom."

He smiled. "He's a great guy, so thanks. Gotta love a writer."

"Yeah, he's got writing on the brain."

"So, did you go to college?"

Anna thought. "I lasted for about two years at the university here. Had a tuition discount because of Tom. But, I was a party girl. My grades were terrible."

"That happens. What did you study?" He sipped his bourbon, the ice clinking in the tumbler. An older woman from the next table was watching him.

"Pre-med, biology, if you can believe it. I thought I wanted to be a doctor, but that flew out the window with the dissection labs and chemistry. Plus, I hate the sight of blood."

"Yeah, blood is freaky. I used to think I wanted to be a nurse, but I'm just too curious about writing, although I still have this weird nagging feeling that I should be helping people. I suppose talking about great fiction is useful, but it can't cure cancer, except maybe in fiction. It is what it is." He nodded to the woman watching him and smiled. She looked away.

"My two older sisters graduated, one in English, the other in history. They both have pretty good jobs. I kind of got left behind, but that's my fault."

"You're fine. You're . . . beautiful, and smart. Your mom and Tom adore you." He finished his bourbon.

"Thanks. That's very nice, sweet."

Just then Jackie appeared with the cheese tray and the wine. There were four cheeses, pecans, apples, and homemade crackers on a wooden platter. She stood back. "So, just to be clear. For two, right?"

"Yes, for two. By the way, this is Anna." He nodded toward Anna. He took a sip of wine.

Jackie looked at him. "Anna?"

"Yes, Anna," he said.

"It's okay," said Anna.

"It's, uh, nice to meet the both of you. Would you like to order your entrée?

He consulted with Anna. "Sure, but no hurry. I'll have the winter vegetables. I love rutabagas, and she will have the Springer Mountain chicken."

Jackie nodded and took the menus. "Make sure you save room for dessert." She backed away and bumped into an older gentleman on his way to the restroom.

Michael stifled a laugh. "I think we've got her number. The wine is pretty good." He scooted the cheese plate closer to her.

Anna took the small knife and spread some chèvre on a piece of apple. "Looks great. Thank you."

"As they say, 'My Pleasure.'"

They ate in silence for a moment, sampling the cheeses, drinking red wine. More people were arriving than leaving. There was a main dining room and a bar. He and Anna were seated behind a low partition in front of the tinted windows. There were paintings and wood. Not overly fancy, but well appointed. You could wear jeans if you wanted or perhaps a flannel shirt now that the weather had cooled.

"This one is smoky like the air," he said. "Try it." He cut a slice and placed it on a cracker for her.

"Yeah, smoky." She nibbled and smiled. "I have to go to the restroom. Do you mind?"

"Not at all. I shall await your return."

"Silly." She left the table.

"Everything okay? The cheese?" said Jackie. She examined the full glass of wine sitting in front of the empty chair. The small plate with a cracker and cheese.

"Very nice," he said.

"And your friend, your date?" The other waiter wanted to know more.

"She's in the restroom."

"More wine for you?"

"We'll have a bottle with dinner. Probably a white, a chardonnay. I think it's called Dreaming Tree."

"Yes, Dreaming Tree. That's a great pair with your entrées. Okay, your plates should be out within twenty minutes." She hurried back to share the latest with the waiter Jess. She knew Michael, knew his ex–wife. Was very curious.

Anna had to wait and follow a woman with red hair into the restroom. A few minutes passed.

"Ah, you're back," he said, and stood halfway.

"Don't stand. That's so old fashioned."

"And so is courting," he said.

"So you're courting me. Is that it?" She smiled.

"Yes, I am. Is that okay?"

"Yeah, I like that. Courting. I'm having a good time."

"I'm having an excellent time. Anything you want to talk about?"

"Hmm, well I'm wondering about mom, how she's doing with all of this. She's been kind of nervous all week. She comes to my bedroom and talks to me. She sits on the bed."

"I think that's a good thing. What does she say?"

"She just wants to know that I'm still there. She even put my meds on the bedside table with a glass of water. But, I suppose I don't need them anymore."

"Treated for depression, right?"

"Yeah, that and anxiety. I took Prozac for a few years, but it stopped working and I moved to another drug, Cymbalta. I took an antipsychotic. They say my depression is atypical, whatever that means."

"I take Cymbalta, too, the generic form. Five bucks copay. I think atypical means that your depression is resistant to treatment. Pretty serious stuff."

"I mean I woke up every day thinking about death. It just wouldn't go away. I couldn't function, couldn't hold a job. My last job was working in a gift shop downtown. It was pretty easy, mostly tourists, but I couldn't get out of bed. Mom and Tom did their best. I stopped taking my meds and didn't tell them. Bad idea."

"I think I'm divorced because I quit my meds for a few years. I'm just a completely useless asshole without them. I'm surprised it lasted as long as it did."

"I can't imagine you being an asshole."

"Not unkind, just belligerent, paranoid, ready to pounce. I was desperate and went back on meds about a year ago. Racing thoughts, death, death, death."

"Yeah, racing thoughts, like rockets in your brain."

Jackie appeared, carrying their plates. "Here we go. Winter vegetables and the chicken." She placed the plates on the table and took the cheese plate. The waiter Jess was behind her with the wine in a granite cooler. She smiled.

"Looks great," said Michael.

Jackie uncorked the bottle, poured a taste, and handed it to him.

"I'll let Anna do the honors." He held the glass for her.

"I hate this part," said Anna. She sniffed the bouquet and sipped. "Mmm, nice, vanilla."

Jackie and Jess stood there, eyes wide, with their hands folded. "Uh . . . okay?" said Jess.

"Yes, perfect," said Michael.

"Great." Jackie wrapped a clean white cloth around the bottle and poured two glasses. Should I take this glass?" She pointed to the full glass of red.

"Just leave it for now," he said.

"Okay, well enjoy your dinner. I'll come back soon and let you see our desserts."

He nodded. "We've already discussed that, so we're in."

Jackie and Jess backed away, glancing at one another.

"Your chicken looks great. The cranberries," said Michael.

She cut a piece of chicken, a breast with the wing attached. "Mmm, pretty good."

He took his fork and prodded his roasted vegetables. Turnips, rutabagas, potatoes. "I hope I can eat all of this."

They ate and talked further about their common ailment, the black dog of depression. He confessed that he'd overdosed once, many years ago. She wanted to know more, putting her fork down. He had been thirty-three when he did it, fresh out of graduate school, which he'd stumbled through in a state of quiet rage and despair. Afterward, he'd quit his high-paying administrative job at an HMO and found himself at a mental hospital. He'd taken a bottle of Paxil at midnight, swallowing them one at a time with sweet tea.

"I'm sorry," she said. She let her knee touch his.

He recounted the night. He hadn't died but had lapsed into a kind of frenzy, pacing, hitting the walls, staring at himself in the bathroom mirror, his pupils blown, his mouth dry, his voice turned to a squeak. The next day, he somehow had managed to drive to the hospital and was checked in immediately.

Anna looked teary eyed. "I'm sorry," she said.

"That was the bottom, but I'm okay now. It took a while, years, for me to recover. You know, I've probably lost fifteen years of my professional life to depression. I should have a PhD, be a tenured professor, but at least I've made it to lecturer. It's something I can't explain to most people. That I've worked so hard to be where I am. I just feel like I'm so behind, that I have to catch up."

"I know that feeling," she said.

They ate, drinking the Chardonnay, and the talk turned to more cheerful things. She loved the holidays, and he confessed that he didn't.

"I'm worried how mom will be," she said. "This will be the first Christmas . . . without me."

"Yeah, but you're here. She knows you're here."

"I guess so. I'm just not so sure."

"You just have to believe."

"I'd like to."

"Mind if I take the last of the wine?" His hand fumbled, and he hit his glass.

"No. I'm fine. Are you okay?"

"Perfect." He poured.

Jackie had checked on them, taken their plates, and now brought the large tray display of desserts. They gazed at the sweets already knowing what they wanted.

"For me, the bread pudding, and for her, the crème brûlée."

"Excellent choices," said Jackie. "Coffee?"

"Anna, would you like something to drink? I think I'll have the coffee and some Frangelico."

Anna thought. "Coffee is nice, with cream. What would you suggest, to go with crème brûlée?"

"How about a sniff of Grand Marnier," he said.

"Okay."

"So, Jackie, we'll have coffee. No cream for me, but cream for her, a Frangelico, and a Grand Marnier." He tapped his fingers on the table, admiring Anna's shoulders.

"Very good," said Jackie. She looked tired but her voice was brisk.

"So, after tonight, what do we do next?" said Anna.

"I'll definitely want to see you again. You up for that? I can call."

"I mean will we just keep going out to eat? I mean, I like it. You're good company."

"Don't forget I'm courting you."

The desserts and drinks arrived within ten minutes, and Jackie bowed out, promising to bring coffee soon.

"Yeah, I guess I'm okay with that. Gosh, where to start?" She tapped the crust of her crème brûlée and took a small bite. "Wow, that's so good. And then a sip of this."

Michael sipped his Frangelico. "It's hard not to drink this in one gulp. Tastes like vanilla cream cake." The lady who had been watching him stood with her husband and left. She glanced back. "Get a life," he said. "Not, you, but that woman who just left. She was staring."

Anna laughed. "Can't blame her, right? What if the shoe was on the other foot?"

"I guess you're right. Damn, this bread pudding is to die for. I want to eat slow but can't." He polished off the Frangelico.

"So, how do you feel? You can drive, right?"

"I'm buzzed, but that's it. So much food, plus the coffee will help."

"How long have we been here?"

"Going on an hour and a half I think. But, it's good to take it slow. I enjoy talking with you."

"Same here. We have a lot in common. I only remember you from when you brought that crockpot with the dip in it."

"There were no plugs, but you found an extension cord. You were being a good hostess."

"Mom and Tom have great parties, but it seems they've slowed since . . . well you know. I want them to have people over. Especially for mom's sake. She stays in that house all day, wandering into my room, adjusting things. Did you know that she keeps my cell phone charged, that she answers it? It's usually a collection agency, with my credit cards and all, but sometimes it's someone who hasn't heard and she gets into a long conversation with them. She just wants to talk about it so badly, needs to talk about it, and that makes me super sad."

He thought. "That's a little bizarre, but I get it. Maybe she thinks you will call."

"I wondered about that." She swirled her Grand Marnier making legs inside the glass.

"Huh, well that means I can call your cell phone, and you can call me. Maybe at the end of the day, but I'd like to take you to a movie. How about Thursday night? There's still some Halloween movies playing. See something scary." He finished the bread pudding, and Jackie was there with the coffee and the check.

"No hurry. I hope you enjoyed your dinner."

"It was lovely," said Anna.

"Thank you, Jackie. It was lovely, as she says."

Jackie murmured.

"I think a movie would be grand. I haven't been to a movie in over a year. At home I watched Ingmar Bergman films with Tom."

"My favorite director of all time. And Max von Sydow. What a team. So, great, I'll see about the time and let you know. I'll have to check with Mandy, though, run it by her, right?"

"Yeah, that would be a good idea. You want the rest of my coffee? I'm so full."

"Sure," and he took the cup. He laid his credit card in the tray.

The drive to Anna's took about twenty minutes and he pulled up in front of the house. Anna was silent.

"Walk you to the door?" he said.

"Of course. Mom will want a full report." She laughed.

On the front porch they stood, the breeze, the stark white moon beginning to rise. Anna turned and hugged him. "Thank you."

"You're welcome." He blushed and rapped on the door.

Mandy was there in a flash. She opened the door with a look of surprise. "You're back. Come inside. Can you come inside?"

Anna put her hand on his shoulder, smiled, and went to her room.

Tom was at the dining room table typing. He waved.

"Sure, but I do have a lot of grading, so maybe not for long." He took a seat on the old-fashioned couch, the cushions deflated. "We had a great time."

"What did you do? Did you eat? Did . . . she eat?" She was sitting beside him, her hands in her lap.

"Yes, she had the Springer Mountain chicken. We split a bottle of Chardonnay. We just talked. She adores you and Tom."

"So she ate . . . and drank?"

"Of course she did. We were at a restaurant, right?"

"This is maybe too much. I so want to believe."

"It's your calling, to believe. She's a great person, a little shy, but a great person to talk with, hang out with. Would you mind if we went to a movie on Thursday?"

"A movie. Tom, he wants to take Anna to a movie."

Tom shifted his ballcap. "This sounds like a movie. I just want you to be happy is all." He turned back to his computer. He was typing an email to send to Michael.

"Okay, did you ask Anna?" said Mandy.

"Yeah, and she would like to go. Maybe the three of us should go out sometime?"

Mandy's eyes widened at the thought. "Okay, I would like to."

Anna appeared in the doorway to the hall. She waved goodnight. He waved back.

"You waved? Did she wave?"

"Yeah, she's saying good night."

Mandy turned and stared.

"I should be going. Most of my classes are online, but still lots of grading." He touched Mandy's knee and stood.

"Okay, but I might call you. Is that okay?"

"Sure. And we had a great time. Thank you for understanding. I know it's strange. I feel lucky that you're sharing her with me."

"You're a good man, Charlie Brown." She looked small sitting on the sofa.

"Okay then, good night. Night, Tom."

Tom waved, having sent the email.

Three

On the drive back to his apartment, Michael ran a red light and cursed. He wondered about the concept of courting, what his next move should be. Should he call her the next day? Would that seem too rushed? He wondered when her birthday was, what he could do that would be special. The phone rang inside his car. It was his oldest daughter Claire.

"Hello?"

"Hey, Dad."

"Hey, what's up?"

"Oh nothing. Just bored. Mom and Yancy are fighting, and I told them to shut up and now mom's mad at me."

"Oh Lord. You got homework?"

"Studying for a Spanish test. I really like my teacher."

"Yeah, you've said that. I'm glad." He noticed he was going too slow and sped up.

"What are you up to?" she said.

"I've been out to eat with a friend."

"Have you been drinking? You sound like you've been drinking."

"Ha. Well a little bit."

"A girl or a guy?"

"You're nosy."

"Oh my God, then it's a girl. I'm telling mom. Mom!"

"Hey, we're divorced. Calm down."

"Yeah, but this is your first date, right, since you moved out?" she said.

"Actually the second. We had coffee last week."

"OMG. Mom!"

"Hey, no yelling. That's one thing I don't miss. All of the yelling."

"Sorry . . . Hey, I just told mom, and she rolled her eyes. I think she's jealous. This is juicy. You're not gonna bring her over here are you? Although, I would like to meet her. She's not a college student is she?"

He laughed. "No, no. Younger than me, but not a college student."

"Did you kiss her?"

"No, not yet. That takes time."

"Such a gentleman."

"Always," he said.

"Okay, just called to check in. Gotta go now. Bye, Dad." Laughter.

"Okay, bye. Love you."

"Love you."

He was nearly home and turned onto his street, pulling into the apartment complex. The smokiness in the air had lifted in the coolness, but the fires were still burning. Even NPR had run a story that morning about the area fires, all on the tops of mountains. His cat Leonard met him at the door, looking up with his big yellow eyes. The other cat, Tweezer, the black one, was on the dining room table. He scratched their heads. "Kitty, kitty." He walked to the couch and Arty was there, turning on his back for a belly rub. "Hey, buddy. Take you outside in a second." Arty's tail beat the couch.

He sat in the recliner, feeling the alcohol, the food, and leaned back for just a moment to gather his bearings with his eyes closed. The outfit Anna had worn. Her arms. Her long brown hair. He had to clean the litter box. *Shit.* And he had to take his meds. He relaxed for a few minutes, reliving the dinner and went to his bedroom, fumbling in the drawer for his pills. In the kitchen, he popped a Heineken and downed the meds. He found a plastic bag from the grocery store and went to clean the litterbox. As usual, Leonard hopped in, as if he had to go at that precise moment.

"Leonard, you crazy cat." He scooped around him. Instead of covering up his mess, Leonard pawed the air and the wall as if that would help. "Leonard?" He added new litter to the box, noting that he'd need to drop by Walmart for more.

"Come on, Arty. Go outside?"

Arty tumbled off the couch and did a play bow and a single yip. His adoption papers had identified him as an "Eskimo mix."

They headed through the sliding glass door onto the small porch. A road ran just below a steep embankment twenty feet away. With Arty in the lead, he navigated down the slope, taking the last two steps in a run. Arty darted to the other side, looking for squirrels, dragging Michael with him, looking up into the trees with a hopeful grimace. Nothing said happy better than seeing a squirrel.

They eventually walked a slow circle, meeting no one, parking spaces filled, windows in apartments blazing. Back inside he unleashed Arty. "Good boy, Arty." He rubbed Arty's head and scratched his neck. "I had a date tonight, Arty, with a pretty girl. You'd like her, buddy. I bet you would." He searched for the open Heineken and

put on his shabby black Polartec, his smoking jacket.
"Outside, Arty?"

He grabbed an H. Upmann 1844 Reserve from his
small humidor, clipped it, and stepped back onto the patio
with its two plastic chairs, lime green. He tethered Arty on
a ten-foot cable and with his laptop settled in to grade a
few assignments before beginning his nightly writing ritual.
As usual he checked his email, hoping that no students
wanted feedback, at least not now. He checked his Gmail
and then his university account, and saw the email from
Tom. The title line was "Is this…"

*…a good idea? I mean, you are awakening in Mandy
some kind of delirious obsession. I'm not sure that she can
properly grieve if she thinks that Anna is going on dates
with you. You have to admit that it's crazy. I just don't
want her to get hurt is all. Best, Tom.*

He replied:

*Tom. I totally understand, but we have to think of
Anna as well. If you could have seen her tonight, looking
so alive and well. We really have a lot in common, and I'll
admit to you that I consider that I'm courting her, not
dating. I just don't want to rush things, plus there is the age
difference, which I'm worried that you care about. I think
that taking good care of Anna is also a way of taking care
of Mandy. If she tells me to back off, then I certainly will,
without any hesitation. I'm with you. I definitely don't
want to bring any harm or make her suffering worse.
Michael.*

He hit send. Next, a student had emailed asking for
an override for the following semester. He replied that the
class was full and to try back later, that perhaps someone
would drop the class. He felt bad about not letting him in,
but otherwise the classes would get out of hand if he said
yes to everyone. The other emails he deleted:

announcements about theses being defended, a blood drive, a seminar on Title IX.

It was ten, and he spent an hour grading essay responses to the next day's reading assignment. Finished, he called up the document he was currently working on for a paper about the current state of depression in the United States, with a focus on drug company rhetoric. It seemed that there was this notion that America was a happy-go-lucky lot of pill-popping imbeciles, obtaining artificial joy through meds such as Prozac and Paxil. But, suicide rates were up and serious depression, even though dulled by the new class of antidepressants, the SSRIs, was nothing akin to engineered happiness. The endless thoughts of doom and death, who wouldn't want to take a pill to relieve the agony? It wasn't like getting a nose job or a new haircut; it was life and death—dear, dear life and death in all of its somber glory.

He worked till two in the morning, going through two cigars, the Heineken, and then a Diet Coke. He had begun taking Adderall a year ago and found that he could work late into the night. He wasn't taking it for ADHD, but as a complement to his antidepressant, of which he took the maximum dose. He never felt high or wired, but just didn't get tired, or hungry, although it was still hell getting up in the morning. He couldn't thank enough the nurse practitioner who had prescribed it for him.

"Come on Arty. Inside." Arty scratched at the glass door and bounded inside as Leonard tried his usual escape act. "No, Leonard! No." He scooted him back with his foot, sliding the door closed.

To transition to bed, he sat in his recliner with his eyes closed and kicked off his shoes. He thought about watching an episode of *House Hunters* , but held off. He was thinking about getting rid of his cable due to the cost.

His ex-wife was still paying his phone bill, and he would have to add that expense. He thought about how he had made twice the money more than two decades back at the HMO. But, he was where he belonged, in a world of books and paragraphs and sentences and words and letters. He was surprised that he could function as well as he did, considering his history. *Anna.* He had to do right by Anna. She deserved it. He felt a dull ache, as if he had swallowed a cold stone.

The next day, Wednesday, he woke in the usual funk, feeling worthless, and hit snooze on his phone. Briefly he thought about running his car into a bridge abutment, about buying a gun, about hanging himself. He shook his head. He had to get up and walk Arty, who was in bed with him, had to dress and get over to the house to take the girls to school. And then there was class at noon. A quick panic surged through him, imagining standing in front of the class. Last semester he'd had a panic attack, a full body cramp, and had nearly doubled over in front of the students. *Anna.* Bread pudding. Frangelico. He would call that evening, perhaps around six. That sounded good. He wound up hitting snooze twice more, the maximum, and piled out of bed, throwing on jeans and a long-sleeve t-shirt. His meds. And he took them with orange juice.

Yancy went to a creative arts high school, and Claire attended a STEM school. No two sisters could have been more different. Yancy was first, and then he'd come back for Claire. He popped the trunk, and Yancy let her stuffed backpack drop with a thud followed by her large water bottle.

"Anything going on today? Gonna stay late?" he said.

"Nope," said Yancy. She finagled her iPhone to sync with the radio. She wore black tights and a loose light-blue top. She had dark brown hair and a smooth oval face with perfect eyebrows.

"Panic! at the Disco. What a surprise," he said.

Yancy laughed. "Yep."

"Your makeup looks nice. It always looks nice."

"Thank you, Father." She gave him a mock smile.

It was just a drive of five minutes, and he pulled into the drop-off line, inching forward.

"There's Simone. I hate her. The bitch." Yancy scowled. "Everyone's like, she's so nice, she's so talented, but she makes me sick."

"Whoa, early in the morning for that?"

"Whatever, pop the trunk?"

He pulled up to the crosswalk and released the trunk. She was out the door. "Have a good day. Love you!"

Back at the house, he had twenty minutes before Claire would be ready, and he ate a piece of chocolate. His ex, Suzanne, had already left. "Hey, I'm here!"

"Okay!"

As usual he lay on the couch, resting his head on a pillow and closed his eyes. He cherished those twenty minutes, drifting into a haze. It seemed like only a minute had passed, and she was ready, wearing brown khakis and a white button-up shirt, part of the school uniform. She was tall with a happy face, a touch of mascara, and dark brown hair, maybe a tinge of red.

"Come on. I'm late again."

He stood too quickly, his vision going blank. It was a twenty-minute ride, listening to NPR. He sped up, coming off the ramp, and merged over two lanes to take the left.

"Most dangerous part of the day," he said.

"I'll be driving this time next year," said Claire.

"Wow. And we're late by four minutes."

"Ugh, at least all of my homework is done. I think I'm the only one who ever does their homework.

"Slackers."

"Makes me look good."

He pulled up and stopped. "Okay, have a great day. Love you."

"Wait a minute, you had a date last night. But, I gotta go. You can tell me when you pick me up." She walked but not in a hurry.

His thoughts turned to his creative writing class at noon. He would go home, walk the dog, drink a cup of coffee, and then review the material for the day out on his patio, smoking a cheap cigar. Nighttime was for the expensive ones. He couldn't really afford them, but he had cut down on his bourbon habit. A year ago he'd been doing 1.75 liters every week, three or four drinks a night, and then he'd suddenly lost his taste for it, gravitating to beer, so maybe he could afford the cigars but didn't want to do the math.

Precisely at eleven, he showered and dressed. He brushed his teeth and did the combover the best he could. He'd shaved the night before, so he was good to go. He picked from his teaching clothes, a pair of gray cotton pants and a purple and green plaid shirt. He pulled on his walking shoes, without untying the laces, and had ten minutes. As usual, he went around and pet each of the animals, telling them that he would be back. He leaned back in his recliner with his phone in his hand and closed his eyes, gathering the strength he needed to teach. And there was Anna in her dress, her shoulders showing, her shy smile. He shifted in the chair, a longing in his chest and throat. He was going to call at six. That was the plan. Hopefully Mandy would let him talk to her. Maybe she would give him her cell phone number. That would be even better. He checked his phone, eleven-thirty-five, and he headed out the door with his backpack.

He walked into class with exactly three minutes to spare. "Hello!"

The five or so students looked up, bewildered, stuck inside their cell phones. He let the screen down to use the overhead projector. He was there, ready, breathing, and one by one another seven students dribbled in. He nodded, waited until noon and then silently checked roll.

He walked in front of the tall lab table. "So, today we're talking about genre versus literary writing, which is an elitist contraption, I think. But, there is now a trend to think of literary writing as a genre versus being in its own special category . . ." He felt okay. He could do it, and then one by one they went through the readings, identifying literary trademarks. A poem about meeting a blind woman, an essay on writing, an absurd story involving physics. At twelve-fifty he was done, and that was that, free for the day and the next day as well. He sighed, excited, deflated, elated, the phone call coming at six. He slowly packed his things, being the last out of the room. He had three hours before he had to pick up Yancy and then Claire.

Back home he undressed into his jeans and t-shirt, his go-to outfit, and pet the animals. He picked up Leonard and rolled him onto his back, getting a yowl and then a purr as he scratched his ears. He dropped Leonard and ran his hand down Tweezer's back as she arched and mewled. Arty was on the couch, waiting for his turn.

Later, at five, back from dropping the girls at the house, he busied himself to kill the hour or so until he would call, eating a frozen dinner and apple pie straight from the tin. He grabbed a beer and with Arty on his tether sat outside in the waning sun, checking his email, and there was a message from Tom.

Hey, this is Tom. Mandy has been a wreck since last night. I don't think it's a good idea to continue this. So for now, let's just give it a rest.

"No." He gazed at the empty road, the trees on the other side. He couldn't break the momentum. It would turn out all right, glorious even. What to do, though, about Tom?

Tom, it's early, perhaps too early to give up just yet. I'll call Mandy, at six, and talk with her. I'll respect her wishes, but I just need to talk with her first. I appreciate your concern and don't forget Anna.

He guzzled his beer and then another. Five minutes. He felt like the mercury in a thermometer, rising slowly to a fever. He had to. He just had to. *What if? What if?* He counted down the seconds and dialed.

"Hello? Is that you?" said Tom. "I'm afraid I'm just going to have to intervene here."

"Tom, no," said Mandy. "I need to talk to him." Michael could hear her in the background and held his breath.

"Look, this is the last time you call, okay? I hate to be blunt," said Tom. "Here she is. For God's sake."

"Hey, it's me," said Mandy. "I've just been crazy since last night. I want to believe. I really do, but Tom thinks it's a bad idea, and maybe he's right."

"Mandy," he said. "It's going to be okay. I think we have to just take this one step at a time. She wants to go to the movies on Friday, but I do need to talk with her, if you approve, just for a minute is all."

"But, how can you talk to her? This is so confusing."

"Just let her have the phone. Go to her bedroom and tell her it's me. I'm sure she wants to talk. Please?"

"I've been in her room a hundred times today, but she's not there. But you talked with her on your date. You saw her?"

"Yes, and she is lovely as ever."

"Okay. Hold on."

He waited, his heart pounding. He could already hear her voice, not quiet, but not loud, polite would be a good way to put it.

"Okay, I'm putting the phone on the table. Will that work?"

"Yes, that's fine. Give us five minutes, that's all I'm asking."

"Okay, here . . . she is."

"Anna?"

"Hey. I can't pick up the phone."

"Don't worry, that will come. How are you? I just wanted to hear your voice, make sure you were okay."

"In my room most of the day as usual. Watched a little TV. It's still so smoky outside."

"Yeah, right. Still on the national news."

"Mom's really upset. I tried to talk with her, but she can't see or hear me."

"Not yet, but she will. I promise. We just have to, uh, draw you out is all. I've got a good feeling. Still want to go to the movies on Friday?"

"Tom says no, but I think mom is okay with it. I would like to. I need to get out. You're the only one. You know what I mean."

"Great, fantastic. That's such a relief. I mean I've just been thinking about you." Leonard jumped into his lap, purring.

"Thank you. It's nice."

"My pleasure."

"As they say . . ."

He laughed. "Exactly."

"I better let you talk to Mom. She's standing here staring at the phone."

"Okay, great. I'll wait for her to pick up. I'd like to see you sooner, but maybe that's not a good idea."

"Probably, take it slow. Okay, here she is."

He held the phone to his ear waiting, rubbing Leonard's ears. He wondered if Leonard had fleas, but he was on flea medication.

"Hello? You there?" said Mandy.

"Yeah, here. Thanks for letting me talk to her."

"What . . . what did she say?"

"Well she's worried about you most of all, but really wants to go out on Friday. She needs to get out of the house."

"She said all of that?"

"Yeah, she did. Heck, you could even go with us, if she thought it was a good idea. I didn't ask her."

"That sounds doubly weird. I don't know. Let me think about it, okay?"

"I understand. I'll pick her up at six. We'll probably get a bite too, after. I hate eating before I go to a movie. Makes me fall asleep."

"Yeah, right. I just want the best for her is all. She was my youngest . . ."

"I will take very good care of her. I promise."

"Okay. I'd better go. Tom is giving me the stink eye."

He laughed. "I understand his concern, but this is great for her, the best medicine."

"I'm not sure what that means, but I trust you. She did like you even though you'd only met a couple of times."

"She's a great person."

"Yes. Yes she is. Okay, gotta go for now. Bye."

"Bye, Mandy. Would it be okay to call again, maybe tomorrow? Just to check in?"

"I don't know. I don't mind, but then there's Tom. You can call, though, and talk to me if you like."

"Sure, that sounds like a plan."

"Okay, bye."

"Bye." He turned his attention back to Leonard. "Leonard, such a good boy. Where's your girlfriend? Where's Tweezer? Gotta get up, though," and Leonard jumped to the rug.

Four

On Thursday, he called again at six and Tom answered, told him to leave Mandy alone, and hung up. Michael had to get Anna's cell. He felt desperate to see her, a longing, an ache like stepping on a nail and that moment of truth before pulling it out. He went for a run after that, later than he would normally, and ran farther than usual, running as if to purge himself of something unclean, something unholy. *What if? What if?* He showered, ate, and had a Facetime session with Claire. She was bored and sick of arguing with Yancy. He listened, trying not to offer advice, just listening.

"So, Dad, any more dates?" said Claire.

"Uh, tomorrow night in fact. I think we're going to a movie."

"Mom says you're a freak."

"Maybe she's right. Do you think I'm a freak?"

"But you're not going out with a real person, Dad. Come on, that's just weird."

"You may doubt me, but I am. She's very real. I spoke with her on the phone yesterday. She's bored and needs the company."

"Dad?"

They spoke for a few minutes more, and she had to get a shower.

He needed to grade papers, but was upset over the brief conversation with Tom. Tom didn't understand what was at stake. Anna was at stake, and maybe Mandy too. It was his duty, and he couldn't wait to see Anna again. He wondered what she would wear, what she would smell like. He paced the apartment. He opened a beer and sat on the patio in his green plastic chair, staring at the road below with no traffic. On the other side of the woods a housing development was being built. He wanted to buy a house, but he'd been turned down for a mortgage. He was 53 for Christ's sake, but his years of depression and paranoia had cost him in more ways than one. His salary as a lecturer was pitiful, and he could barely pay his bills. He hadn't ever had a retirement plan until he was hired at the college two years ago. He hadn't had a car payment, but then the student had totaled his Honda. He loved his new Corolla, but there was the payment. He thought again about canceling his cable. He figured he would be a renter for the rest of his life, a renter on Social Security. Or maybe he could rent a trailer like his parents had for so many years. They had never had money.

He turned on the TV, restless, and found *House Hunters*. Tweezer jumped into his lap and settled on his outstretched legs. There was something soothing about watching other people inspect houses, commenting on the outdated kitchens. "This is a total gut job." The unexpected pool. "I wouldn't know how to take care of it." The distance from work. "That's a long commute, but the price is right." John and Stephanie were looking for a colonial in the Buckhead neighborhood of Atlanta. They had three kids and wanted five bedrooms and five bathrooms. The houses were going for a million plus. He changed the channel to *How It's Made*. A ship's propeller, molded in sand and filed down with a graphite grinder. At commercials he went back and forth, drinking his beer. *Anna. Anna. Anna.* He wanted to scream. *What if?*

Finally, around ten, he found the energy to write. His epic novel series about famine in Ethiopia, he was on book five. The first book had been picked up by a small press, but they hadn't responded to his latest email. It had been two weeks, and he worried that they'd gone out of business. Book five had entered a surreal realm, the villages replaced by futuristic towns where everything was free, except for sex and information. There was no food, just buster, a nourishing liquid sold at bars. He was lost in that world and wrote, pecking away at his laptop in the dark, his keyboard backlit.

At two in the morning, he reached a stopping point. He was well beyond 100,000 words in book five and needed to bring the whole thing to a close. He dreaded finishing, knowing that he would feel empty, knowing that he would plow forward into a new project, and that the pages would accumulate as if by magic. He gathered Arty and lay him on the bed, set his alarm, and crawled beneath the cold sheet and comforter, rolled into a ball, and soon slept.

The next day, Friday, he taught as usual. The next week was Thanksgiving break, and he had canceled class on Monday to give everyone a longer holiday. He could barely contain himself, thinking about seeing Anna again. He had decided on *Goosebumps* for that night, worrying though that something scary might not be Anna's cup of tea. He worried that he'd show up and that Tom would meet him at the door. That something would happen. He didn't want to create a scene, for the sake of Anna and Mandy.

He decided to go casual and wore his freshly washed black jeans. Usually he wore them for at least two weeks before washing them. The evenings were cool now, in the low sixties, and he opted for a thin green pullover, wearing his light hikers. He examined himself in the mirror, muttered, and took a squirt of lotion to his hands, which he felt showed his age. He brushed his teeth and was ready to go. The movie started at seven. It was six.

He pulled in front of the house and both cars were there. He took a deep breath and found himself on the porch. A cactus there, nearly three feet tall. A windchime that sounded like Gypsy bells. The smoke in the air he could taste, but it seemed to have lifted with the onset of evening. He knocked.

It was Mandy. She put her hand to her mouth. "You're here. I didn't think you would come."

"Who is it?" said Tom from the dining room.

"It's, it's . . ."

"Hey, Tom, it's me!"

"Well, come in," said Mandy.

Tom met him in the space between the living room and dining room. A clock on the wall ticked, a pendulum swung.

"For Pete's sake, I thought—"

"Please, Tom. Just give this time. Anna wants to go out. It's good for her."

Tom turned red. "Can't you just listen? Nothing good can come of this."

"Tom," said Mandy.

Anna appeared from the hallway. "Please don't argue with them."

He turned. "Anna, tell them what you want."

"Good God," said Tom.

"She's there. I swear it," he said. "She's wearing tan pants with a black belt and a blouse with a flower print. She's wearing a cream-colored sweater and brown loafers. You still want to go—"

"Stop it!" said Tom.

"No, Tom, please!" said Mandy. "He makes sense. That's exactly what she would wear. The tan pants I hated, the sweater . . ."

Anna folded her arms.

"Please for her sake, for yours. I hate to beg, but I will," said Michael.

Tom stared at him. "Mandy, just this once, I'll listen to you. But you have to understand that this is just plain . . . wacko. Anna is gone."

"No, she's not," said Michael.

"Mom, Tom, I want to go," said Anna. "Just please don't fight."

"I heard her, I swear," said Mandy.

"She asked you not to fight," he said.

"My God," said Mandy.

"Look, I didn't hear anything," said Tom.

"That's because you're not listening," said Mandy. "Anna? Are you here?"

Anna looked at Michael. What should she do?

"It's okay. She's here," said Michael.

"Mom, I love you," said Anna.

Mandy turned toward the hallway. "I can feel her."

"Good God," said Tom. "Okay, I'm in. Just let's quit talking like lunatics. Go. Go to the movie with Anna. Take good care of her. Be home before midnight. There, I said it."

"Thank you," he said. "I'll bring back a full report."

Anna moved across the room and took his arm. "I'm ready. I'll be fine, Mom. And thank you, Tom." She smiled.

"Okay," said Michael. "We're on our way." He put his hand on Anna's shoulder.

"Oh my God, she's here," said Mandy. "Be safe, please."

"Will do," he said, and they were out the door into the waning daylight. He opened the car door for her, feeling Mandy's eyes on them through the curtain.

"Wow, that was a bit of a scene," he said.

Anna sighed. "You have to understand that they can't see me like you can. It's hard for them, especially Tom. He just doesn't want Mom to get hurt."

"I get it. I'm just so excited, though, to see you. I get carried away. I would have died if they hadn't let you come tonight. I've been thinking about you all week."

"I don't think you would have died, silly. Don't be so dramatic."

"It's been over a year since my divorce, and I haven't had the energy until now to even consider dating. You're the first. You're special."

"I wonder if I'll be the last?"

"That's not a good way to put it. Right now you're the only one, and that suits me just fine." He was headed toward downtown to the Cinema Deluxe. "Warm enough for you?"

"Yeah, I have the sweater. What movie are we seeing? Hopefully nothing gruesome."

"Oh no. It's *Goosebumps*. Lots of special effects. Kind of like watching a scary *Scooby Doo*."

"Can I get popcorn? And don't say no."

"Ha, I'll buy you the popcorn machine. How's that?"

"A little over the top, I'd say."

He began to look for parking spaces, but the streets were full and he turned toward the parking deck. He drove up two levels before finding a spot. "Walk or take the elevator?"

"Maybe walk. I've just been in the house all day."

He opened the stairway door. "Whew, smells like pee."

"I don't smell anything. I can taste but not smell. Strange." She walked in front.

They passed a middle-aged couple coming up the stairs. The man was drunk, his face red. "Wonderful night!" he said. "How are you young people!" He laughed.

Michael could smell the alcohol. "Doing great," and they continued down the stairs, exiting onto the street across from the theater.

Inside, the theater lobby was crowded, and they headed to the ticket line. The room was vast, lined with life-sized movie posters. "Two for *Goosebumps,*" he said and paid with his debit card.

"Thank you," she said.

"You're welcome. Thank my students. They pay my bills." He escorted her to the popcorn line. "I like your pants. Your mom said she hated them."

She edged closer to him. "Ha, she was with me when I bought them."

"What will you have?" said the teenager behind the counter. He had sloppy black hair and an earring.

"Um, one large popcorn. You want butter? A drink?"

"What's that?" said the teenager.

"Yes, butter, please," said Anna, "and a small Diet Coke."

"Okay, the popcorn with butter and two small Diet Cokes."

"The large drinks are only a dollar more."

He looked at Anna, and she nodded. "Okay, make them large."

"Alright, two large drinks and a large popcorn. Thirteen even."

With popcorn and drinks they headed to the line. He handed two tickets to the young lady dressed in black pants and a black shirt. She handed one ticket back to him.

"There are two of us," he said.

She frowned. "You're good," she said.

"No, two," he said.

"They'll need the ticket to get in."

"I'll give the ticket to her," he said.

The young lady tore the two tickets and handed him the halves, looking for the next person.

"That was funny," said Anna. "You certainly make me feel real."

"It's my duty," he said. "Need the restroom? Powder your nose?" He moved through the crowded hall.

"No, I'm fine."

They entered the dim room with its tall ceiling.

"I don't like to sit too close. How about the middle?"

"You lead the way," she said.

In their seats, they settled back. The previews had just started. He took his cell phone out and silenced it.

"Mind if I take a picture?" he said.

"That's weird, but okay."

He held up his phone and clicked. "You're very photogenic."

She laughed and raised the arm that separated them. "I might get scared," she said.

"Me too." He loosely put his arm around her. "That reminds me. Can you give me your cell phone number? I hate to keep bothering Mandy and Tom." She told him, and he typed it in.

The first preview, *Star Wars: The Force Awakens.*

She sipped her drink. "I'd like to see this."

"Cool," he said. "For sure. Me too."

After twenty minutes, the lights fully dimmed and the movie began. Anna snuggled closer into him. "Do you mind?"

"Do I mind? Hell no."

Halfway through the final credits, with most of the crowd gone, he stood. She stood. He gathered the empty containers, and they exited, holding hands. He dumped the trash on the way out.

"How about a bite to eat? Did you have dinner?"

"I haven't eaten since we went out Tuesday, so sure."

"Wow, I need to tell Mandy to make you a place at the table."

"Maybe, but I don't get hungry."

"Need to eat. How about we grab a burger at Five Guys? I need to stop by the restroom first."

She stood against the wall. "Yeah, that sounds good. I love their fries. You go ahead."

"Sure, you'll be okay?"

"Yeah, go. I promise not to run away."

He smiled and was soon back, leading her through the lobby. They headed down the street to Five Guys, the sidewalks alive with people. Inside it was crowded, with five in line, other moviegoers with the same idea. There seemed to be dozens of middle schoolers all dressed in formal attire as if they'd been to a wedding. He overheard them talking about a Model UN conference.

Soon it was their turn. "What'll you have?" said Michael.

"Just a little hamburger, all the way, no pickles though, and a drink."

"Okay." He turned to the cashier, a young man with a mustache and acne. "We'll have two little hamburgers all the way, one with no pickles, and an order of large fries. And two regular drinks."

"The large fries will feed about three. You sure?" said the cashier.

"We'll manage," he said, handing him the debit card.

"You're number sixteen."

They got their drinks and took the last table for two.

"Want some peanuts while we wait?"

"Sure."

He went to the crate of peanuts and filled a small paper tray.

They talked about high school. He had hated high school and so had she. It seemed that they'd both suffered from serious depression but hadn't been diagnosed until much later, she in her twenties and he in his thirties. They took their time eating their burgers and fries and walked back out onto the busy sidewalk, the air crisp, a light breeze blowing, bumping into one another as they strolled toward the parking deck. It was ten.

"Gosh, we have a couple of hours before you need to be home. Want to come and meet my animals, at my apartment?" He opened the door for her.

"Sure."

His cell phone rang, the car's Bluetooth taking over.

"Hello?"

"Hey, Dad." It was Yancy.

"Hey, what's up?"

"Just bored. What're you doing? Writing?"

"I just saw a movie with Anna. We're going over to meet the animals."

"What? You're kidding? That same girl?"

"She's not exactly a girl," he said.

"Dad, I'm worried about you. Mom says that you've lost it."

He laughed. "I lost it a long time ago tell her." He reached over and patted Anna on the leg.

"Hey, Yancy," said Anna.

"Look, Dad, I know you're lonely, at least that's what Mom says, but you should date *real* people."

"I am seeing *real* people." He headed onto the bridge across the river, the grooved metal humming the tires.

"Look, Dad. Okay, I'll let you go, Dad. Make sure you come over tomorrow, okay? I miss you."

"I miss you too. Yeah, I'll come over. Probably around one or two. How's that?"

"Okay, Dad. Love you."

"Love you," and the radio resumed, Def Leppard's "Hysteria."

"That was sweet," said Anna. "But she doesn't think I'm real."

"Yeah, they're both good kids. She'll come around. I promise."

He pulled into the complex. "Here we are." He jogged around and opened her door and walked her down to the ground level. Leonard met them at the door and darted away, seeing a stranger. Arty was on the couch, already on his back, waiting for a belly rub.

Anna walked in, gazing around the combo living room and dining room. "Looks nice, for a bachelor."

"Hey, buddy," he said. He rubbed Arty's belly. "This is Arty."

"Well hey," said Anna.

Arty growled.

"Arty, no growling. He just has to get used to you. I need to let him out to pee. Outside, to pee?"

Arty jumped off the green couch, the cushions covered with a blanket, and stretched. Arty liked to dig into the cushions.

Leonard reappeared, and then Tweezer.

"They're so cute. Hey, little girl," said Anna. She reached down and rubbed Tweezer's neck. She arched and began to purr. "Aww."

"Let's sit on the patio. I can put Arty on his tether. Do you mind if I smoke a cigar?"

"Lord. You smoke cigars? I don't mind."

"Want something to drink? Beer, wine, Diet Coke?"

"Maybe a glass of wine. Do you have white?"

"Yep. I'll have one with you."

Outside, with Arty sniffing the grass, they sat in the green plastic chairs. The street below was quiet as usual. A neighbor on the top level and over one unit was on her patio talking on the phone. She always talked to her dad who had lost his wife the year before to cancer. Michael enjoyed listening to their conversations.

"Wine okay?" he said. He lit his cigar with his fancy butane lighter.

"Yes, perfect," she said.

"Good. This is where I write."

"I'll have to read something. You have a novel don't you?"

"Yeah. I've written seven, but only one is published. Have a lot of stories published. I'll give you a copy of the book. It's called *Sprinkle Cheese*."

"Sprinkle cheese? That's a weird title."

"You know, the powdered cheese you shake on spaghetti?"

"Yeah. Mandy calls it sprinkle cheese." She sipped her wine. "What's it about?"

"About this guy who jumps off a bridge in Thailand. He goes back home and moves in with this old man who's had stroke. They help each other recover. Has a happy ending."

"Sounds interesting. Yeah, I'd like to read it."

Arty barked, straining at the thin steel cable.

"Arty, no!" he said. He looked and saw it was a baby opossum in front of the neighbor's patio. "Hell, look. A opossum."

Anna stood. "He's so cute."

Arty barked and barked as if a pack of wolves were descending.

Michael stood and walked toward the opossum, which froze. It was the size of a kitten. "Go, shoo, go." He clapped his hands, and the opossum turned and walked away, taking its time. "Arty, hush!"

Anna was behind him. "Brave little sucker."

He took Arty and soothed him, telling him to be quiet. Arty settled down, and they took their chairs, talking into the night. When he checked his phone, it was twelve-twenty.

"Hell, I have to get you home," he said.

"So soon?"

"Yeah, I promised. They'll be worried." He opened the sliding glass door and let Arty in.

They walked to the front door, very close to one another. At the car door, she paused.

"This was great." She moved in and hugged him.

He embraced her, feeling a thrill, wanting to kiss her when she looked up at him. "Okay. We do have to go. My car will turn into a pumpkin." He closed her door and jumped in.

"It'll be fine," she said.

He drove her home and walked her to the porch. There was a light on inside.

"Should I say something to Mandy?" he said.

"Well—"

The door opened, and it was Mandy.

"Hey, you're back. I was worried."

"Yeah, we just got to talking and time slipped away. But, she's here. We had a great time."

"She's here?"

"Yeah, right here."

"I can't see here, but I feel her."

"Mom," said Anna. "I want you to see me." She reached and touched Mandy's arm.

Mandy's eyes grew wide. "Someone touched me. Anna? Come inside. Tom is in bed. You have to tell me all about it."

They followed her inside, and Anna went to the bathroom.

"Here, on the couch," said Mandy. "Tom is asleep."

He sat, his elbows on his knees. He told her all about the movie, about the popcorn, about the hamburgers, and meeting his cats and dog, about the opossum, that Anna wanted to see the new *Star Wars* movie. Anna had rejoined them, sitting in a high-back chair, listening and smiling. An hour passed.

"I should be going," he said.

"This means so much to me," said Mandy. "I just want her to be happy in her life."

"She is happy," he said. "Maybe we could all go and get coffee together, tomorrow?"

"The three of us?" said Mandy.

"Yeah, the three of us."

"Okay, what time? Ten or so?"

"Sure, I'll come at ten. I have to go over to the house around one, though."

They said goodnight and stood. He walked toward Anna and said goodnight, and then he was gone.

Five

He slept better that night, having had his time with Anna. She was letting him put his arm around her, and it was a matter of time before they kissed. He didn't shower, wanting to affect a rumpled Saturday look with jeans and a ballcap. It was nine, and he decided to call Anna, just to make sure she would be ready. He couldn't find his cell phone, *Dammit*, and remembered he'd left it in the car. He ran up the steps to the parking lot to get it. He typed in Anna and hit the call button. He was counting the rings, one, two, three . . .

"Hello? Is it you?" said Anna.

"Hey! Yeah, it's me. Just wanted to make sure you remembered about coffee today with your mom.."

"She did come in my room and remind me. She wasn't so sure that I heard her. So, at ten?"

"Yeah, ten. Maybe we'll go somewhere different, maybe over here on the other side of the bridge. Can't wait to see you."

"Silly, it's been less than twelve hours. Mom is here. I think she heard the phone ring. Hold on. Mom, it's me. I'm on the phone . . . I'm back. She's just staring at the cell phone. Uh oh, she's picking it up . . ."

"Hello? Hello? Who is this?" said Mandy.

"Hey, Mandy. It's me. I was just talking with Anna about coffee at ten."

"You're kidding. How did you get her number?"

"She gave it to me last night." He sat on the couch and rubbed Arty's head.

"That's so bizarre. Yeah, I'll . . . we'll be ready at ten. I'm curious to see how you handle this. Is Anna in the room? Anna?"

"Mom, I'm here."

"Yes, she's there. You just can't see her yet, but you will. I promise."

"Tom's not happy at all about us going out, so be ready for that. Maybe he'll run out to the store. I'll send him to buy some eggs. We need eggs."

"I totally understand," he said. "He's just trying to protect you. Good intentions."

"Okay, you're right. I'm going to hang up now."

"Let me say bye to Anna. Just put the phone back down."

"Sure," and she laid the phone on the bedside table beside a box of tissues.

"Anna?"

"Hey."

"Just wanted to say goodbye and see you soon. I'm not dressing up, so you can see my sloppy side." He laughed.

"Can't wait. Maybe I won't comb my hair."

"Yeah, don't. We'll both have bed hair, except I'm wearing a cap."

"Maybe I'll wear one of Tom's. He has a dozen."

"Okay then, see you soon," he said.

"Bye."

He brushed his teeth. He felt that he could really be himself with Anna. She was so . . . not pretentious. He would have to be careful and not push too hard against her kindness. He drank half a cup of warm coffee and bid the animals goodbye. Leonard followed him to the door, gazing at him with his big yellow eyes. Michael reached down and scratched his ears. "Bye, buddy."

When he arrived, Mandy was ready. She had dressed up, wearing a long slim dress over a mauve long-sleeve shirt. Her graying hair had been brushed out. He leaned against the wide entrance into the living room.

"So, is she with us?" said Mandy. "Tom is at the store. He knew what I was up to, though."

He gazed inside toward the hallway. "Not here yet. I'll call her. Anna!"

Anna knew he was there but had decided to freshen up and put on makeup. She blotted her lips on a tissue. It was her favorite Burt's Bees lipstick, a dull red that tasted like fruit. "Coming!" she said from the bathroom.

"She's coming," he said.

"You heard her?"

"Yep. Here she is. Hey," he said. "You look great."

"Thanks," said Anna.

"Anna? What is she wearing?" said Mandy.

"Gray sweatpants and a Tennessee Vols sweatshirt."

"I forgot the ballcap," said Anna.

"She's going to get a ballcap."

"Why a ballcap?" said Mandy.

"I think because I'm wearing one," he said.

"Oh."

Anna returned wearing an Adidas hat. "Okay, I'm ready. Let mom sit up front."

"Are you sure?" he said.

"Sure of what?" said Mandy.

He laughed. "She wants you to sit up front."

"Oh . . . thank you, Anna." She looked around the room as if hunting for a mouse.

At the car he opened the door for Mandy and then for Anna. "She likes soft rock," and he hit the channel selector. It was "Cool Rain" by the Little River Band.

"Did she say that? I mean, that's what she liked . . . likes."

"Yeah," he said. He drove to the main road and headed toward downtown and then across the river. He found a space right in front of the coffee shop and parked. The haze from the fires on the mountains was visible in all directions.

Inside there was a short line with plenty of empty tables. He asked Anna what she would like.

"I think a caramel macchiato."

"Okay, maybe I'll have that too." He squeezed her shoulder, and she looked down at her feet.

"What will it be?" said the barista. She was young and wore a tight, low-cut sweater that outlined her large breasts.

"You go first," he said to Mandy.

"Okay. I'll have a vanilla latte."

"Regular or large?"

"Regular is fine."

"And we'll have two caramel macchiatos, large," he said.

The barista looked confused. "You want two caramel macchiatos, large, and a vanilla latte?"

"That's right," he said.

Mandy brightened. "The other is for my daughter."

"Okay, sure. Just swipe and sign." Behind her another barista was making the drinks.

"Thanks, Mom," said Anna.

Mandy looked puzzled. "I swear I heard her voice." She looked around the large open room.

"You did," he said. "She thanked you."

"You're welcome, Anna." Mandy looked afraid.

"You guys get a table, and I'll bring the drinks," he said.

"Okay," said Mandy. She walked toward the window and took a table there and sat. Anna followed her. "Anna?"

"I'm here, Mom. Right beside you."

Mandy put her hand to her mouth.

"You guys look quiet," he said. He carefully placed the cups on the table.

"She's here. I can feel her," said Mandy. "Is she sitting here?" She stared at the cup in front of the empty chair.

"Yep, right there," he said. "So, how is it?" he said to Anna.

"It smells nice," said Anna. "Mom, I just want to say that I'm sorry, for what happened."

Mandy looked perplexed.

"She says that she's sorry for what happened." He put his hand on top of Anna's.

Mandy took a deep breath. "I was always so afraid that it would happen for real. She was just so depressed, but I thought that things were looking up. She'd started using makeup again, had gone out with a friend. She'd even gone with me to the yarn store and started knitting a hat for winter."

"Everything was so dark," said Anna. "The thoughts wouldn't go away. I couldn't take it anymore. It wasn't my first time to try. I just hate myself."

"No, don't say that. It's all good. I've been there. It's overwhelming," he said.

Mandy just listened.

"I quit taking my antipsychotic a month before and my antidepressant too. It's all my fault. The meds made me gain weight, made me lightheaded. I just wanted to eat all the time. Those damn thoughts, of death, over and over, day and night, like voices but not really voices."

"It's okay. Things have changed. It can only get better, right?" he said.

"How can I say that I love Mom when I did that? It's just so selfish, right?"

"No, no. It's a disease, like cancer, except for a lifetime sometimes."

Mandy hadn't touched her drink. "You're . . . talking to her."

"Yes, she was overcome, desperate to make the thoughts go away. At some point they take over. It's like there's no way out except to end it all."

"I hope she understands," said Anna. "I hate that I've hurt everyone."

"It's okay. Everyone loves you. It's so obvious, especially your mom."

Mandy spoke. "Her sisters really took it hard. They wanted to have a big ceremony, a funeral with everyone, but Tom and I decided to have a private service. She was . . . cremated. I still have her ashes. I don't know what to do with them."

"Mom, tell them I love them. That I'm truly sorry," said Anna.

"She feels really bad," he said. "But everything is getting better, right?"

"I just want her back," said Mandy. Tears flooded her eyes, and she wiped at them.

He handed her his napkin.

"Mom, don't cry." Anna put her hand on Mandy's shoulder.

"Oh," said Mandy, reining in her tears, taking a deep breath. Others had begun to watch. "I can feel her. I can feel her."

"Yes, you need to feel her," he said. "She's here, with us. We're having a grand old time, drinking fancy coffee drinks." He smiled.

"Thank you," said Mandy. She wiped her eyes. "I love her so much."

"I love you too, Mom."

He felt a warm surge pass through his chest and a hiccough in his soul. He examined Anna's face, her perfect skin, just a touch of worry around her eyes that seemed to tell a thousand stories. When she smiled, her face creased, making her look older, wiser, tired.

They recovered and sipped their drinks. Mandy asked him about his ex-wife and daughters, about where they had moved from, and how did they like it here. They had come from a small college in Eastern Kentucky, where he'd been off his meds and on the verge of insanity. How he'd held his job, he didn't know. Things were much better now after the divorce, after he had begun taking his meds again. He felt normal. The racing thoughts of death a rarity now. He was running two to three times a week, which helped as well. She wanted to know who his doctor was.

"I see a nurse practitioner at a mental health center," he said. "I couldn't get in with a psychiatrist. No one was taking new patients. But it's worked out. I even have a social worker." He laughed.

"We tried a handful of doctors over the years," said Mandy. "But it was always the same. She would get better, and then have a huge setback. She was so sick, and no one seemed to know what to do. We had talked about ECT, but we decided that was too radical. Maybe we should have tried it."

"You did what you thought was best. You did everything you could," he said.

Anna nodded.

"That's good of you to say. Is there anything we could have done differently? Can you ask her that?" said Mandy.

"She heard you," he said. "Anna?"

Anna thought. "Well, if I'd never been born. No, they did everything they could, and I'm appreciative."

"She said you did everything you could, that she's appreciative," he said.

Mandy sniffled, a look of relief. "Gosh, you're better than the psychiatrists."

He laughed. "It took me fifty years to get straightened out. I'm just lucky. My grandparents were the ones who kept me alive during the roughest times. And then having children has made a difference. Things change when you have children, at least for me."

"I wanted to have children, but could never stay in a relationship. The depression was just too powerful," said Anna. "It was like God."

"Do you still want to have children?" he said.

"That seems impossible, right?" said Anna.

"Nothing is impossible. It's like writing fiction. You can make anything happen."

"Or like poetry," said Mandy. "Tom says the same thing."

"Or like poetry," he said.

They talked for another half hour, and it was time to go. Mandy had errands to run. He had assignments to grade and had promised to drop by the house and see his daughters. He drove them home and walked to the porch. He hugged Anna, and then Mandy.

"Okay, bye you two. Mandy? Is it okay if I call Anna on her cell phone? That way I won't have to bother you or Tom."

"It sounds crazy, but I'm fine with it. I'm beginning to see the possibility."

"Okay, great. Anna, I'll call. Maybe we can do something tomorrow?"

Anna smiled. "Sure, I'd like that."

"Okay, then I'll call. See you guys." He turned and left. It was noon.

He drove down the alley and pulled into the driveway behind the house. The wood from the old deck was stacked against the cement retaining wall. Craig had sawed it into four-foot lengths so it could be carted away. He'd finally finished and had headed to his mother's house in Florida. Arty jumped out wagging his tail, eager to see the family and the dog that everyone called Mr. Spritely, a tiny mutt that looked like a miniature Jack Russell. Michael examined the new flooring of the deck, the new rails. Craig had done a great job, even though it had taken weeks.

Inside there was yelling. "My God, unload the dryer!" said Suzanne. She was upstairs. "You guys are so sloppy! It drives me crazy! Is that you? Did someone come in?"

"It's me!"

"Hey, Dad," said Claire. "She's being a bitch. I've gotta get out of here. Can we go somewhere?" She hugged him and left her arm hanging around his neck.

"Um, okay. Need to see if Yancy wants to go. Where is she?"

Suzanne came down the stairs, wearing jeans and a Kent State sweatshirt. She looked stressed. "Gonna suck up to your Dad, huh?" Her graying hair flipped back and forth as she moved.

"Jeez, why is everything so negative around here?" said Claire.

"So, how are you?" said Suzanne. "Could you help me do one little thing?"

"Lord," he said.

"Never mind. Do it myself. I pulled my back yesterday."

"No, no, what? I'll help."

"Hey, Dad," said Yancy, wearing black tights and a loose gray sweatshirt. She was taller than Suzanne, and had parted her dark hair on the side. Her subtle makeup was perfect.

"Hey there," he said. He patted her on the back.

"I need to move some stuff from the garage back into the house. Take us about five minutes, if you're up for it," said Suzanne.

"Okay, sure," he said. He sat on the couch and put his feet up.

"What've you been up to?"

"Who me?"

"Yeah, you," said Suzanne.

"I had coffee with, uh, Mandy and Anna this morning." He looked her in the eyes.

Suzanne looked alarmed. "Look, you can't be messing around like that. God, what does Tom think? You can't piss him off. So what do you exactly mean when you say that Anna was there?"

"She's there. I can see her. I talk to her. She talks to me. She wants to get out of the house." He yawned.

"That's swell," said Suzanne. "You're dating a ghost. You know she was cremated a few months ago. And Mandy went with you? God, what was that about?"

Yancy and Claire listened, glancing at one another.

"I know it sounds crazy, but I'm obligated. Anna needs me. Mandy needs her. I'm having a good time with her. Mandy is fine with it, still a little confused, but that's to be expected. I just have to keep working with Anna. Everything will work out."

"So, why you? Are you sure you're just not having some kind of psychotic episode? Are you taking your meds?"

"Yeah, Dad, are you taking your meds?" said Yancy. She was making a butter sandwich.

Claire was smiling, sitting on the loveseat. "I think it's cool that he's dating a ghost. I'd like to meet her."

"She's not a ghost," he said. "She's very real. We might do brunch tomorrow. Y'all could come."

"No thank you," said Suzanne. "That's just too weird. What does Tom think? He could get you fired. Jesus." She was unloading the dishwasher.

"Can I come?" said Claire. "You have to take me. We could go to the Squirrel Tree. You could get that cocktail you like. The purple one."

He laughed. "Sure, be ready around ten. I'll call you, though, to make sure. I'm going to call Anna later and confirm."

"How the hell are you going to call her?" said Suzanne.

"I have her cell phone number. Mandy's kept her account active," he said. "I need to take a nap."

"Huh, you always need to take a nap," said Suzanne. "I mean, are you really okay? Are you going to class? Don't fuck up your classes."

"I'm fine. Never been better," he said. "Classes are swimming. Got Thanksgiving break next week. The mountains are on fire. Couldn't be better."

"Yeah, the mountains *are* on fire. Claire, you gonna make us some lunch, maybe some rice? We have leftover chicken."

"Yes, Mother. Anything else? Wash the car?" said Claire.

"I'll be in my room," said Yancy. "Dad, you're nutso."

He laughed. "I am that. Certified. But, we're two peas in a pod, right?"

"Brothers in arms!" said Yancy. "Peace out." She hurried up the stairs.

"I just don't want you to lose your job over this," said Suzanne. "You understand that? You have to think of the girls, and not just your fantasy life."

He sat up. "Look, I'm in control, and this is real. I'm the only one who can do this. Anna is counting on me, and so is Mandy."

"You're impossible sometimes, but I still love you. Okay, enough. How about helping with the moving?

Craig moved the stuff out by himself, to varnish the floor, but I need help moving it back in. Boxes mainly."

"Ugh, okay. Let's do it." He stood and leaned over, catching himself from blacking out. "Stood . . . too fast."

"You okay, Dad?" said Claire.

"Yeah, fine. Okay let's do it. Heavy lifting."

Suzanne closed the dishwasher, and he followed her down the stairs and into the garage.

"Wow, you really cleaned this up," he said.

"Yeah, everything was mildewed, too much humidity in here. The stuff in the driveway is what I need to move."

"Okay."

"But really, are you okay? You're not losing it are you? I'm worried about you."

"Never been better. I need this. Anna needs this. We're good for each other."

"You have to admit that it's kind of creepy. You could really hurt Mandy too. It's not just about you."

"I get that. I'm committed, though. I'm taking it slow. I'm uh . . . courting her, Anna that is."

Suzanne stared at him. "Courting her?"

"Yeah, taking it slow." He picked up a box filled with framed photos. "Where does this go?"

"In the spare bedroom, back in the closet. You are a wonder of surprises."

"I'll take that as a compliment."

Suzanne laughed.

"So how did it go?" said Tom. He stood with his hands on hips, following Mandy to Anna's room.

"It was, well, nice." Mandy examined the room, ran her hand across the pink bedspread. "We talked."

"Who's we?"

"Mostly with him, but he talked with Anna, ordered her a caramel macchiato." She adjusted the cell phone on the bedside table.

"I think he's lost his mind, and maybe you too. This is just going too far." He took off his ballcap and scratched his head.

"Anna's happy. I can feel it. I could feel her there, and maybe even hear her, but it's stronger when he's with her. He's going to call her later."

"How's he gonna do that?" He spoke with an accent, just a trace.

"Anna gave him her cell phone number."

"Oh for Christ's sake, really?" He turned and walked away.

"Honey, it's okay. I know you miss her too. It's hard to understand." She followed him into the kitchen. On the fridge was a photo of Anna at SeaWorld, her arm around Tom, a bright smile.

Tom leaned against the sink. "It's been so hard. I mean, it's just too much, bringing her back like this. It's sacred ground. He barely knew her, and now he's, he's dating her. Did I just say that?"

"Tom. Just do this for me. I need this." She rubbed his back.

He turned on the water, washing a fork. "Just leave me out, though, for now. It's just too much."

"I can do that."

Anna watched from the doorway, tears in her eyes.

Six

Growing up, Anna was bright and often tearful. Her dad sold insurance the old-fashioned way, door to door, but he was quite good at it and made a decent living, enough to buy the girls thigh-high boots for Christmas and always a gift of jade for Mandy—necklaces, rings, even a small vase. When Anna was twelve, when she had just started her period, her father fell in with a client, "a floozy from Memphis," and left the family. Four years later, just as Anna was about to enter eleventh grade, he walked into his backyard and shot himself with a .38 through the temple.

Tom had entered their lives some three years after her father left, but Anna had already slipped into the grips of a serious and unrelenting depression. Unable to get out of bed, she missed days of school at a time, but never with a visit to the doctor, until she was sixteen, when she first tried to kill herself, a half-crazed raking of her wrists with a razor blade that hit only veins. That was the ticket to the ER and a series of trips to see a therapist who diagnosed her with major depressive disorder as well as bulimia. The year was 2003 with Prozac all the rage, and she'd been put on 40 milligrams a day and then 60, the drug addressing both of her diagnoses. It was her deep immersion in the medical continuum that nurtured her desire to major in pre-med at the university. She truly felt that she'd been helped and wanted to do the same for others.

She managed to gain control of her bulimia, although she remained paranoid about gaining weight and refused to eat sweets. Thoughts of death still occurred but were not persistent, and, except for the winter months, she managed fairly well. But that final year of high school, her dad killing himself, and starting her freshman year at college conspired against her. She continued to take her meds but threw herself full on into a life of parties, drinking, marijuana, and cocaine. She was very attractive and usually could get the drugs from admirers versus having to buy them. Of course, her Mom worried, and Tom too, but there was little they could do to reel her in without pulling her from the college. She did go to class, usually, and made an effort, but it never resulted in more than Cs and Ds. During her last semester, just as the fall semester was ending, she escalated out of control, and in an unusual burst of energy, hopped into a rusted Cadillac with a guy named Rob, headed for California. During the trip, she'd become psychotic, ranting about government spies, and Rob had dumped her in Bossier City, Louisiana, 600 miles from home.

She wound up wandering the streets until an off-duty police officer picked her up and checked her wallet. As soon as they heard, Mandy took the first flight to Shreveport and picked her up at the station, where she was being held in a cell with three other women.

"Mom, Mom! They're trying to kill me! Mom! Oh God!" She shook the bars.

"Yes, Baby," said Mandy. "I'm going to take you home. We're going home."

"Good riddance," said one of the women. "Crazy bitch."

"Okay, now keep her under control," said the officer. "I wouldn't recommend flying back." He unlocked the door and Anna clutched her mother, sobbing, her eyes dark, her brown, shoulder-length hair a mess. She wore torn jeans and a dirty short-sleeve t-shirt airbrushed *Panama City!* in rainbow colors.

"Anna, calm down, Baby. I'm here, it's okay. Oh my God, I found you. I found you."

"Follow me, ma'am. Need to sign some papers."

Mandy followed with Anna clutching her leather jacket, sobbing.

"Those women were spies, Mom. God, why does it hurt so bad? Why? Mom, please help me."

"I'm helping you, Baby. I'm helping. It's gonna be okay." She took off her coat. "Here put this on." She draped it over her thin shoulders.

"Does she take medicine?" said the officer. He held a door for them.

"Yes, but I've never seen her like this, on or off medicine."

"Mom, please don't talk to him. Mom . . ."

"Shh, it's okay. I'm here. I have to sign some papers. I have a car. We'll get in the car and go home. You need rest. Tom is so worried."

"Okay, ma'am, the clerk here will help you. Just keep her under control. It took two of us to get her in the cell."

The clerk opened a folder. There was a mug shot of Anna, a look of terror, a hand holding her face toward the camera.

Mandy didn't bother to read what she was signing. "Why didn't they take her to the hospital?"

"I'm not sure ma'am. One more, right here." He picked up a ringing phone.

The station room was crowded with four desks, no windows. It was cold as ice.

"Is that it? We can go?"

The clerk nodded and pointed toward the door. He hit a metal button, and the door buzzed. Mandy managed to open it and ushered Anna into a sterile lobby, an old church pew up against the wall. The mesh-glass doors were just ahead, and she struggled Anna through them into the humid air, a chill breeze blowing. The sun high overhead, unconcerned, casting few shadows.

"Mom, Mom, what is this place? How did I get here?"

"Honey, I don't know. Just relax for now. We're walking to the car. You can rest, can sleep. You need to sleep. Are you hungry? I'm going to go through a drive-through anyway."

The car was two blocks away at a metered spot. She hadn't had any change, and there was a ticket on the windshield.

"Goddammit," said Mandy. She just left it there. "Okay, into the car, Baby. I'll turn the heater on. Here we go. Door's open."

"Mom, do you love me?" Anna dropped into the seat of the Ford Focus.

"Of course, I do. I love you more than ever. I'm closing the door." Mandy hurried around and jumped in. "Thank God. Thank you, God. We thought you were dead, Honey."

"I am dead. Mom, I am dead." She burst into tears.

"No, you're alive. You're with me."

Mandy leaned and buckled her in. She fumbled the keys in the ignition and ground the starter. She tried to turn on the signal and the windshield wipers came on. "Dammit!"

"Mom! Please get me home, away from here!"

"I'm trying, Honey." She backed and bumped the car behind her. She eased out and kept going, wondering how to get on the interstate, but soon saw it and drove back and forth until she found an on-ramp heading east.

The car was warming, and Anna had fallen asleep, her head against the window.

"Oh, Baby," and Mandy drove.

They arrived home nine hours later. Anna had slept for six of those hours, going in and out. She had only eaten half of a hamburger but drank a large Coke as if it was her last. When she bought gas, Mandy had bought her Gatorade, but she had fallen asleep again.

Back home, Tom had met them, Anna still speaking of spies but with less energy than before. A great weight seemed to have fallen over her, and she slept the entire night in her mother's bed, Mandy by her side.

The next day, after a phone call to her psychiatrist, they'd admitted her as an inpatient to an acute mental health ward at the hospital near the university. Within the space of twenty-four hours, Anna had gone from raving to severely depressed, obtunded, and barely speaking. After ten days, she'd been diagnosed as manic-depressive and sent home on an antipsychotic in addition to her Prozac.

Mandy drove, her hand on Anna's knee. The sun was bright, clouds scattered the sky. "We're glad to have you back, Sweetie."

"Mom, I'm so much trouble. I swear I'll be better."

"No, you were sick. A very sick little girl. You still have a ways to go."

"I guess I failed my classes. Jesus I'm such a fuck up!" She slapped the dashboard.

"No, no. Don't say that. You're my girl, my baby girl. We're gonna take care of you. I have to ask, okay? How are the thoughts of hurting yourself?"

Anna sighed and adjusted her seatbelt. "They're still there, but not so bad. That new pill is pretty good, although I get dizzy when I stand."

"That's a small price to pay. You have to let us know, though, if the thoughts . . . well you know."

"I know," said Anna. "I will. Just keep asking."

"Do you want to get some Indian food for lunch? The buffet?"

"I just want to go home. You can make me a sandwich, anything and I'll be fine. I don't have the energy. Plus everyone would stare at me."

"Why would they stare at you?"

"Because I'm crazy."

"Honey, we're all a little crazy. Even your sisters are crazy. No one can tell by looking at you that you are the way you are. Get that out of your head." She turned, headed toward their neighborhood of winding roads and steep hills.

"If you say so. But, I just need to be away from people for a few days. Those other patients creeped me out, not all of them, some were nice. Just so many people asking me questions, and those tests they gave me."

"We have to thank Dr. Kincaid. She's been so good with you. The tests helped with your new diagnosis."

"Great, another diagnosis." She laughed.

"Ha. Embrace your diagnosis!"

"I will, Mom. I will."

Seven

Sunday dawned with just a hint of smoke in the air. According to the news, the fires had been contained but were still burning. Michael made a pot of coffee but only drank one cup. He wanted to go for a quick run before he showered and went to Anna's. He'd called her the night before and settled on having a late lunch with her, after the church folks had had their fill. He fed the animals, walked Arty, and then drank two glasses of water, otherwise he'd get cramps in his calves. He settled down to let the water percolate throughout his body and Tweezer jumped into his lap. He rubbed her sleek back, making her arch, tail erect.

He stretched on the stairs outside and decided it was too cool for his ballcap and went back inside for his toboggan, one he'd bought in Seattle at a conference. He descended the embankment to the street and started off, painfully slow, but gathering some steam after the first small hill. He wondered if smoking cigars affected his ability to run, but he didn't inhale, right? He'd gotten into a habit of smoking cigars when he wrote and couldn't seem to break it, enjoyed it immensely. The weather was getting too cold to sit outside, though, and he pondered buying an air filter so that he could smoke inside.

It was flat and then a long steep downhill before he hit the walking bridge. He waited and then sprinted across the busy street. The bridge was just shy of half a mile across. He enjoyed weaving in and out of the Sunday strollers, some with kids, some with dogs. He wound up past the art museum, through the small art district, and then around to an adjacent bridge to head back for the strenuous uphill climb, which he sometimes walked, especially when it was hot. But, he plodded, panting, jogging as slow as some people walked and felt like a million dollars when he reached the plateau and the flatter roads back to his apartment. He'd always liked to run, especially since his taste for the gym had waned.

He showered with lemongrass soap he'd bought at Walgreen's. He called Anna to see if she minded going half an hour earlier.

"Hello?" It was Mandy.

"Hey, I was calling for Anna."

"I forgot you might call. It's just a habit, me answering her phone. Sometimes I think it might actually be her calling." She sighed.

"No problem. I'm sure she's there. You can just place the phone on the table there."

"Yeah, right. So you're coming over?"

"A late lunch, but I wanted to let her know that I'd be a bit early, to see if that was okay?"

"Do you want me to tell her?" said Mandy. She looked around the bedroom.

"Sure, that would be fine. Just let her know that I'll be there about one-thirty."

"Okay, I'll tell her."

"Great, bye."

Mandy laid the phone on the bedside table. "Anna?"

Anna stood on the other side of the bed. "Yes, Mom? I overheard the conversation."

"Anna? I guess you overheard me talking. He says he'll be here at one-thirty. He hopes that will be okay."

Anna smiled. "That sounds fine. I'm ready. Thank you, Mom." She walked toward her and touched her arm.

"My God," said Mandy. "Anna, is it really you? I can feel you. I really can."

Anna laughed. "It's crazy isn't it, Mom?" She sat on the bed.

"Anna, can you touch me again?" Her voice cracked.

Anna stood and put her arm around her. "I'm here, Mom. Right here."

Mandy flinched then relaxed, melted. Tears came to her eyes. "Anna. I miss you so much. I just want you back, Baby." A tear dripped from her nose.

"It's okay, Mom. I'm sorry I went away. I'll never do that again, I promise."

Mandy sat on the bed, her face in her hands. Tom stood in the doorway.

"You okay?" said Tom.

"Yes . . . yes."

"What happened? Just thinking about her? Did he call?"

"She's in this room, Tom. I just know it. He's coming. They're going to lunch." She wiped the tears from her face.

Tom coughed. "If you believe, then I believe you. I want to believe it, but you know how hard that is. Are you okay with him coming over? If not, I'll call him myself."

"Don't Tom. I want them to go out. She's getting more real every day. This is a good thing." She stood, her arms folded.

"Come here, Honey." Tom hugged her. "Just don't get carried away. Stay in the moment. It could be an impossible thing you're wishing for. You know that."

"But it's impossible that she's gone, right? What could be worse than that? If I can only believe, just a little bit even."

"I get it," said Tom. "You know you were thinking about going back to the counselor. Have you thought more about that?"

"Yeah, I've thought about it. But she'll think this is crazy, right?"

"Probably, but it would be good for you, I think. You should call her, set up an appointment." He let her go.

"Okay, maybe tomorrow. Maybe Anna could go with me."

"Mom, I'll go with you," said Anna.

"Tom? Did you hear that? Did you feel something? She's in this room."

"If you say so, then I believe it."

"Thank you, Tom."

"You're welcome. I'm going on the porch to smoke. Want to come out with me?"

"No. I just want to sit here for a while. She's here. Is that okay?"

"Yeah, sure, of course." He turned and left.

Michael drove the speed limit, feeling serene. The day was gorgeous, white puffy clouds, the sun peeking through. Jimi Hendrix on the radio. Claire was going with them, and he dropped by the house.

Suzanne was outside pulling weeds from the beds around the deck.

"Hey."

"Hey. Claire ready?"

"You'll have to check. Do you think this is a good idea? Dragging her into this?"

"I'm not dragging her. She wants to meet Anna. It'll be good for them both." He walked to the back door.

"Whatever."

He let himself in. "Claire!"

"Hey, Dad! I'm coming. Just putting on a little makeup."

"Hey, Dad!" said Yancy.

"Hello! You want to go with us?" he said.

Yancy came to the railing above. "No, I'm going over to Julia's. Study for a math test. You look nice."

"Thanks. Have fun."

"Yeah, math, fun, right. See you!"

Claire came down the steps wearing jeans and a CBGB t-shirt that he'd given to her. "Dressed up aren't you?" said Claire.

"It *is* Sunday." He wore gray slacks and a black button-up shirt, long-sleeve. He hugged her. "Ready?"

"Let me grab my purse." She ran back upstairs.

He walked outside. "Deck looks great."

Sweating, Suzanne said, "Yeah, Craig did a good job." She pulled up a wad of Johnson grass. "The long cold winter is upon us."

"Ha. Yeah, I'm already feeling it. Went to bed at nine last night, slept for twelve hours. Still feel tired."

"So, you doing okay?"

"As well as I can. The meds keep me alive and kicking. Plus it's not so cold"

Claire was outside.

"Okay, y'all have a good time, on your date." Suzanne rolled her eyes.

"Gonna meet a ghost," said Claire. "Dad, you're insane."

He laughed. "Let's go."

He drove down the alley, turned down the radio.

"So, you really believe this, right?" said Claire.

"Yep. You'll see. Maybe you'll see."

"So, what is she like?"

"She's younger than I am. She's twenty-eight."

"Dad, you're fifty-two. Is that a problem?"

"It doesn't seem to be. I like her company. She's a good person. We get each other."

"Wow, you talk about her like she's real."

"She is real, very real. Mandy gets it, her mom. Her dad, her stepdad, is a little skeptical, well a lot skeptical."

"Never a dull moment," said Claire.

"Life is strange," he said.

"Very strange."

They drove and talked. He pulled up in front of the small three-bedroom house. "We're here. Just be cool. Mandy knows you're coming."

"Should I wait here?"

"No, come with me."

"Okay."

Mandy met them at the door. "Hey, and this must be Claire."

"Hey," said Claire.

"Yep," he said. He gazed beyond Mandy and saw Anna in the hall entryway. He waved.

"Is she here?" said Mandy.

"Yeah, over there," he said. "Hey, Anna. You look nice." Anna wore a long blue dress and her cream-colored sweater.

Mandy stepped onto the porch.

"Hi, Claire," said Anna.

"Claire, Anna says hi."

Claire looked around. "Yeah, okay."

"Okay, we're off to the Squirrel Tree. The crowd should be gone by now."

Mandy looked around. She waved to a neighbor passing by. "You guys have a good time, okay? I'm eager to hear how it goes. "Bye, Anna."

"Bye, Mom," and Anna followed them to the car.

"Claire, let Anna sit up front." He opened the door.

"Thanks," said Anna, and she sat. He closed the door. Claire climbed in the back.

He pulled out and waved to Mandy on the porch. Tom had joined her there, his arm around her.

"Okay, let's do it," he said. He slowed and stopped. "Gotta buckle you in." He secured the seat belt for Anna.

"Thanks," said Anna. "I think I can do it now, though."

"My pleasure!" He laughed and navigated the narrow streets back to downtown and drove down Central Avenue. Parking was still tight, and he drove around until he found a space or rather a space he could make. There were a few people sitting outside drinking mimosas.

He held the heavy wooden door for them, and a hostess greeted them.

"Table for two?" she said.

"Uh, three," he said.

Claire smiled.

"Right this way." She led them upstairs to two padded benches with a low table in between. The acoustic band had finished up and was packing up gear, but it was still crowded.

"We can't lean back," he said. "But that's okay."

"I've never been here," said Anna. "I'd heard about it."

"It's great for brunch," he said. "You like mimosas?"

"Dad?" said Claire.

"Just talking with Anna."

Anna smiled. "It's okay, Claire. Yes, a mimosa would be fine."

"Or a cocktail. They have great cocktails." He held the drink menu. "This one, the Ms. Beauregard is pretty good. I'm getting that."

"The purple drink?" said Claire.

"Yeah, the purple one. It has a violet liqueur in it."

"That sounds good," said Anna. "I'll have that."

The waitress appeared. "Hey guys, I'm Melody. Can I get you started with some drinks?" She wore black jeans and had long black hair with a barrette for her bangs.

"Sure," he said. "Two Ms. Beauregards. Claire, what would you like?"

"A Diet Coke with lemon, please."

"Someone else joining you?" said Melody.

"You could say that," he said.

"Okay, sounds good. I'll be back and then get your orders."

"Dad, will she drink it?" said Claire.

"Just say her name. She's right here. You can talk to her. She doesn't bite."

"Oh . . . okay," said Claire.

"Do you mind if I use the restroom?" said Anna.

"Of course not," he said. "It's downstairs. Should I come with you?" He stood to let her pass.

"No, I'll be fine. Be right back." Anna stood and walked toward the stairs.

"She went to the restroom."

"Really? That's just weird. What does she look like?" said Claire.

"Really pretty, long brown hair. High cheekbones, brown eyes, not as tall as you are, slim."

"And you can hear her when she talks?"

"Sure can. She has a soft voice, not really an accent. What're you gonna get? The pork belly?"

"How did you know?" She laughed.

"Thought so. I think I'll just get the eggs Benedict with ham."

"What's Anna having?" said Claire.

"Not sure. She didn't say." He looked around the open room with the slanted wood ceiling, the walls windows of light.

"Dad, this is just really the most bizarre thing you've ever done. This beats riding your bike to work in the rain. I know she, um, killed herself, but how did she do it?"

"Let's not talk about that. That's done. Let's focus on now. Have to think about the future not the past."

Melody was coming up the stairs with their drinks. She maneuvered through the low tables and backless couches. "Here we go, guys."

He took the cocktails and placed them on the table.

"Still waiting?" said Melody.

"She's in the restroom," he said. "Should be coming back soon." He looked toward the stairs, worried.

"Do you want to wait before you order?"

"Yes, please," he said.

"Okay, I'll check back in a few minutes."

"Thanks, Melody. Gosh, I hope she's okay."

"How can she open the door?" said Claire.

"I didn't think about that," he said. "I should go check on her. Be right back."

"Okay," said Claire.

Midway down the stairs he scanned the open room, the tables, the long stainless steel bar. He saw her and broke into a jog, pushing his way toward her. Anna was in the floor, leaning against the wall, her face in her hands.

"Anna? You okay?" He squatted beside her.

"I'm lost. I got lost. I can't remember where I am." She wiped tears from her eyes.

"It's okay, I'm here."

"Sir, you okay?" said a waiter.

He looked up. "Yeah, it's just my friend here. Here let me help you up. Did you make it to the restroom?"

Anna took his hand, trembling. "No, I don't think so. I couldn't find it. So many people, and they can't see me. I'm sorry to be . . . so much trouble."

"No. It's just over here. I'll open the door for you, but you'll have to follow someone out, right?"

"Gosh, I'm not sure. Maybe so."

People were staring, whispering. He opened the door, and she went in.

"I'll wait here," he said.

Melody saw him. "Everything okay? I saw you in the floor."

"Yeah. She just got lost. She'll be fine now. Just waiting." He leaned against the wall, realized he was too close to the door and moved back.

"Okay, just wanted to be sure."

"Thanks." He waited, gazing at his feet, feeling the looks of others. A woman passed him going into the restroom. He nodded. She looked back, puzzled. He waited, wondering about how much time was passing, watching the door from the corner of his eye. It opened, closed, and then opened again. It was her.

"Anna, thank God," he said. "Gosh, you opened the door."

"Wow, I guess I did. That was weird."

He put his hand on her shoulder. "Okay, this way, back upstairs."

Melody was watching from across the room, talking to the bartender.

They walked to their table.

"Everything okay?" said Claire. She looked at Anna's drink.

"Yeah, a little mishap, but all's well. Anna, did you get a chance to look at the menu?"

"Right." She perused the menu.

"Dad?"

"What?"

"The menu is floating in the air. Oh, my God."

"I'm sorry," said Anna. "I didn't realize . . ."

"No, no," he said.

"Dad, this is freaking me out."

"Just go with it. It's fine."

Anna put the menu down. "I'll have the biscuit and gravy, I think. Not too hungry. It's warm up here." She took off her sweater and folded it on the seat beside her.

Melody appeared, looking askance at Claire. "She's not back yet?"

"Yes," he said. "She's here. She would like the biscuit and gravy. Claire?"

"Right. Um, I'll have the pork belly, and some more Diet Coke."

"Okay," said Melody.

"And I'll have the eggs Benedict with the ham," he said.

"I'll get these orders in," and she left, looking back.

"I guess she thinks we're insane," said Claire. "Sorry."

"It's okay," said Anna. "I understand."

"Dad?"

"Yes?"

"I can feel her. Anna." Her eyes were wide.

Anna laughed.

"Of course you can. She's right next to you." He sipped his cocktail. "Anna, try it."

Their eyes were on the fluted glass as it rose from the table. It tilted.

"That's good, sweet, and strong."

"Jesus," said Claire.

"Yeah, it has cucumber-infused gin," he said. "Last time I had two and got a little woozy. I'll get us some waters when Melody comes back." He sipped.

Claire was on her phone. "Okay if I Snapchat this?"

"Gee, I don't know. Maybe just that we're here, okay. That's all." He smiled.

"Okay." She snapped his photo.

"Is it okay if I tell my friends?" said Claire.

"It's okay," said Anna. She reached for her glass.

"Oh my God," said Claire.

"She says it's okay, but just be respectful. This is a special situation. Got it. We can't alarm anyone. Mandy needs this to be Anna's experience and not your friends'."

"Who's Mandy again?"

"Anna's mom. We're doing this for Mandy, right?"

Anna smiled. "It's sweet of you to say that. I just want her to be able to give me a hug. That would be worth it."

They chatted and passed the time. It took about fifteen minutes for their food to arrive. Melody had their plates on a large round serving tray. She placed the plates on the table.

"Okay, look good?" said Melody.

"Looks great," he said.

"Thank you," said Claire.

"Yes, fine, thank you," said Anna.

"Could we have two glasses of water?" he said.

"Sure," said Melody. She stared at the vacant seat and stumbled with the large tray. "Oops." She laughed.

They sat for a moment, looking at their food, and then a forkful of biscuit was rising to Anna's lips.

Claire stared.

"Claire?" he said.

"Right." She took her knife and cut into the pork belly.

They ate, no one around seeming to notice and soon were finished.

"I wish these seats had backs to them," he said. "Kind of uncomfortable."

"It's okay," said Anna. "Different."

"You guys ready?" he said. "Maybe we could take a walk on the bridge. Would you like that, Anna?"

"Sure. It's not so cold, and the smoke has cleared up."

"Dad, can you drop me at the house first? I've got some stuff I need to do."

"Sure. Okay, let's do it." He waited for Anna to stand.

He drove and let Claire out at the house.

"Bye, Dad . . . Bye, Anna." She ran to the house.

"She's sweet," said Anna.

"Yeah, they're both great girls." He backed and turned around, drove, and parked along Frazier near the walking bridge. It was Sunday, and parking was free.

They walked to the intersection, waited, and crossed.

"Do you mind if I hold your hand?" he said.

"No, I'd like that." She slipped her hand into his. Bikers passed them coming and going. A woman with a baby in a stroller, a kid on a skateboard. The cool breeze from the river. "Can I ask you a question?"

"Sure, as long as it's not about math."

She laughed and nudged him. "Oh nothing like that. At the restaurant, you said you were doing this for Mandy. Is that true? I mean, what's in it for you?"

"It just makes me happy. It's for you, too. For you and Mandy, and Tom, and your sisters."

"Yeah, but what about you?"

He thought. "Gosh, I get to hang out with a pretty girl, I mean woman."

"Aww, thanks. That's what I wanted to hear. I mean we'd only met twice before. Remember the crockpot?"

"Yeah, the spinach-artichoke dip. You had to get an extension cord."

"So, did you know then?"

"Know what?"

"That you'd be holding my hand walking with me on a Sunday afternoon?"

He blushed. "I wanted it turn out like that. I wanted to ask you out, but was worried about me being older, what Mandy and Tom would think."

"I knew it. I really did. I've always dated older men, though."

"Um, so are we dating?"

"According to you, you're courting me, which is sweet. I've never been courted before." She pulled him over to a bench. "Let's look at the river."

They sat, and he put his arm behind her.

"Yeah, courting. I didn't want to seem to forward. I think mainly for Mandy's sake. She's in a delicate situation."

"Because of me. Do you think I'm selfish, for what happened?"

"No, not at all. I know what it's like to be severely depressed. I've been treated for over twenty years. I've been there. I mean, I actually tried once myself. I mentioned that, right? I was at my wit's end. It was the only option. I couldn't take it anymore, and then I wound up in the hospital."

"It wasn't my first time to try, either. The world just seemed so cold. It was almost like a voice telling me over and over to do it, to get it over with. I think Mom blames herself, but she did everything she could: meds, therapists, knitting. I was just a hopeless case."

"But, you're back. This can work, right?"

"So far, it's working. I'm happy, happy to see Mom distracted. You're doing a good thing. I appreciate it." She moved closer.

He felt a knot in his chest, his pulse rising. He faced her and then they kissed. He looked away. "Was that okay?"

She laughed. "Silly, of course. Just don't tell Mom, or Tom. They'll freak out."

He hugged her to him. "I won't. That was nice. I feel like a million dollars."

"You deserve it. I can tell you're lonely. How long has it been since your divorce?"

"I moved out two years ago. The divorce was final a year ago this month."

"Have you been on any dates since then?"

"Actually, no. I had these grand ideas that I would be out there dating, but I haven't had the energy. I feel like I'm in limbo. I tried one of those online dating sites, but it was a scam. I had women from Nigeria contacting me, pretending to be from here. It was weird."

"I never tried that. Why did you get divorced? Can I ask that?"

A large sightseeing boat was approaching the bridge, music playing over a loudspeaker. A deep horn blew three times.

"Sure. Sometimes it seems like we haven't divorced. I mean I'm over there all the time, to be with the girls. I still cook dinner there. I guess the main reason was my depression, if you ask Suzanne. She couldn't take it anymore. We just fought all the time, which wasn't good for the girls to see. It's much better now."

"I hate fighting. It's the worst. The last guy I dated, he was impossible. So, was that your first marriage? I mean, your kids are pretty young."

"Ha. I was married in my twenties to another woman. I was totally fucked up then, pardon my language. It was before I was diagnosed as bipolar."

"There you go. That's my diagnosis too. Imagine that."

"Really? I wondered. Want to walk some more?"

"Sure, to the end and back, then maybe I should go home. I feel strange, like I'm going to disappear."

"Don't do that." He waited for her to stand.

Hand in hand they strolled. A huge Great Dane was pooping a truckload, the owner looking on in horror.

"Yuck," said Anna.

He laughed.

"So, what will you tell Mandy?"

"About our date? Claire could see my glass moving around, my fork. That was totally new. Mom would freak out, I think, if you told her." Shadows from the trusses crossed them as they walked.

"Gosh, I don't know. I think maybe it's best if she sees it for herself. Does she make you a plate at the table when they eat?"

"No."

"I'll have her do that, tell her it's important for the process."

"I am starting to get hungry, and using the restroom. So weird, like I'm some kind of baby learning to walk again." She smiled and squeezed his hand.

"So here's a question," he said. "Before I came to court you, were you in the house? I mean did my interest cause you to appear or were you just waiting?"

"It's fuzzy. It's like I was there but not really. Like I was on the way to somewhere else but my foot was stuck in that house. I think that was because of Mom, her sadness. I couldn't leave, not as punishment but just as a matter of course. Does that make sense?"

"Yeah, I think so. I knew that I had to come, that you were there. I was called in a sense. I kept thinking, what if I had asked her out, how would that have changed things? It was my fault. I'm so damn shy. And there was the age difference. There's always something that makes me hold back. Once, I didn't have sex with this girl, woman, because I hadn't brushed my teeth."

"Really? She wanted to have sex?"

"She had spent the night at my apartment. We woke up and she said that she loved to have sex in the morning. I totally collapsed. The moment was lost, all because of my damn teeth."

"Was she pretty?"

"She was gorgeous. Her parents were from Pakistan."

They reached the end of the bridge. There was an ice cream shop there. Or they could go left and up to the art museum across another footbridge.

"Need to turn around? Want some ice cream?"

"That might attract too much attention. An ice cream cone floating through the air. I think maybe we should go back for Mom's sake. I know she worries."

They headed back, their hands falling apart. She took his hand and put it on her waist. "Such a nice day. The sun makes me feel stronger, like I'm just going to burst open like a flower."

"Huh, earlier, you said you felt like you might disappear."

"Yeah, pushed and pulled."

"So, I have a serious question. I guess it's a serious question."

"What?" she said.

"Did you actually . . . die? I know there was a service, that you were cremated. I know this is hard, but did you leave, did your soul . . . go to heaven?"

"It's like I went to sleep in a dark room, and I just stayed there. Nothing happened. I don't even think there was time there. Gradually the dark space became my room and then the house. And then you came and the outside became real. It's like the world is reforming around me."

"Wow, that's just too hard to digest. I stopped believing in heaven and hell, God, Satan, after my breakdown. I think that was part of my breakdown, that I had to unload so much of my life into a dumpster. It ripped me apart. No medicine could have prevented it."

"When did that happen?"

"It was just before my first wife divorced me. I had done some volunteer work in Haiti just before we were married. Duvalier had been exiled. It was chaos. That's where it started, the great rip I call it. I couldn't justify the world I lived in anymore. Too much disparity, too much pain and suffering."

"That sounds terrible. I mean for you. But now you're here because of all that, right?"

"Yeah, with the most beautiful woman in the world."

She stopped and looked up at him. "Kiss me when you say that."

He leaned down and kissed her, lingering.

"That was nice," he said. "I feel like I'm going to fly." He looked around but no one seemed to have noticed.

She laughed. "I wonder what keeps me on the ground? I mean am I subject to gravity? When I first came back, I kind of floated around and through things. I guess I'm getting more solid."

"You're solid to me. It just takes time."

"You keep me on the ground."

"Ha, you're grounded," he said. "Your mom is going to freak when she sees you eating at the table. I bet it won't take long."

"What about Tom? He's not buying into any of this."

"It could be that it happens later for him. He'll have to believe, at least until you're in full control."

"You know you can't leave me. You're stuck with me, right?"

"Don't put it that way. I'm honored to be stuck with you. This is my life right now. I'm yours."

"That makes me feel better. I mean what if you meet some hot chick, and she throws herself at you?"

"I'll tell her I'm courting a ghost, and she'll run screaming."

She laughed. "Don't call me a ghost."

"I'm sorry. That's just what I would say, not what I mean. Looks like a family reunion."

They passed through a large group, all wearing the same t-shirts, some fat, some skinny, kids and adults. Two boys tossing a Frisbee. They walked and talked until reaching the end of the bridge. It was time to leave, the wind picking up, the air chilling down. He drove and soon arrived at her house.

His heart was in his throat again. Without speaking, he leaned across and kissed her on the cheek. She turned and her lips met his for a long kiss.

"That was nice," she said. "Okay, time to go."

"Right," and he walked her to the door. Before he could knock, the door opened.

"Come in," said Mandy. "You were gone for a while. Everything okay?" The house smelled of something fried.

"Mom," said Anna. "We walked on the bridge." She touched Mandy's arm.

"I can feel her. She touched me," said Mandy.

"She did," he said. "She said that we walked on the bridge, after we ate. It was so sunny. We had a great talk."

"Sit down, sit down," said Mandy. "Tom, they're back!"

He sat on the couch with Anna beside him. Tom appeared in the hallway and stepped into the living room. He was drinking a glass of wine.

"Like a glass?" said Tom. "It's a red cuvee, un-oaked. Light and crispy."

"Tom and his wine," said Mandy. "Can he get you a glass?"

"Sure," he said.

"So, tell me about lunch, the walk on the bridge."

He told her that Anna had ordered the biscuit and gravy, that they'd had a cocktail. He left out the part about Claire seeing the menu, glass, and fork move. He recounted the walk across the bridge, leaving out the kisses.

"I guess we need each other," he said. He sipped his wine. Tom had taken a chair, listening without comment.

"We had a great time, Mom," said Anna. She put her hand on Michael's thigh.

"And what did she wear today?" said Mandy. "I have to know. I have to know everything."

He looked at Anna. "She's wearing a long blue dress. It has short sleeves. And the sweater, cream-colored." He looked at her feet. "And her boat shoes with blue socks."

"I can just see her." Her eyes welled with tears. "Anna, I love you so much." She stared at the empty place on the couch.

"I love you too, Mom."

Mandy's eyes widened. "She said that she loves me. Tom, did you hear that?" She wiped a tear.

Tom sipped his wine. "Um, no, but . . . We have to be reasonable, right?"

"To hell with reason," said Mandy. "I want Anna back. She's coming back, in pieces."

"That's a good way to put it," said Michael. He put his arm around Anna and gave her a hug.

"Mom, I'm going to surprise you. I promise," said Anna. "And you too, Tom."

Mandy's eyebrows lifted.

"I should probably go. Have some papers to grade as usual," he said. He removed his arm, gazing at Anna, and she stood.

"Don't go," said Mandy. "Stay as long as you like."

"Thank you," he said. "But I'll leave her here with you. You should talk to her. And she wants you to make a plate for her when you eat."

Tom drained his wine. "Really?"

"Tom, don't roll your eyes. Don't interfere. Of course we'll make a place for her. Is she hungry now?"

"I'll leave and let her tell you," he said.

"Okay," said Mandy. "Anna, just let me know, okay, dear?"

"I will, Mom," said Anna. "I'll walk you to the porch." She stood.

"I'll say goodbye to her on the porch, if that's okay."

"Of course, go ahead," said Mandy. She was wringing her hands.

On the porch, he hesitated, looking down into Anna's big brown eyes. "Can I call you?"

"Of course you can call me. Any time." She looked back. "Here, a quick kiss." She leaned up and kissed him on the cheek. "Thanks for a wonderful time. Maybe I can see you tomorrow?"

"Yeah, I'd love that. Every day would be nice."

Eight

That evening, Mandy made vegetarian lasagna, one of Anna's favorites. As requested, she made a place at the table for Anna. Making the salad, she couldn't help but check to see if the chair had moved, to see if the wine glass was lifting. She suspected that more was happening with Anna than Michael had let on. She measured out oil and vinegar and added dry basil and black pepper. Tom studied the wine bottles in the mishmash of racks in the pantry, selecting a California Chardonnay.

In her room, Anna sat on her bed, feet out, leaning against a pillow. She was beginning to feel objects, in the absence of Michael, to feel their pressure against her. She picked up her cell phone, but it slipped through her hands. She could still answer it, though, pressing the button. She wished it would ring, wondering if she should call him, but she decided to be patient. She could at times smell the lasagna, but then it went away, replaced with the stale smell of envelopes or paper. Things were much more alive when he was there.

"Dinner's ready. Anna?" Mandy stood in the doorway, wearing a small apron with cookbooks on it. "Anna, we made you a plate. Come and join us." She hesitated there.

"Okay, Mom," said Anna. "I'll wash my hands." She stepped past Mandy into the bathroom. She couldn't turn the knobs, though, her hands going through them. "Damn."

Tom was sitting, spinning the wine in a bucket of ice.

"Pour a glass for Anna," said Mandy. She stood with her hands on the back of her chair. "Anna, are you here? We're sitting down now."

"I'm right here, Mom." She managed to squeeze into the chair. "Tight fit."

"Let me pull the chair out a bit more," said Mandy, and she did. "It feels heavy," she said to Tom. She approximated her hands to where Anna's shoulders might be and held them there. "Tom, pour the wine. She needs a glass of wine."

Tom sighed and poured. "Shall I serve everyone lasagna?"

Mandy sat. "That would be nice. Nice big portions."

"Right," said Tom. He maneuvered the hot glass pan with a pot holder then scooped with a large metal spoon onto matching plates painted with tomatoes and garlic. He examined the plates, waiting for something to happen. Anna's wine had not moved.

"Maybe we should say a blessing?" said Mandy. She pushed a bowl of shaved Parmesan cheese toward Anna's plate.

"What?" said Tom. "We never say the blessing."

"But we did when the girls were little. Maybe it's a good idea. I'll say it. Let's all hold hands. She took Tom's hand and extended the other across the table. "Tom?"

Tom did the same but with a tiny scowl. Anna took their hands, smiling, and bowed her head.

"Tom, do you feel it? I can feel her hand." She stared at the empty chair.

"I'm trying," said Tom. "I want to believe but maybe it's just my job to support you. If you feel it, I believe you."

"But, you really have to believe in her, Tom, not just me. It's not enough. We have to really want her here, just like he does. Michael can see her, can tell what she's wearing."

"Okay," said Tom. "I'm trying. It's just hard, but I'm glad it makes you happy."

"Tom, you're sweet," said Anna. "Mom, he's trying."

"Okay, let's pray. Dear God, it's been a while, but we want to thank you for Anna. We want to thank you for bringing her back to us. She is very precious and deserves the best in this life. And thank you for this food. Amen."

Tom mumbled an amen.

"Amen," said Anna. She squeezed their hands.

"Oh my," said Mandy, and a tear was in her eye.

"Okay, no crying at the table," said Tom. He took the first bite. "Good as always." He sipped his barely chilled wine.

Anna tried to pick up her fork. It moved just a bit, but she couldn't do it. She tried the wine. "Mom, I guess I need a straw. Today at the restaurant, it was different. I could do it. I swear."

Mandy was listening, discerning, as if tending to puffs of air, seeking out a pattern, a rhythm. "It's okay, Anna. We know you're here. Tom, what if we put a straw in the wine? Perhaps she's too weak?"

"Wine through a straw?" said Tom.

"Yeah, some people drink red wine that way to keep from staining their teeth. Remember that student who did that at one of the parties? She'd had her teeth whitened."

Tom nodded. "Yeah, Angelica. A provocateur, I would say."

"I'll get it." She fetched a straw from the kitchen. She kept them for her granddaughter. "Here we go. Anna, there's a straw. Will that help?" She sat, her eyes on the wine glass.

Anna held her hair back and tried the straw. She managed a sip with great effort.

"My God," said Mandy. "Did you see that? She did it. Anna, oh my. Tom?"

Tom frowned. "I must have missed it. I'm sorry, but I believe you."

"Tom, you weren't watching. Anna?"

"Your lasagna is getting cold, Mom," said Anna. "I'll try it again." Nothing happened. "I'm sorry, Mom. I think I need him here with me. He makes things happen."

Mandy took a bite of lasagna, watching, waiting. A full minute passed, and she sighed and took a bite of salad. She seemed as if about to burst into tears.

"Honey, don't let this upset you. I mean we can't just gawk at every meal, right? Either she's with us or not. It doesn't matter if she eats or drinks, right? Just that you know she's here."

"He's right, Mom. I think the harder you look, the harder it is for me. Kind of like stage fright. I can't remember my lines."

Mandy tried to take another bite, but let her fork drop. Fresh tears welled and dripped down her nose. "Oh . . . I'm sorry. I'm so sorry. For everything bad that I've ever done, for every argument. Anna . . ." and she left the table, hurrying to her bedroom.

"Mom!" and Anna followed her, gazing at her mother prostrate on the bed.

"My Anna!" and Mandy cried, heaving.

"Mom, no," said Anna. She sat on the bed and brushed her mother's hair with her fingers. "Mom, I love you. No more tears. There have been too many tears." She felt her own tears appear, making the room look liquid.

Mandy turned over and propped herself against the headboard, gripping a throw pillow to her chest. "Anna? I know you're here, Baby. Thank you, Anna." She put the pillow to her face, wiping away the salt.

"You okay?" said Tom. "You promised that you wouldn't let this upset you. I have to protect you. I want Anna back as much as you do, but we have to keep moving forward. I mean, you were doing so well until . . . he came along with this dating idea."

"Not dating, courting. It's different," said Mandy. "He's courting her, courting her back to life. I believe it. I think he loves her."

Anna blushed, rubbing her mom's leg. "Love is such a strong word, Mom. I just think he really cares, maybe more about you than me. He just wants you to be happy is all."

"Thank you, Honey," said Mandy. "I know you're here. I know you want to eat the lasagna. It's your favorite. It's just not time yet. I understand. Tom, I'll try to be more level-headed but we both have to believe, okay? You have to believe with me, otherwise it won't work. Here, help me up."

Tom helped her stand. "Are you taking the pills still? For the depression?"

"Yes, I'm taking the pills. They help, but this is even better." She hugged him.

"Okay, let's finish dinner." He adjusted his ballcap and led her by the hand back to the dining room with the table too big for the room, a mahogany buffet against the wall.

Mandy took her place. "Thank you, Tom."

"You're welcome."

"Thank you, Anna."

"I love you, Mom."

Michael dropped by the house, just in time for a quick dinner of chili with gluten-free crackers. Yancy was allergic to wheat. Claire had already told them all about brunch at the Squirrel Tree. She had seen the fork move, the food disappear, the cocktail going as if to a mouth, the story about Anna getting lost going to the bathroom.

"So," said Suzanne. "I don't know what to make of all this. Are you guys just in this together, or what?"

"Mom, I saw it," said Claire. "She's real. I Snapchatted about it. I took a picture of her plate, before and after." She grinned.

"I believe it," said Yancy. "Dad wouldn't lie. Crazy things happen to Dad."

"It's not crazy," he said. "It's true. Anna is real."

Suzanne tapped her spoon. "Sounds like you're in love. I haven't seen you this way in a long while, maybe not since we were dating."

"It's . . . kind of like that. I told you I'm courting her, for her and Mandy's benefit."

"Dad says she's really pretty," said Claire. "And she's much younger."

"Well, there's that," said Suzanne. Her shoulder-length graying hair bounced as she talked.

He coughed. "She's just a beautiful person. I'm just the right person at the right time."

"And you're not missing your classes, right? You haven't bought a one-way ticket to Brazil or anything like that, right?" Suzanne was stern.

He laughed. "Not yet. Although I have wondered about taking a trip, maybe some place not too far away. The beach maybe."

"In November?" said Suzanne.

"Dad, can I go?" said Claire. She wore an old Yale t-shirt.

"If she goes, I go," said Yancy. She had her hair pulled back with barrettes.

"The beach is magical in winter, although it's not really winter. The water is always so rough. I wouldn't get in the water," said Michael.

"Just long strolls on the beach with this Anna," said Suzanne.

"Hey," he said. "You've been on dates with that guy from philosophy. Are you jealous?"

Suzanne thought. "You know, maybe I am just a little bit. You seem so happy about this, and I only went on two dates and that's done anyway."

"But, you have to wish me the best, right? We want each other to be happy."

"Yeah, Mom," said Claire.

"How's the chili?" said Suzanne.

"Changing the subject," said Yancy. She laughed.

"Yeah," he said.

"I just don't think you realize how bizarre this is. I mean an invisible person actually drank a cocktail, in a public place, and nobody called the evening news?"

"It was just natural. No one really noticed," he said. "The more I see her, the more real she becomes. Mandy gets it. She's totally on board. I couldn't do this without her blessing."

"But when, and it's a matter of when, this gets around your department, what will people say? They're going to think you're bonkers."

He laughed. "But, I am bonkers. I mean I'm medicated, but I'm always on the edge. I think that's part of it. If I were some rational person, maybe this wouldn't work. I mean I write fiction. I make things happen. Anything can happen in a story. I believe in that. Lock, stock, and barrel."

"Oh the figurative language emerges," said Suzanne. She pushed her chili around with her spoon.

"Okay, well look at it as a miracle. You believe in miracles, right? And the chili is good, thank you. It's like ambrosia . . . with beans. More figurative language for you."

"Just keep on keeping on, I guess. Just do not hurt Mandy. Promise me that. Tom would never forgive you. You're not tenured and that would sink your boat in a hurry."

"Posh. I've lost years of my professional life to my 'disorders.' The worst is over. Things are looking up for the first time in a long time. I feel great!" He slapped the table for effect and said, "Ha!"

Yancy and Claire laughed.

"You guys always gang up on me," said Suzanne. "I'm just trying to protect you. I guess I have to let that urge go. You're on your own now. I mean we were married for what, fifteen years?"

"Yep, and you politely asked me to move out. You wouldn't toss someone out of the lifeboat who couldn't swim would you?"

"Let's just say I had faith in your life vest, in your meds. If you had been treated twenty years ago, who knows. I think it's ironic that we split up after you leveled out. I guess I like punishment."

"Huh, you enjoyed the old me, the crazy me more than you thought?" he said.

"When we were dating you never told me the whole story, about your diagnosis, about your *diagnoses.*"

"I didn't want to scare you off."

"That's honest. I might have had second thoughts."

"But we wouldn't have these two," he said.

"Yeah," said Claire. "Okay, may I be excused?"

"Yeah, me too," said Yancy. "This is getting too serious."

"I think Yancy is right, keep it simple for now," he said.

"So, what's next, flowers, a ring?" said Claire.

"I told you we're courting, nothing serious."

"You can't wait to see her again, can you? I can just see it in your eyes. You really believe this," said Suzanne.

The dryer upstairs buzzed and Yancy and Claire took off.

"So, you *are* jealous," he said.

"You used to think about me like that."

"We both changed. We went from lovers to parents. It's a deadly transition," he said.

"Oh you always say that. We could have still been lovers. Other people do."

"Name one, with kids."

"Don't put me on the spot," she said.

"You put yourself on the spot. I know I can't think of anyone. Marriage is all about having kids, has nothing to with love. We got married to have kids. Being lovers became secondary. I mean we're handling the divorce pretty well. We still feel like family but without all of the tension and fighting." He munched a cracker, his eyes bright.

"You're no romantic. Both Yancy and Claire say they'll never get married. We could have done better for them. Although, it could be worse I suppose." She collected empty bowls, taking them to the sink.

"Yeah, we could still be trapped in a legal relationship, yapping at each other like angry dogs. The girls don't need to see that. They say they're glad we're divorced. The wisdom of children."

"Bring your bowl," said Suzanne. "Not to change the subject, we need to talk about Thanksgiving next week. Are we going to see your dad? You know your cousin Dane invited us down for dinner on Thursday night, and we should definitely do that. The girls need to see their cousins. It's been three years."

"Well," he said, "a year and a half if you count mom's funeral."

"Forgot about that." She rinsed and loaded dishes into the dishwasher. "Check the dog's bowl for food, would you?"

He walked that way, toward the fireplace. "Yeah, I'll call Dad tomorrow. He'll probably invite us to eat." He dipped the bowl into the dog food canister.

"Don't tell him about going to Dane's. He wasn't invited. I'm afraid he'll find out."

"Yeah, wonder why? Probably because of Shirley. I think maybe she makes them uncomfortable. But, we should go to Dad's if we're invited. Come here, Buddy, got your food." The dog, Mr. Spritely, jumped off the couch, wagging his tail, showing his teeth.

"She snagged him the weekend after your mother was buried," said Suzanne.

"Or he snagged her. He said, 'Shirley's the one for me!'"

Suzanne laughed. "I guess I'll get to meet her, not that I want to."

"Right," he said. "She wants me to be a part of her giant family, but I don't have the energy for another fifty relatives. I can barely keep up with what I have."

"So, do you think you're in his will?" She dried her hands on a dishtowel with a trefoil pattern.

"God, I have no idea. I mean he's never had anything, except the house he inherited from his parents. He's sunk a shitload of money into the house that he and Shirley fixed up. I'll be lucky to get a spare tire."

"Maybe not," she said. "Didn't your uncle have him get a pre-nup?"

"I think so, but he can retract that at any time. I need to get home and walk the dog." He sauntered to the bottom of the stairs. "Bye, Claire!"

"Bye, Dad! Love you!"

"Bye, Yancy!"

"Love you, Dad!"

Suzanne smiled. "At least the girls love you."

He grinned. "You're my jealous ex-wife."

She slapped his arm. "Go, go home. And don't get in over your head with this Anna? Got it?"

"Whatever, bye," and he was out the door, standing in the driveway, the sun setting, the shade drawing down the chill of evening.

Nine

He'd called Anna around ten the night before and talked for nearly an hour. She'd told him all about her sisters. Spring, the oldest, worked at a health food store. Spring had two small boys. Tiff, the middle sister and single, worked at a disability insurance company and had one daughter.

Class was cancelled, an early Thanksgiving treat for his students, but a student in one of his online classes wanted to meet at noon and discuss a research paper. He'd taken the girls to school and walked Arty, and it was ten-thirty. He read for an hour, showered, and drove to campus, walking to his office in the library. The student's paper was about how to prevent ACL tears in female athletes. The hypothesis was that female athletes experienced a higher rate of ACL tears than male athletes, a popular topic it seemed. He grabbed a large coffee from Starbucks and walked up to the fourth floor. With three of his four classes being online, he spent little time in his office, doing most of his work from home.

He was ten minutes early and began to read, doing his own research on the rhetoric of depression, specifically Prozac. No other drug had ever garnered so many books in the popular press: *Listening to Prozac, Prozac Diaries,* and other books like *Comfortably Numb.* He was convinced that Americans were not the doped airheads that some books were making them out to be. Severe depression deserved a magic pill, if that's what it could be called. Life was too short to be miserable, to have zero joy. "Prozac," he said, "because Zoloft is for pussies."

The student arrived. She was young and attractive. As he got older, there were fewer and fewer ugly people in the world. He propped the door open with a wastebasket.

"Hey, Samantha?" he said.

"Yeah, nice to meet you," said Samantha. She wore ripped jeans and a baggy sweatshirt with her bra strap showing. She held out her hand for him to shake, and he did.

He settled into his chair. "So, what do we have?" His mind drifted to Anna. This Samantha had long brown hair like she did.

"I just have a few questions. I brought what I have so far." She handed him ten pages.

He glanced at it. "You have all of your sections here. One thing I notice right away is that you need more paragraphs to ease the reader along. For example, your entire introduction is this long two-page paragraph. You need to break it up." He glanced at the references page. "Make sure you alphabetize your sources and review APA style. I see that some of the journal titles are not italicized."

Samantha wrote hurriedly in a notebook. "Okay, thanks. One thing I wanted to know is whether or not I establish the importance of the topic like you said to. I used statistics."

He read over the introduction. "Yeah, I think you have good stats here. You might include some cost data about what the cost is of ACL injuries, among women if you can parse it down to that, perhaps compare it to men. That would make a good graph. I notice that you only have two graphics so far, and you need three."

"Right, yeah that sounds like a good idea." She was leaning forward. "Is my hypothesis okay?"

He scanned the abstract and introduction. "It's in your introduction, but we need that right up front in the abstract too, but what you have is clear."

"And I had a question about the in-text citations. Do I have enough?"

"You want to cite all of your stats and any statements of fact that you can attribute to a source. It looks like you've been doing that here. One thing about punctuation. It goes inside the quote mark. Check those."

"Okay, great."

"Anything else?" he said.

"I guess that's it. Thank you, professor."

"You're welcome. Looks like you're off to a great start here. You still have about three weeks to finish up." He handed her the paper.

"Thank you." She just sat there, kind of frozen.

"You're welcome. It looks good so far."

"Thank you again." She stood.

He stood. "Have a good day."

"Thank you," and she left.

He had nearly four hours before he picked up Yancy. He knew he should keep reading, but wondered if Anna might like to grab a cup of coffee. He was having dinner with the family that night. Suzanne was making pesto. He pulled out his cell phone and dialed.

"Hello?"

"Anna?"

"Hey. I was wondering when you would call."

"You okay?"

"Yeah, but I feel like I've faded since yesterday. Mandy's making a place at the table for me, but I'm not able to eat like I did at the restaurant. I guess I need to spend some more time with you." She laughed. "Mom is in the doorway, staring at the phone. It's okay, Mom."

"Gosh, I'd love to see you. I have some time. Would you like to get some coffee? I can be over in twenty minutes."

"Sure, I'd love that. I'll let Mom know, the best I can."

"Maybe I'll call her, just to give her a heads up."

"Okay. Come on over. I'll be waiting."

"Okay, bye. I'll call her right now."

"Bye."

He dialed Mandy's number. "Hey, Mandy. I just talked with Anna."

"Hey. I heard her phone ring." She wound the cord around her fingers.

"Would it be okay if I dropped by and took Anna out for coffee?"

"Sure. You know I've been making a place for her at the table, but I can't really tell if she's there. Am I doing something wrong?"

"No. She's there. Just have faith. She actually mentioned that you were doing that."

"She did? That's good."

"Yeah, okay, I'll be over. I'm on campus now. I think we'll go to the Angry Mug."

"To the what?" said Mandy.

"It's a coffee place on Main Street."

"Right. Okay, I'll see you soon."

"See you," and he began the walk to his car in a light breeze. The sky was shot with white clouds. The fires had been contained, and there was no smell of smoke, but there had been no rain and the ground was still parched. He wended his way between buildings, passing students along the way. He rarely met other faculty walking on campus, and he wondered if they used secret tunnels.

Traffic was heavy but he arrived and parked, and Mandy met him at the door as usual.

"Come in. I want you to see." He followed her to the dining room. "See." On the table was a plate with a tuna salad sandwich and a glass of ice water.

He looked around. "That's perfect. I don't see her here, though."

"I'm coming!" said Anna.

"She's coming," he said.

"I think I heard her," said Mandy. "It's only when you're here, though, although I can feel her."

"I guess we need to spend more time together." He turned and saw her and smiled. His heart quickened and his palms felt dry.

"Hey," said Anna. She wore a short paisley dress with black leggings, low heels, and her sweater.

"Wow, you look great," he said.

Mandy strained to see. "Anna?"

"I'm here, Mom."

"What is she wearing?"

He told her.

"I can just see her. The dress may be too light, though, but she has a sweater you say?"

"Yep," he said.

"Okay, good. That makes me feel better. Maybe she'll eat at the coffee shop. Will you buy her something to eat?"

"Of course. They have pastries. Shall we go?" He held his hand out for Anna, and she took it. "Okay, Mandy, we're off. Should be back in less than two hours."

"Okay . . . have fun." She looked like a single snowflake, floating. "I can tell when she leaves."

He walked Anna to the car. "You're wearing perfume?" He opened the door.

"No, I don't think so."

He slid in and cranked it, gazing at her. "You're so damn pretty."

She laughed and blushed. "Thanks, Romeo."

Off of Main he found a spot in a small lot, but had to pay five bucks. The bell on the door jingled, and there was a short line. The coffee bar was on the right with two tables in front and more tables to the left and in the back. Art covered the walls, all for sale.

"What will you have?" he said, pulling out his wallet.

"Maybe a café latte and a cinnamon bun."

"Okay." He held her hand until it was time to order.

"Take your order?" The guy had a bushy red beard. Beards were all the rage.

"Yeah, a café latte, a regular coffee, and two cinnamon buns."

"For here?"

"Yeah, for here," he said. "Let's take the table here."

"What's that?" said the guy. He swiped the debit card.

"Nothing. Just talking to her." He smiled and took his card.

"Receipt?"

"No, thank you."

The guy handed him two buns on a single plate. "I'll bring your drinks."

Michael waited for her to sit. He wanted to kiss her right there.

"Looks homemade," said Anna. She broke off a gooey piece. "Look, I'm doing it."

"Yeah, you are. Is it good?"

"De-lish. I was hungry. I wasn't hungry until you started coming over."

"That's a good thing. I'll come over more often."

"Fine by me." She smiled.

He took a bite. "Need some napkins." He grabbed two.

"So, I'd like to see your dog and cats again. Maybe we can do that today?" said Anna.

"Hmm, I guess we would have time. Yeah, they'd like to see you. They get bored, especially Arty."

The guy came with their drinks.

"Thanks," he said. "Yeah, we'll just finish our buns and head that way." He felt a light airiness in his chest, as if yarn was being pulled from his heart.

"Tom got a little upset with mom last night."

"Why?"

"Well she set the table for me and nothing happened. He's just worried about her. I'm afraid he'll stop you from coming over."

"Gee, I hope not. It's really important that we spend time together. I'm not trying to smother you, but it's necessary for now."

"I don't mind. It's a good thing. I'm really happy. I'm glad you're courting me. It's very romantic." She sipped her latte.

"Yeah, it is. I get chill bumps thinking about you." He stared at the plate.

"Really? I miss you as soon as you leave. Look." The coffee cup went to her lips. "Mmm."

He noticed a man at the next table staring. "That's so cool. I think someone is watching, though."

"Should I not do it?"

"No, just be yourself. The world will never be ready, I'm afraid." He sipped his black coffee.

"Ha, good answer," said Anna. "I haven't asked you yet, but what is the tattoo? I can see the bottom of it, peeking out."

"Lord, my tattoos. I have five, and that one I did myself."

"You did it yourself? How? What is it?" Her hands were folded in her lap.

He raised his sleeve. "It's pretty ugly, just two circles intersecting with a couple of triangles in there. I call it my map of the universe."

"Wow, that's pretty cool. I can tell you did it yourself, though."

"Yeah. Did it with a needle and stamp pad ink. I was living with this old man who had been in a car wreck, paralyzed from the waist down. He went to bed early, and I had all night to stare at the walls. It just came to me that I had to do it, and I did."

"What happened to the old man?"

"He actually improved quite a bit. There was a community pool, and I'd take him there and let him float in an inner tube with his legs dangling. He loved it. Before I got there, he was lying in bed and had sores on his backside and hips." He finished his cinnamon bun and wiped his fingers.

"Is he still alive?"

"No. I went home on the weekends, and he died while I was gone. Had a heart attack. It was sad. We were good for each other. I'd been through my first divorce, and a breakdown. We helped each other."

"That's so sad but sweet too. Don't look so sad, though."

"Yeah. We should go if you want to see the animals. I have to get the girls at four."

"Okay, just one more bite."

He watched her eat and drink, smiling.

"Ready?" He helped her to stand and pushed the chairs back under the table.

"Come back," said the guy.

"We will!" he said, stepping through the door, the bell jingling.

They drove across the river to his apartment. Leonard met them at the door with Tweezer hanging back in the hallway. Arty was on the couch, thumping his curly tail.

"Baby, you're so sweet." Leonard rubbed against her leg. She scratched his head and neck.

"Arty, you okay, buddy?" He rubbed Arty's tummy.

"Come here, little girl," said Anna. Tweezer raised her tail, looking apprehensive. She walked toward her and sat. "Pretty girl." Tweezer sniffed her hand, but backed away.

"She's the shy one," he said.

"They're all so cute. My cat is great, but he's so old. He scratches everything."

She stood, and they were very close together. She put her arms around his waist and pulled him close. His heart thudded as her lips parted. He leaned down and kissed her, and she kissed him back. They stumbled, laughing, and with Anna against the wall, he kissed her long and deep, and their breath quickened.

"Oh," said Anna. "I need this. It's been so long," and she leaned up into him, drawing his head down, taking his mouth with hers.

For several minutes they kissed, groaning. His hands were on her back, squeezing the top of her hips. He withdrew.

"My God, you're such a hot kisser." He kissed her again.

"It takes two," she said. She led him to the loveseat and made him sit there. "Can you hold me and kiss me?"

"Of course."

She sat in his lap, her head even with his. She looked into his greenish eyes. "I'm so glad you came along. I wish it had been sooner."

He felt a pang of guilt. "Better late than never."

She moved his mouth toward hers, her hand rubbing his chest. He tried not to squeeze her too tightly but wanted to melt into her. They kissed, looked at each other, and then kissed again. His hand moved up and down her back, brushing her neck.

"That feels good," she said. "Maybe give me a back rub?"

"Um, sure."

"Maybe on the bed?" she said. She seemed flush with energy, bright, cogent, alive.

She followed him to his bedroom. There was no closet door, just clothes hanging there, his shoes on the floor. She crawled onto the bed, on her stomach, and put her hands beside her head.

"Come on. Don't be shy," she said.

He carefully worked his way on top of her, on his knees, straddling her, sitting on her legs. He used his thumbs, going up and down her spine.

"That's super." She moaned.

He used his imagination, putting pressure with his knuckles in different spots, not really knowing how to give a proper massage. She was soft, fragile, but solid. He lingered on her neck, gently rubbing. He was most definitely aroused and that fog of unreality was settling over him. He was the luckiest man in the world.

"You know what would feel good?" she said.

"What?"

"If you massaged my behind, my backside. You can push my dress up. Here, lift up." She pulled up her dress exposing her firm butt encased in leggings.

He stared as if in a dream and put his hands there, pressing the flesh, moving his thumbs in a circular motion. He was imagining having sex with her, but couldn't remember where he'd put his condoms. She made little sounds, helpless sounds of pleasure.

"Pull my leggings down, get to the skin."

He felt that he would come in his pants and peeled the leggings down, exposing thong underwear. The skin there was perfect, alabaster, and felt like silk beneath his fingers. Time seemed to stand still. He glanced at the clock, and he would need to get Yancy in an hour.

"Mind if I take off my shirt?" he said.

"Of course not," she said.

He peeled off his long-sleeve t-shirt. Wanting to feel her against him, he lay down beside her, pulling her close and finding her mouth, his hands on her soft butt cheeks, almost frantic, pushing up her dress until her warm stomach touched his. He tried hard to hold back, closed his eyes, and imagined . . . picking mushrooms, taking out the trash, washing his car. He breathed deep, their mouths searching.

"I think we should do it," she said. He could smell her, her scent of steel and skin.

"Jesus, I want to bad," he said. "But, I'm courting you. It feels too fast." He moved a hand to her breast, searching and exploring.

She laughed. "You're quite the gentleman. But, I feel like I need it so bad, for you to come inside me." Her hand was there, undoing his belt.

"God, I'm at your service."

They entwined, kissing madly, clothes coming off until they were naked. He kissed her body from her breasts and all the way down to where she was wet and waiting. He lingered there in full ecstasy as she thrust her hips.

"Hurry," she said. "I'm coming."

He focused and eased inside her, an explosion of warmth. They moved with one another, grabbing for the sheets, for skin, for dear life. Together they climaxed, sweat on their chests, moving as one primitive being.

She panted, arching into him for more. For another five minutes they struggled with one another, the bedspread now on the floor, the wetness on the bed, the smell of sex in the air, and Leonard jumped onto the bed, mewling with wide eyes.

"Oh, my God," said Anna. "God, that was perfect. Just hold me."

He pulled her close and gripped her, kissing her forehead. "You know . . . I think I'm . . . falling in love."

"I knew it. The looks you've been giving me. I'm the same way, although that's a hard thing to say just yet." She relaxed onto her side and pulled his arm over her. "This is just so cozy. I could stay here forever."

"Me too," he said. "I'll need to get you home soon, to go pick up the girls. Do you need to shower?"

She laughed. "No, I'll just tidy up in the bathroom. Maybe I can go with you to pick them up? Mandy won't mind. Maybe I can call her and let her know."

He massaged her breasts slowly, relishing their softness. "Wow, it would be cool if she heard you. Do you think it would freak her out? Maybe I should call."

"No, I feel like I'm ready to make that leap. I feel like it's time, that it will work." She turned over and kissed him. "Thank you. I guess we're not courting anymore?"

"Maybe not. Dating?"

"Yeah, that suits me. You're sweet."

"You're fucking precious."

"That makes me want to do it again, but I'll save it. I won't be able to sleep tonight thinking about it."

He laughed and kissed her. "Okay, we better get ready. You go first." He found her bra and handed it to her. He pet Leonard, and he jumped off the bed.

She gathered her things and walked naked to the bathroom, her figure a perfect hourglass shape.

He lay back on the bed, feeling complete but sleepy. He wanted to just fall asleep with her and hold her for hours. Soon, she emerged dressed, and he headed for the bathroom. She slapped him on the bottom.

"I meant to walk Arty, but I can do that after I get Claire. I'm supposed to have dinner with them tonight. Maybe you could come?"

"I don't know. Let me call Mom. I'm excited."

He handed her his phone, and she dialed.

"Mom?"

"Hello? Who is this?" said Mandy.

"Mom, it's me. Anna."

There was silence of five seconds. "Anna? My God. I can hear you. Where? How?" Her voice cracked.

"Mom, it's okay. I'm fine. I'm with Michael."

"Michael? Michael. Come home, will you? Tell him to bring you home. I want to see you. I want to see you. Your voice, it's so real."

"It's real, Mom. It's me. I wanted to tell you that I'm going with Michael to pick up his girls. Is that okay? And then he'll bring me home."

"Anna, I guess that's okay. I need to tell Tom. He'll be home soon. I need to call him. Just come home soon, please, Anna?"

"I will, Mom. I love you so much."

"I love you too. More than . . . I can say."

"Mom. Don't cry. It's a happy thing." She smiled at Michael. He was sitting in the recliner, tying his shoes.

"I love you so much . . ."

"I love you too. Okay, Mom, I'm going now. But we will see you soon. Okay?"

"Okay, Honey. I love you."

"Love you too. Bye."

"Bye."

Michael stood and hugged her. "She must be overwhelmed."

"I think so. Ready?"

He patted Arty on the head, and they walked to the car. On the way they met his neighbor, an elderly woman named Ellen, who lived alone. She was sweeping the sidewalk and looked surprised.

"Hello, and you have such a pretty friend with you. Who is this?"

Michael laughed. "This is Anna."

"Nice to meet you, Anna. I wondered when he would have a lady friend over. I worry about him."

"Nice to meet you," said Anna.

"It's a lovely day isn't it?" said Ellen. "I just had to get out and get some exercise. You know me." She was bony with perfect yellowish hair, wearing a colorful Christmas sweater.

"It's a perfect day," said Michael. He took Anna's hand. "We're off to pick up the girls from school. Only one more day, and they'll be out for Thanksgiving."

"Do you have big plans?" said Ellen.

"Not really. Just drive down to see my dad and some friends."

"That sounds like a good time. You tell your dad I said hello. I know you said he had cancer. Is he doing okay?"

Michael maneuvered closer to the car. "Doing pretty well, considering. It's like he just doesn't acknowledge it." He opened the door for Anna.

"Nice to meet you," said Anna, beaming.

"Nice to meet you. I'm glad you've found a friend," said Ellen. "I *was* worried about you."

He laughed. "Thanks. She's special for sure."

"Oh my!" and she winked. "Bye. I'll keep sweeping. Can't keep me down."

"Bye," and he hopped in. "She's so nice, but she's a talker sometimes."

"Seems sweet, and she actually saw me! Oh my God. We have to have sex more often. By the way, that was great."

He smiled. "Any time, my dear. I still have chill bumps. I wonder what your mom will think, if she sees you for real."

"Oh gosh, who knows. She'll burst into tears."

"I guess that's to be expected. Let's see what happens with Yancy. Her school is just down the road. You've been there."

"Oh yeah, Yancy was very skeptical if I remember."

"Maybe we'll cure her today," he said.

He drove and pulled into the lower lot, backing in. It was five till four. He turned on NPR. It was the news, a story about the weirdness of Donald Trump.

"Have you heard about this guy?"

"Just from Mom and Tom. He wants to build a wall to keep the Mexicans out."

"Yeah, very strange. There's no way in hell he'll get elected." He turned the volume down. "So, we just wait."

"Were you surprised?" said Anna.

"About?"

"Us having sex, silly."

"Oh my God, yeah. I was considering myself lucky to just hold your hand. You are stunning . . . in the nude . . . and with clothes on."

"Ha, you think so?"

"I know so. You don't regret it do you? Not too fast I hope. I guess I could have held back but it would have been near impossible. God, once my hands were on your body."

"You have great hands. But I could tell you were being shy." She reached over and squeezed his thigh.

Kids were starting to trickle down the stairs.

"Thanks. My pleasure."

"As they say . . ."

Yancy came bounding around the white Explorer that was beside them. She paused, slowed, looked, and opened the back door.

"Dad?"

"Get in. This is Anna, in the flesh."

"What? Dad you're creeping me out. No offense, ma'am." She slid in, her eyes wide.

"Anna, this is Yancy. You've met once before, under different circumstances."

Anna turned around. "Hey, Yancy. You're beautiful."

"Hey," said Yancy. "You're Anna?"

"Yep, that's me. Your dad has transformed me."

"Dad?"

"Yeah?" He pulled out into the exit line.

"I mean, it's like I can see through her."

"Oh no," said Anna.

"Really?" he said. "Huh."

"I do feel less . . . material."

He pulled onto the street, driving slow, glancing at Anna. He could only see her, in all of her raw beauty. He drove Yancy home, and she hopped out, staring at them as they drove away to pick up Claire.

"Maybe, it doesn't last?" said Anna.

"Maybe. Maybe with time," he said.

It took fifteen minutes to reach Claire's school, which was on the campus of the community college. He pulled into the parking lot.

"Yeah, the sex had a powerful effect," he said.

"In more ways than one," said Anna. She brushed back her hair. "I need a hair tie."

"There's probably a dozen in the backseat, along with a hairbrush and some eye shadow. Want me to look?"

"No, that's fine. I'm fine." She bit her lip, folded her hands in her lap. "God, maybe we should do it again."

"In the parking lot?" He felt himself aroused.

"Just in theory." She laughed.

It took about five minutes for the stream of students to emerge. Claire was one of the first out. She walked toward the car, smiling, and waved. She opened the front door.

"Hey, hold on. Anna's up front," he said.

"What?"

"Just jump in the back. Anna's in front."

Claire looked puzzled but opened the back door. "Dad, are you okay?"

Anna turned. "Hey, Claire. I like your hair."

"Oh my god," said Claire. "I heard her. Anna?"

"Yeah, she's right here. Yancy actually saw her, but she's . . . faded."

"This is just too weird, Dad. I mean I guess the restaurant was weird too. My friends didn't believe me."

"She's holding out her hand for you to touch," he said. He reached back and guided Claire's hand.

"Oh!" said Claire. "I felt it. Oh my God."

"See."

"Maybe this isn't good for her," said Anna.

"She's fine. She believes in ghosts."

"Am I a ghost?" said Anna.

"Not to me, just to other people. You know." He pulled out and was soon on the four-lane.

"Dad. Did I really touch her? Is Anna living with you?"

"No. She's at her parents."

"But I need to spend more time with him," said Anna.

"I can't understand what I'm hearing, but it's a voice," said Claire. "Geez."

They drove to the house.

"I'll let you out. I have to take Anna home, but I'll be over around five-thirty or so," he said.

"Yeah, okay. Be careful, Dad," and she hopped out.

"She's so pretty," said Anna. "And tall."

"Yeah, they're both lookers. I guess Mandy will be disappointed, that she can't see you." He headed for the bridge.

"I was so hoping to surprise her. Maybe we should have sex in front of the house."

"I'd like to but maybe not." He reached and took her hand. "You are something to behold."

"Thanks," she said.

Soon they were at Anna's and walking to the porch, hand in hand. Michael looked transformed, almost beaming. She rapped on the door and opened it.

"Come on," she said.

He followed her inside and met Mandy.

"Oh," she said.

"I just followed her inside, sorry. But here we are."

Tom came in from the kitchen. "Hey, Michael."

"Hey, Tom. We had a great time, but we didn't eat lunch proper, just some cinnamon rolls and coffee." He looked at Anna. "Are you hungry?"

"I should be, but not really. Mom?" and she moved toward Mandy, taking her hand.

Mandy stepped back. "Oh! What just happened?"

"She's holding your hand," he said.

Tom folded his arms. "Mandy? It's okay. Michael, maybe it's time to go."

"No, no," said Mandy. She wiped a tear from her eye. "Anna, I feel you. Can I hug you?" She held open her arms.

"Mom, I love you," and she embraced her, burying her face into her shoulder.

Mandy gripped what was there and began to shake, tears now jetting from her eyes. Tom moved in and put his arm around her.

"Mandy, it's okay. Just stay rational. I know you believe, but . . . it's impossible. Can't you see?"

"No, Tom, you can't see! She's here, with me. She hugged me."

Now Anna was crying, sniffling, trying not to fall over.

"Okay, I guess I should go. Have a dinner to be at. I'll call."

Mandy was lost in a world of sorrow and joy, her body limp and her arms collapsing. She sat in a chair and sobbed.

"Anna, I'll call you, okay? Take care of Mandy."

"Okay," said Anna. She walked toward him. He hugged her, and they kissed.

Tom scowled, confused.

"Bye y'all," he said.

"Bye," said Anna. "Call me."

"I will," and he left, feeling exhausted, liberated, crushed, and elated.

Ten

He drove to the apartment, reliving the afternoon with Anna. He ran a stop sign and had to focus on driving, nearly hitting a crow. Home, he leashed Arty for his walk and struggled down the steep hill. He'd checked his bedroom, and the sheets were tangled, the spread on the floor. He tried to convince himself that it wasn't real, but it was. He walked as Arty tugged him along, sniffing every bush and clump of grass. The chill of evening was there, and he shivered. They walked down the road to the apartment entrance and up the road. Arty stopped and glanced into the trees, looking for squirrels. An acorn dropped, and he rushed for it, ears erect.

"Just an acorn, Arty." He dawdled, letting Arty scan the perimeter as cars passed. "Come on, boy."

They made the top of the hill and walked back to his building through the long snaking parking lot. It had just been refinished and smelled of asphalt. Leaves scurried, rattling across the pavement. He turned and down the stairs they went to the bottom floor on the back side of the building. Leonard met them at the door, asking with his big eyes where they had been. His one goal was to get outside, and Michael had to be vigilant. He'd lost one cat that way.

With Arty walked and the trash taken out and the litter box cleaned, he was ready to have dinner with the girls and Suzanne. He put two Heinekens in a plastic bag.

"Come on Arty. Let's go see Mr. Spritely."

Arty spun in a circle, yapping twice.

He took his time driving, a Primus tune playing. He knocked and opened the door, using the code, which was 1984. That had been his idea. He let Arty loose to consort with Mr. Spritely.

"Hey," said Suzanne. She was still in her glove dress, kind of with a hippy flair. She was putting fresh basil into the food processor. Water boiled on the stove, two pots, one for gluten-free pasta and one for regular.

"Hey." He could hear the girls upstairs. A vacuum cleaner. He thought he could hear the dryer.

"Are you really okay?" she said. "Yancy told me this crazy story. So, Anna was with you but she went invisible?" She packed the basil and reached for the olive oil.

"That's a good way to put it. When I'm with her, she's started to appear to others. But to me, she's always there. Good enough?" He leaned on the counter.

"I'm fine, I guess, with you playing out this fantasy, but don't get the girls involved. You're freaking them out." She opened a bag of pine nuts.

"But Anna needs to be around other people. I think that's helping too."

"You know what I mean. Sure, she's harmless. She passed away four months ago. But, you can't involve them."

"She's back. I'm bringing her back. Whether you believe it or not. Yancy saw her at first. How do you explain that?" He watched her open a bag of Parmesan cheese and dump it in the food processor.

"Yeah, that's tough. Unless she's playing along with you, which I suspect. Claire didn't see her."

"But she felt her, touched her arm."

"Okay, look, regardless of what happened, which I can only chalk up to inherited hyperactive imagination, just keep a low profile with this Anna. Do your thing, but leave the girls out. Got it?"

"Are you jealous?" he said.

Suzanne laughed. She was wearing an agate necklace he'd given her several years ago for Christmas. "No, I want you to have a love life, just not with a ghost."

"Can she come to dinner? Would you like to see for yourself?" He opened a Heineken.

"What? Tonight?" She dumped pasta into the boiling pots.

"No, another night, maybe Friday. I could grill out. The more time I spend with her, the more real she gets to others. My plan is to see her every day."

"Will Mandy let you come over every day? Is she not freaked out at this point?"

"A little. And, of course, she'll let me come over. Tom is the problem. He doesn't believe, just like you. You should have seen Mandy today. Anna hugged her. They were embracing, and Mandy was so . . . happy . . . crying."

"That doesn't sound good. She's going to be a nervous wreck. You have to be careful. What, do you want to write about this? That's it, isn't it? This is your next writing project. Hold on." The food processor ground and whined, started and stopped, started again as a thick pesto formed.

"Ugh, not a writing project. I haven't even thought about that. I'm doing this for Mandy, and Anna."

"And yourself." She removed the blade from the processor and scraped the pesto into a bowl that he'd bought in Mexico.

"Okay, for me too. But what's wrong with that? I mean, I need affection. I need to love someone. I have to move on with my life. I think you are jealous." He swigged his beer, wiped at his goatee.

Suzanne laughed and shook her head. "You are one bizarre dude. Are you taking your meds?"

He flushed. "It always goes back to my damn meds. Yes, I'm taking my meds. Otherwise, I can't function. Anna is good for me."

"Is she your therapist? Can you put out the silverware and place mats?"

He moved to do that. "Maybe she is. She gets it. She was severely depressed. She's bipolar too. Once I was diagnosed, I think you gave up on me, a slow letting go, even though I was getting better and better and still getting better. I haven't felt this good, ever."

"Did you use our marriage to work out the kinks? I feel that you did."

Yancy came barreling down the stairs. "Hey, Dad!" She ran and hugged him tight. "I love you."

"Oh sweetie, I love you too." He stood back and looked at her. She was already in her PJs.

"I told Mom about Anna. I still can't figure out how you did that, or maybe I'm as crazy as you are." She examined the pots bubbling on the stove.

"You are a chip off the old block," he said. "You're taking *your* meds, right?" She was on the same antidepressant and antipsychotic as he was. It had caused her to gain thirty pounds, and she had threatened to quit the meds.

"Yes. Like father, like daughter." She smiled.

He laughed. "Just keep taking them." He narrowed his eyes and glanced at Suzanne then back to Yancy. "You're not cutting are you?"

Yancy frowned, sitting at the table, rubbing Mr. Spritely's head. "Can we not talk about that? My counselor says I don't have to talk about that with you, just her."

"Honey, we need to know," said Suzanne. "Are you, cutting? You seem so much better on the new meds."

"No, and that's all I have to say. Don't ruin a good evening. Come here, Arty! Good boy!"

"Anyway, let's a have a good dinner together," said Suzanne.

"Right." Michael went to the couch with his beer and leaned back, thinking about Anna, about her shoulders, the curves down her back. He closed his eyes.

Claire came down the stairs. "Where's Dad?"

"Back on the couch, his favorite spot," said Suzanne. She stirred the pots. "This is about ready."

"Hey, Dad! Resting your eyes?" Claire stood behind the couch.

"Ha, yeah, resting my eyes, always resting my eyes."

"Did you take Anna home?" said Claire. She was in tight jeans and a sweatshirt, footie socks that didn't match.

"Uh, yeah, I did. You told mom about touching her?"

"Yep." She glanced back at Suzanne. "She didn't believe me."

"Do you believe?" he said. He crossed his legs, his feet dangling off the couch.

"If you do, I do. Hey, I got a hundred and ten on my museum project. Highest grade in the class." She flipped back her long hair. She'd had bangs cut, but was letting them grow out again.

"Good job," he said. "And I need all the help I can get."

"Okay, pasta is ready," said Suzanne. "Claire, you mix the regular pasta, and I'll do Yancy's."

Soon they were all at the table. The kitchen, small dining room, and living room all ran together.

"I forgot to make the Texas toast," said Suzanne.

"Too late," he said. "This is plenty." He took a forkful of the pasta. "Mmm. Yum dillyishus." He gave a rigatoni noodle to Arty.

"No table food. It gives them diarrhea," said Suzanne.

"Gross, Mom," said Yancy.

Claire rolled her eyes.

"Can I talk about work for just a minute?" said Suzanne.

"Sure," he said.

Suzanne was dean of the Honors College at the university. She told them about how well the new AA was doing. How everyone just loved her. But, a student was causing trouble in the program, making unwanted advances on female students. Several had complained to the Dean of Students, saying that the Suzanne's program was creating a hostile environment. Everyone listened, nodding.

"Can't you just tell him to settle down, or he'll be cut?" he said.

"It's not that simple. He's on the spectrum, so it's complicated. I've talked with him, laid down the law, but he seems impervious to advice. He could get me fired if this keeps up."

"That's a tough one," he said.

Talk turned to the girls, how their days had gone. Yancy was bitter about a classmate who was always making sexist remarks. Claire was indignant over the laziness of fellow classmates with whom she was working on a project. They finished eating, Suzanne having had two glasses of wine, her face a bit flushed. She'd quit smoking again and always drank more as a result. He helped clear the table and load the dishwasher.

"Okay, guys, I'm headed out," he said. He put Arty on his leash. "Have to have some cuddle time with the kitty cats. They get lonely."

"Dad, that's so sweet," said Yancy. "Love you."

He hugged Claire. "Love you guys too."

Back at the apartment, he could smell the cigar he'd smoked the night before. He figured it was better than smelling the litterbox, but he'd ordered a wall-mounted air filter so that he could smoke inside on a regular basis. The pairing of his writing with cigars was his true pleasure. He rummaged in the fridge for a Heineken. He checked the stove clock, eight-thirty, and dialed.

"Hey there, Sexy," said Anna.

"Oh my God, if I'm sexy then you're sexy squared." He grabbed a cigar, a robusto, good for thirty minutes, his cutter and a lighter, and stepped onto the patio.

"God, I want to see you right now," said Anna. She was lying on her bed.

"I guess that could be arranged, but I am looking at a long session of grading assignments. I generally give more work for my online classes."

"I imagine Mom wouldn't approve, or Tom, since we've had our quality time already today. Mom's standing in the hall, listening. Hey, Mom! It's Michael."

"Anna?" Mandy entered the doorway, straining to see in the dimness. She turned on the light. "Anna? Are you talking on the phone?" The phone was canted on the bed, as if something was holding it up.

"Mom, I'm right here. It's Michael."

"I heard you." She wiped her hands on her pants.

Anna sat up, and the phone moved with her.

Mandy screamed. "Anna? Tom!"

Tom ran from the dining room, where he was sending emails. "God, what is it?" He looked past her into the bedroom. The phone was on the bed. "What happened?"

"She's on the bed. She was holding the phone, to her ear. It was just floating there, but now it's not."

"What's going on?" said Michael.

"I just dropped the phone. It slid through my fingers. I've got my head on the mattress now. Mom screamed when she saw it. Tom's here now."

"Mandy, settle down. It's nothing. You're imagining things." Tom embraced her.

"No, no, I'm not," said Mandy. "I think you made the phone fall. You don't believe. Tom, you have to believe. For my sake, please. Anna?" She moved toward the phone and picked it up. "Hello?"

"Hey," he said. "You okay? I was talking with Anna."

"I saw it, the phone, floating. She was holding it, but Tom made it fall. God."

"Mandy, you have to understand how bizarre this is," said Tom. "I don't want you led on like this."

"No one's leading me on! Dammit! Just do this one thing for me, please." She put the phone back on the bed. "She's talking to Michael. Let's give them some privacy. I'm sorry, Anna."

"It's okay, Mom." She put her ear to the phone. "They're gone. She yelled at Tom. She never does that. I feel bad, for them both."

"It'll just be a matter of time before Tom has to believe. I get it, though. Just give him time." Arty was scratching at the door. Michael put down his cigar, slid the door open, and leashed him. Arty trotted onto the small patch of grass in front of the patio and peed.

"Can we have sex again? I felt so alive. Right now I really do feel like a ghost."

"Wow," said Michael. "I mean if it's a good thing, sure. I kept thinking about you all day, your body."

"You were a gentleman, though, not like an animal. Do you teach tomorrow?"

"Yeah, just one class from twelve to one. I have about two hours on either side before I drop off and pick up the girls. Want to do a late breakfast or late lunch?"

"A late breakfast would be nice, although mom is setting a place for me. I think if you were here with me, I'd be able to eat. Then Tom could see that I'm real. Maybe you can come back for dinner tomorrow too?"

"I think I can. I'll have to check. So, we'll do a late breakfast. I'll pick you up at ten? I have to walk Arty after I drop the girls. Wait. I don't have class tomorrow. Thanksgiving break."

"Super. But then we can go back to your place, right? Hey I can hold the phone again. You're magic." She sat up on the bed.

"Sure, my pleasure."

Anna laughed. "I'll dream about you tonight. I just know it. You have such good hands. I want to feel them on my body again."

"Slow down, or I'll have to make a house call."

"You could crawl in my window. I think Mom and Tom will be gone this weekend. Maybe I could try and cook you dinner. You could bring a nice wine, although we have tons. We could go to the grocery store together."

"That sounds like fun. I'll have to make sure the girls don't need rides, but I can work around it." He scratched Arty's head. He could his hear neighbor Sheila one unit over and up on her patio, talking on the phone with her dad.

"What would you like for me to cook? I can do stir fry with lots of veggies. I'm craving vegetables." She leaned back against two pillows, sitting cross-legged.

"Stir fry sounds perfect. I never get my veggies."

"That's so sad. You're such a bachelor, except you have cats and a dog. Most men don't like cats, I think. Mine is getting so old. She just sits in the window and sleeps."

Arty was barking at a woman walking her dog on the road below.

"Arty, no! Get over here."

Arty ignored him, and he had to haul him in by his leash. "Arty, that's not nice. No barking."

"He's just a dog," said Anna. "You take good care of him. That's a turn-on for me."

"Yeah, he's a barker. Listen, maybe I'll head back inside, get some work done, do the dishes, do some laundry. I'll get you at ten."

"Do you have to go? I get so bored. I'm afraid to walk outside. Maybe I'll call you later, after you get your work done. Need to charge my phone."

"Yeah, sure. Just let it ring. Sometimes I can't find it. You can text too."

"Texting's no fun when you can have the real thing. I feel strong when I talk to you."

"You're right, and thanks. Okay, so bye for now and definitely see you tomorrow." He stood from his plastic chair.

"Okay, I'm frowning for now. Bye."

"Bye, Anna."

He brought Arty in and filled up the water bowl. For a minute or so he played with the cats, feathers on a string that hung from a stick. He was still hungry and opened the fridge. Leonard was right there about to get inside. He pushed him away and grabbed a coffee yogurt. Both Leonard and Tweezer began to look up, mewling for a taste. He couldn't sit down to eat because they would be all over him. He ate slowly, small bites, thinking about what he needed to do. He would wash the dishes and then put a load of laundry in and then clean the litter box. He was out of litter and made a mental note to buy more. Maybe Anna could go with him to the pet store.

With his chores done, he settled in to grade assignments, all online. He didn't really like grading, but it came with the territory. He considered himself very lucky to be an instructor, even though it was on a yearly contract basis. There had been a time just a few years back when he couldn't hold a job, being so depressed and disorganized. And the only difference was the damn meds. He thought about his mom and her mental problems. She'd never admitted she was ill and had lived a life of what he considered misery.

By ten he was through grading and reading for the paper he was writing on depression. It seemed that depression was now being recognized as an illness that merited treatment for life. Active depression created changes in neuronal structure that made it harder to treat as it progressed. He'd first been depressed, depressed enough to think about killing himself, when he was ten years old. In his late teens and early twenties, untreated, he'd soared into sporadic fits of mania, getting fired, buying cars he couldn't afford. He'd been told that he was a rapid cycler, one of the hardest forms of bipolar disease to treat. He could go from despair in the morning to elation in just a few hours, sometimes bouncing within an hour.

Time to write on his latest novel, and he grabbed a cigar from his small humidor that held about forty cigars. He chose a fat one, a gordo, good for an hour, and a Diet Coke. Outside with Arty, he settled into his plastic chair, eager to get started. The evening was cool, about sixty, and he wore what he called his smoking jacket, an old fleece number with holes burned into it. Occasionally he got so carried away with his writing that the cigar would slip out of his mouth.

Without thinking, he opened his laptop and checked his emails, his Gmail and his university account. Facebook and Twitter notifications, which he deleted. A student wanted to know how to cite a textbook for her final paper. He remembered that Thanksgiving was only two days away. He laughed out loud. That would give him more time with Anna. He was wondering if he should call, and his cell rang. He'd forgotten that Anna might call and considered not answering.

"Hey," he said. "Still awake?"

"Yeah, just wanted to hear your voice. To be honest, I don't really sleep."

"I'd wondered about that. So what's up? Still thinking about this afternoon? I am."

"And how," said Anna. "I've never had such a perfect experience like that before. I mean I've been with older men. They're the best in bed, I think."

"Anyone as old as me? I am fifty-two, although I really feel the same as when I was twenty, physically that is."

"You know, you are the oldest guy I've been with. I hadn't really thought about it. Has sex gotten better for you, as you've aged?"

"Ha, well maybe. It's certainly less frequent, less of a drive to have it, but my meds have something to do with it. Pretty common."

"They're good by me. Whatever works. I'm gonna try and pick up the phone . . . Hey, I did it."

"Yeah, we just have to find a way to keep you moving forward."

"That means lots of alone time with me. Lots." She sighed.

"I'm fine with that," he said.

They talked for half an hour, the cigar steadily burning, and he felt that he'd run out of things to say plus he wanted to write. He'd been warm, but now felt chilled and feared that the moment was passing.

"Uh, it's late," he said. "Maybe time to go."

"Really? I guess so. More papers to grade?"

"No, just some writing I need to get in. I try to do five to ten pages a day. It's a ritual."

"Your special time? I get it. So tomorrow at ten, you don't have class?"

"Yeah, we won't be in a rush." He opened his laptop again, and the screen blinded him.

"Okay, Soldier. Can I call you Soldier? Not sure why I thought of that."

He laughed. "Yeah, I like that, and I'll call you . . . what, I can't think of anything. Okay, Jane. Sexy Jane."

"Save it for tomorrow . . . Soldier."

"Okay, I will. Goodnight, Jane."

"Goodnight, Soldier." She laughed.

"Okay, bye."

He sat there for a minute, and Arty was at the sliding glass door wanting in. He stood and opened the door, and Leonard bounded out like a leopard.

"Fuck! Leonard!"

Leonard came to a stop at the grass, as if it was precious, and sniffed, crouching. Michael grabbed him and carried him inside where it was toasty compared to outside. He felt his strength to write waning and kicked himself for wimping out. Back on the patio, he gathered his computer and lighter, noting that he was wasting most of a good cigar. He dropped it into a small green bucket and headed in.

Eleven

Michael had bought a shotgun. Augusta, his first wife, had said that the apartment was in a dicey neighborhood. He had blazed through three years of graduate school at Harvard, changing his major from African Studies to public health at her insistence. What would he do, go back to Africa for another health survey and repeat the mistake he had made before, leaving her alone to worry, fret, and write long angry letters? He became Director of Quality Assurance at an HMO and hated it. He'd had an opportunity to work with the World Health Organization in Geneva but had let it slip through his fingers. He was angry, hopelessly depressed, and then manic like a cannonball, undiagnosed and flailing. He sawed off the barrel of the shotgun, harder than he had imagined due to a steel bolt in the shoulder stock. It was in his sock drawer.

Augusta had left for day shift at the hospital. He showered, dressed, and drove to work in his new truck with a Harvard sticker in the window. He walked with his head down to his office, a cubicle until a real office opened up, and typed a terse letter of resignation. He left his things, including his tie, and walked out for forever. His mind raced, thoughts of death mixed with an urge to hike the Appalachian Trail from Georgia to Maine. He'd been to the southern terminus on Springer Mountain three times on day hikes. Now was the time. Today was the day.

He shed his slacks and dress shirt and tugged on jeans and a t-shirt. He needed hiking boots. He stuffed a pair of socks and underwear into his backpack with a sleeping bag strapped to the bottom. He didn't have a stove or water bottle. He needed hiking boots.

He drove toward Roger's Army/Navy in a blur. He couldn't recall the street and found himself halfway up the ramp to I-20. He said, "Fuck," and backed down, cars blaring their horns. He pounded the steering wheel. He needed hiking boots. He got there and went inside. He found the boots but couldn't decide. A guy with a beard offered to help. He picked a pair, and the guy came back. The boots were a little small, but he didn't care. He paid in cash and left his tennis shoes in the store. He needed food for the hike, lots of food. He didn't want to have to leave the trail and trek to grocery stores or mail food ahead. That had always been the plan. He needed food.

He picked the nearest grocery store, again circling until he found it. He'd never been there before. He pushed a buggy down the aisles. Potatoes. Pasta, lots of pasta. A tube of sun-dried tomato paste. Boxes of macaroni and cheese. Cans of Spam and beef stew, chili. The buggy was heavy. An hour had passed but it seemed like six. He paid in cash. He had eighty bucks left.

In the back of his pickup he jammed the food into his framed backpack. He couldn't make it all fit and just left the cans in the bed. He had to get to Georgia. He didn't notice the sky, the warm air, the cars, the people. He had to get to Georgia, get through Atlanta and then north to Amicalola State Park. He drove as if in a blinding snowstorm. He'd left a note on the computer for Augusta, for whoever. "Have left to hike the AT."

The boots were hurting his feet. They were too narrow. He struggled to get them off, driving with one hand. He had to get to Georgia. He drove, looking again for that damn entrance to I-20. He found it, but soon realized he was going the wrong way. "Shit!" He exited at

Twenty-Second Street and began again, searching, circling, turning, the windshield like a magnifying glass, and then he was on it.

He drove in a roar, the window down, the wind howling. He could see the trail, the steep uphill climbs, the pine trees, the oaks, the maples, the shelters, the people he would meet. There would be no others heading out for a through-hike, already having left in April or May. He would be alone and that would be just fine. He hoped he wouldn't meet a single person from there to Maine. There was a tradition to eat a quart of ice cream at Harper's Ferry in Virginia. He would eat chocolate. He made it through Atlanta but needed gas and stopped. He was driving from memory. He bought twelve dollars' worth and told the cashier to keep the change. "Hey!" she yelled as he left. He had to get to the state park before the gate closed. It was getting late.

Two hours later, off the interstate, he recognized chicken houses and barns and followed the brown signs. He felt as if he had been driving all of his life. He arrived and went into the ranger station. There was a logbook that he wanted to sign, to add his name to the others who had gone before him. The ranger was young and attractive and asked a lot of questions. He panicked and left without a word, not signing the book. She followed him to his truck, asking questions. He ignored her, hefted his pack, and headed into the woods. His pack weighed eighty pounds, and he struggled. Dusk was falling, shadows clinging. He kept checking to see if she was following him. His feet hurt, and he walked stooped over. The weight was all at the bottom of his pack it seemed, but what could he do? He had to reach the campground where the real access trail began.

It took him forty-five minutes to walk a mile uphill and when he reached the gouge in the bank that led up to a few wooden ties for stairs, a panic overtook him. He had 2,180 miles to go, and he couldn't get up the stairs. He struggled then let his pack fall to the ground. He would just go without it. He staggered for a hundred feet and fell to his knees, tears streaming down his face. He had to get home and in a hurry. He gathered himself, passed his pack, and took the road down instead of the trail. It was the steepest road he'd ever seen. It was dark. At a piped spring, he stopped to drink the water but it was so cold. He was shivering. He had to get home.

He had to break into short runs and zigzag down the road, feeling as if he was flying. The sky was like purple ink. At the bottom, he ran to his truck and flung open the door. His keys were in his pack. He roared and bellowed, pounding the hood, but there was nothing to do but go back up the hill. It was now black ink, and he took the road, following the glowing white stripes. He leaned into the hills and curves, his brain gasping. He had to get home!

It took him an hour, and there was his pack in the weeds. He looked and looked and couldn't find his keys. Fuck! He picked up the pack and dumped everything out. He searched the top pocket again, and there they were. He stumbled to the road, as if blind, as if swimming in caustic soda, as if trapped beneath a foot of ice. On he went, stumbling down the hill, blisters on his toes.

He could barely swing his legs into the truck. He cranked it. He backed out and hit something, a garbage can platform. He just kept going, ripping off a board. He turned on his lights and that helped. And then he saw the gate was closed. He had to get home so he exited the vehicle and began walking, shaking from head to toe with the cold. He was dehydrated, his kidneys like hand grenades.

He walked facing traffic, but there was none. Walking, everything seemed different. There was no moon, just stars, just enough light to know that his feet were on the ground. He had to get home, and he walked. He passed a brightly lit house. He could see inside. There was a TV and a man in a recliner. On he walked, feeling his way for what seemed like south. There were signs but he couldn't read them. For two hours he walked, perhaps five miles, and there was a motel, but it was boarded up. He tried one of the doors, and it opened. There was a mattress on the floor, and he fell on it, as dead as dead could be.

How he got back home still isn't clear to him. There had been a deputy, a police car, his wallet, and lots of questions. He thought they were tricking him into going to jail. He had kept his mouth shut and moaned for home, home sweet home, back with his grandparents. A bed and a pillow. Fried okra. Cornbread. Pine straw on the driveway.

"Michael, Mr. Murphy, you're in the hospital," said the nurse. "I'm Roxy, and I'm your nurse.

He pulled the blanket from over his head. The room was empty except for the pallet on the floor. The walls were padded.

"I've got your meds." She held a cup with four pills. She was creamy black with straightened hair, wearing street clothes.

"What are these?"

"Your pills." She handed him a cup of water. "Are you hungry? You've been asleep for nearly a day."

"I don't know. What are they?"

She poured them into her hand and pointed. "Haldol . . . lithium . . . clonazepam . . . Paxil. Your doctor ordered these for you."

"Okay," he said, scratching his head. He took the pills and swallowed.

"It's four in the afternoon. Can you wait for dinner at five or so?"

"Yeah."

"Since you took your pills, we'll let you out onto the unit at dinner. We have a bed for you."

"Okay."

She closed and locked the door.

He laid on his back, staring at the ceiling, the recessed light. There were no smells. He remembered what had happened. His grandparents had brought him. He'd begun screaming as they were taking him to his room. In the unit he had struggled with a nurse. He saw a window and a chair and had thrown the chair at the window, but it hadn't broken. He ran as hard as he could and threw himself against it. They'd tackled him and injected him with something. He had moaned like a dying calf, feeling that he was already dead. And now here he was.

He didn't know it but his grandparents were in the lobby, waiting for him to come around. He closed his eyes and dozed, wondering where Augusta was. What she would think. The door opened, and it was Roxy.

"Michael, come on out, back to the real world. Come on. Dinner's here. Salisbury steak and mashed potatoes, might be from a can."

He was wearing his clothes, jeans and a t-shirt, no shoes or socks, no belt. He felt his pockets, and they were empty. He stood and had to grab his knees.

"You okay?" said Roxy.

"Yeah, dizzy."

She took him by the arm. "Walk with me."

She led him to an empty table with four chairs. He looked around and everything was tan and brown, even his nurse. He laughed. Roxy put his tray on the table. There was a glass of unsweetened tea, a small packet of lemon juice. There was an old man sitting on a couch. There was a young black woman sitting at another table. She waved at him. He waved back. In the halls were a few people. There was a guy with a badge like Roxy's. He was changing the TV channel.

"Thanks."

"You're welcome," said Roxy.

Michael poked at his food and chewed. The meat felt like hard foam, and he nearly spit. The old man on the couch had raised his voice and was shadow boxing. Michael laughed. He ate and drank his tea, his eyes still heavy. He'd tried to hike the Appalachian Trail and had failed. What could he do?

"Let me show you your room," said Roxy. She held a clipboard.

"Okay." He followed her past the couch into the hall, which was very bright. There was a guy sitting on a stool at the end by the door.

"Room six, a private room. There's a bathroom, but you have to let us get your soap and such. If you need to shave, we have to be with you. You're on suicide watch, so we check on you every fifteen minutes. The bathroom door does not lock, on purpose. Lights go out at ten, regardless, even if you're reading. There's no smoking, until you get transferred to the regular unit. Any questions?"

"Where are my grandparents?" He sat on the bed.

"I think they're still here. No visitors allowed in this unit. I'll go down and tell them that you're up."

"Okay. Should I just stay in here?"

"No, come out to the unit, watch some TV."

He imagined his backpack, the tumble of cans and boxes. Where was his truck? He'd quit his job. Where was Augusta? He was on the last rung of a rusted ladder, his hands reaching for air.

He walked into the dayroom and saw the old man there on the couch. He sat as far away as he could. The old man didn't notice him at first, but then did.

"I'll fight you boy. Knock you out." The old man raised a fist at him.

Michael stared at him and smiled. "You like to fight? Me too."

The old man took a feeble swing at him, missing by three feet.

"Hey, Mr. Herbert. Settle down," said the guy with the badge. He was Rudy, the psych tech. He had unruly brown hair, long sideburns.

"I'll teach you fuckers," said Mr. Herbert. "I'm Jack Dempsey. I'll knock you out." He swung at air, nearly hitting himself.

Michael laughed. The old man scowled.

On the TV was the news. A grocery store, a car that had plowed through the plate glass.

Michael folded his arms, keeping his eye on Mr. Herbert. He had to use the bathroom and did that, and then he took an empty chair when he returned. Nothing happened. People walking around in a stupor. He felt heavy and sluggish, but bright inside. He went to bed at eight and slept the entire night.

Over the course of the next week, he was moved to the stepdown unit, but still locked in. Visitors entered through a double door controlled from inside the nursing station. He met his doctor, Dr. Hall, and tried as best he could to piece together what had happened. He felt loose and disjointed, hopeful yet dogged. He took several written tests, including an ink blot exercise and a lengthy MMPI. On day three, he was transported across town to have an MRI of his brain.

He didn't know it, but had been diagnosed with bipolar affective disorder, personality disorder mixed-type, and anxiety disorder. The meds made him feel liquid and gushy. He felt an urge to walk and paced the unit's hallway. His grandparents visited every day, and two friends as well. He had barred his parents from visiting him. He took up smoking with some of the other patients, having his friend Keith bring him cigarillos. There was a metal lighter device attached to the wall of the small outdoor courtyard surrounded by high brick walls, kind of like a car's cigarette lighter. Dinner was at five and on his fourth day Augusta came to visit.

He had walked to the dining room and was waiting. He could see the parking lot through the large plate-glass window, saw her car, saw her walking. She looked tiny and alone. His heart swelled, and he held back tears, waiting, and then she walked through the door, carrying her purse.

She sat across from him, eyes vacant.

"Hey," he said.

"Hey," she said.

She told him that she'd moved out of the apartment and back home with her parents. That his truck had been towed back to his grandparents' house.

They mostly sat in silence, Michael picking at his food. He had few answers and no questions, and she left. It would be two weeks before he saw her again. He returned to his room downcast, feeling his failure, feeling the empty void of his new life. That night he stood and banged his forehead against the wall of his room, counting to 153 before he was stopped.

Twelve

After Michael dropped the girls at school, he drove to Anna's house. Mandy answered the door. He walked in, and Anna was on the couch, waiting with a smile. She looked fresh, wearing a yellow print dress that barely reached her knees, some leggings, and one of Tom's ballcaps.

"Hey," she said, smiling.

"So, what's happened? Did you talk to her last night? The phone didn't ring." Mandy was in jeans and a flannel shirt. She put her hand on his arm.

"She called me last night. She's right there, on the couch. Hey, Anna."

Mandy looked at the couch. "Anna?"

"Mom, I'm right here." She stood, smoothing down her dress.

"We're going for coffee, if that's okay," he said.

"Can I come?" said Mandy. "I'd like to come." She looked at the couch.

"That okay?" he said.

Anna thought. "Sure. But I still want to go back to your place." She came up to him.

"Right. Yeah, we can all go, but maybe we'll drop you off after. She wants to see my pets, the dog, the cats."

"Okay," said Mandy. "Just give me a minute. Anna? Thank you, Anna." She looked frail and hurried to the bathroom.

"I missed you," she said. She pressed her body into his.

He hugged her and kissed her forehead. "Missed you too. You look great. I like the ballcap."

She laughed. "Thanks. I want to take a shower, but can't turn the knobs. My hair's a bit of a mess."

"Okay, I'm ready," said Mandy. She held a large maroon wallet.

"Alright, let's go. Maybe we'll go to a diner. How about Longhorn? Anna, have you had breakfast?"

Mandy gazed around the room.

"How about Frankenstein's? They have really good pancakes," said Anna.

"Okay, shouldn't be too crowded."

"What, what did she say?" said Mandy.

"She wants to go to Frankenstein's, across the river."

"Really? That's fine," said Mandy.

Anna let him lead and followed him onto the porch. "Chilly today."

"Hot tamale," he said.

"What?" said Mandy.

"Just a joke," he said.

He opened the door for Mandy and then Anna. He turned down the radio and drove.

"Mom, I'm glad you came."

"What?" said Mandy. "I heard her. Oh my God, I heard her. It's only when you're around. Anna?"

"She said she's glad you came," he said.

Mandy smiled from the backseat. "Anna, I love you so much, darling. I want to spend as much time as I can with you."

"I know, Mom. And we will."

"Thank you, Anna." Mandy wasn't buckled in, leaning forward, staring at the empty front seat. "You buckled her in."

"Yeah, for now," he said.

Soon, they arrived at Frankenstein's. It was an old house, a bar at night. A porch with stools wrapped around the front. A terrace of three tables just below. They ascended the creaky wooden stairs, smells of food. Inside was warm and bustling, and there was one empty table.

"Hey guys," said the lady behind the counter. She was pouring coffee for a patron at the bar.

He nodded and pulled out the chair for Anna. Already, she seemed more solid, more there. A waitress came over with two menus and introduced herself as Tammy.

"We'll need three menus," he said.

"Sure, got someone else coming," she said. She was skinny in tight jeans. Her t-shirt was knotted at the waist. She grabbed another menu from the bar. "Take your time. I'll check back. Coffee in the meantime?"

"Anna?" he said.

"Sure, room for cream," said Anna.

"Mandy?"

"No, I've had my coffee. Just some orange juice will be fine. Did she say she wants coffee? She loves coffee."

"Yeah. So two coffees, one with room for cream," he said.

"Okay, two coffees and a juice. I can wait till your friend gets here for the other coffee," said Tammy. She had flower-vase hips, a rugged face.

"No, just bring them both," he said.

Anna laughed.

"She laughed," said Mandy. "I know her laugh. Anna?"

"Mom, it's okay. I'm glad you can hear me."

"My God," said Mandy. She reached her hand to touch the empty chair.

Tammy returned with the drinks.

"Just put the extra coffee here," said Michael.

"Y'all ready to order?" said Tammy.

"Gosh, I am," he said. "Anna?"

"Yeah, I'm ready. I want the Polish sausage with scrambled eggs and grits."

"Okay. Mandy?"

"What did Anna order?"

Tammy batted her eyes, shifted her hips.

"She wants the Polish sausage with eggs and grits," he said

"I'll have the same thing," said Mandy.

"Okay, anything else?" said Tammy.

"Yeah," said Michael. "I'll have the shrimp and grits."

"That's a lot of food for two," said Tammy.

Anna was laughing.

"That's okay, there's three of us," said Michael.

"My daughter Anna is here," said Mandy.

"Okay," said Tammy. She scribbled on her notepad.

Mandy coughed. "I know we're having a good time, but I really want to ask a question. Anna, do you mind? If you can't answer, it's okay."

Anna opened a cream and dumped it in her coffee. "Sure, Mom. I probably know what it is."

"She put cream in her coffee," said Mandy. "I saw it." She reached and waved her hand over the empty seat, touching nothing but feeling a tug, resistance.

"Yep, she did," said Michael. "She says it's fine to ask, although you may have heard her."

"I was focused on the coffee. She said it's okay? I just want to know why she did it. Anna, why did you take your . . . life? I so very much miss you. I never wanted to lose you, although we knew you were sick."

Anna sighed. "I just couldn't take life anymore. Nothing gave me pleasure. The only thing I could think of was death, and it drove me crazy. It was like a voice, encouraging me to overdose. I quit taking my meds for three months. I hid the pills. You were great to me, so supportive, but I could never explain my misery to you or anyone. It was just too powerful." A tear came to each eye.

Mandy sat stupefied. She had heard every word, although hard to hear. "Anna, I heard you. Baby, I just wish you had come to us and told us. We could have put you in the hospital until you were better. We had even talked about ECT, and you had said you might try it if things got bad enough."

Michael sipped his coffee, gazing from Anna to Mandy.

"I couldn't bear the thought of the hospital again. They take away everything. You can't shower with the door closed, and everybody else in there is crazy. I just let it get too far, and I shouldn't have quit my meds. I thought that I was getting better, and I felt alive when I quit taking them, but then I just melted. I could tell I was going down. I wanted to get it over with before I collapsed from the exhaustion." She lifted the cup to her lips and drank.

Mandy's jaw went slack, her eyes narrowed as if looking at bacteria through a microscope. She looked around to see if others had seen, but it seemed that they hadn't. "Anna, you have to come all the way back. This is your second chance. Tom and I need you to come back. I'll take really good care of you. Maybe you don't need meds anymore."

"I wondered about that," said Michael. "Do you think you're cured, the depression, the mania?"

"I haven't really thought about it. I've kind of just been in limbo. No thoughts of death, but am I really alive? I mean, I'm a shadow of myself. I just drifted back that first day you came by to take me out. You called me back. From where I'm not so sure."

"Anna. I don't care where you've been, just that you're back, you're coming back." She watched the coffee cup rise in the air.

Tammy was hurrying by and saw. "Whoa, what kind of trick was that?" She kept moving, taking an order to another table.

"I guess I should be more discrete, at least until people can see me. Mom, can you see me? I'm feeling stronger, with Michael here. He's like my dynamo."

Mandy stared. "Maybe a faint outline. My imagination is running wild. I want to see you, but hearing you is miracle enough.

"A Thanksgiving miracle," said Michael.

"You'll be home for Thanksgiving, and . . . and Christmas. I was so dreading the holidays," said Mandy. She sipped her juice, smacked her lips. Her eyes wide, taking in everything.

"It'll be nice," said Anna. "But no presents. Just being back is enough."

Tammy was back. "Did I see what I thought I saw?" She put the hot plates on the table. "This one go here?"

"That's fine," said Michael. "Thank you."

"Looks good," said Anna. She waited for Tammy to leave.

Tammy lingered for a second and then went behind the bar, looking back.

Mandy stared at Anna's plate, smoke rising from the fat sausage.

Michael dug in.

"Okay, here goes," said Anna. She looked around and cut a piece of sausage with her fork, juice spurting. She lifted the morsel to her lips, watching the shocked look on Mandy's face. "It's okay, Mom."

"I can see her hand," said Mandy. "I can see your hand."

"That's great," said Michael. "It's just a matter of time, I think."

"But we have to spend lots of time together," said Anna. "That's the only way it works."

"Michael, you can spend as much time with her as you want. Heck, you can move in with us if you want to. If Tom could see this, he would believe."

"Well," said Anna. "What if I moved in with . . . Michael?"

Michael looked surprised. "I had thought of that. But it could be that your home is needed for this process. I think if Tom would believe, you could possibly develop without me. Maybe develop isn't the right word."

"But I can feel it when I'm with you," said Anna. The fork rose.

Tammy was talking with the cook through the order-up window, looking their way.

"I'm willing to do everything I can. We'll work things out." He took a bite of shrimp and grits. "I love spending time with you."

"You better," said Anna with a wry smile.

"We're depending on you, Michael."

"Mom, your food is getting cold."

"Right. I just can't stop staring. I'm sorry."

They ate and talked, Tammy refilling the coffee cups, eyeing the plate at the empty chair, the food that was missing. They finished, and Michael called for the check.

"Let me pay," said Mandy. She hurried to open her wallet.

"No, it's on me," said Michael.

"No, it's not," said Mandy. "I want to pay for my daughter's meal. Okay?"

Michael handed her the ticket. "Just this time, though."

"I love being fought over," said Anna. She laughed.

"I'll always fight for you, Honey." She slipped her credit card into the sleeve.

Back in the car, it was decided that they'd take Mandy home, and then they would head to his apartment to see the animals. By now Mandy could see a vague outline of Anna. She got out of the car and walked nearly backwards to the porch, waving.

Michael waved and drove. "So you really want to see the animals?"

"Yeah, and see more of you." She rubbed the back of his neck. "You have to make me come to life."

"I think some of that has to come from within. You have to kindle it, nurture it. Like oxygen to a fire."

"You are my oxygen, right?"

"Maybe. It seems that way."

He opened the apartment, and there was Leonard to greet them, Tweezer in the hallway, with Arty on the couch as always.

"Hey, guys," said Anna. She scooped Leonard up and scratched his ears.

"He loves that."

After saying hi to everyone, Anna sat on the loveseat. "Gosh, I need to brush my teeth. I need to leave a toothbrush here. Come sit by me."

He sat next to her, putting his arm around her. "You look smashing today, swimming."

She smiled and pulled his head toward hers. He kissed her, and she pulled him on top, running her hands down his back. A thrill shot through him, and he kissed her deeper, his hands wandering. She pushed him away and stood, offering him her hand. She led him to his bedroom and pulled off her dress. She wasn't wearing a bra and her breasts were just perfect. Soon they were on the bed in a flurry of touching and kissing. He kneeled below her and removed her underwear, watching her legs spread. He was naked, except for his socks, and they coupled, him on top, breathing deeply. It was over quickly, both in the rapture of sex.

"Wow," he said.

"Wow is right."

She pulled him close, running her nails down his back. He arched and groaned. She took his deflating member in her hand.

"We have to do it again," she said. "For my development, as you say."

"It'll take a while, I'm afraid. It's my meds."

"Not your age?"

"Maybe that too." He relaxed and tried to laugh.

It took about ten minutes and soon they were making love again. This time he moved more slowly, responding as she began to gasp, and then relaxing. He fell into a rhythm and moved to his side, pushing her leg over him. For several minutes they moved, in and out, but he couldn't come again and was losing his steam. Finally, he stopped and withdrew, a terrible desire to sleep coming over him.

She cupped his face in her hands and kissed him. "I feel so strong, stronger than ever."

Sex is primal. Powerful medicine, it seems." He ran his hand down her thigh and clutched her bottom. "You're so fucking soft."

"You lucky devil." She kissed him.

"That I am." He relaxed and felt the world swallowing him. Tweezer had jumped on the bed, purring. "Need the restroom first?"

"No, you go ahead. I'm so comfy. But don't be long. Maybe bring me towel to lay on."

He rose from the bed, becoming dizzy, and reached for the wall. He stumbled into the bathroom, feeling empty, feeling complete. He cleaned up and washed his face, looking at himself in the mirror. His eyelids had begun to droop, and he had a small sag beneath his chin.

"I'm back." He gave her a towel and laid beside her. "I feel like we should have a glass of wine, but I think I would fall asleep."

"Silly, it's too early for wine." She was stretched out on her back, her hips curving gracefully. "Rub my stomach, and my breasts."

He turned on his side and did just that, circling her brown nipples. "You really are perfect. I wish I had asked you out, you know, before."

"So, do you think you could have saved me?"

"I don't know, but I did feel guilty. Better late than never, I suppose."

"You know you can never leave me. You're stuck." She laughed. "You brought me back. That's a big responsibility."

He looked worried. "I'm in it for the long haul."

"That sounds romantic. So, I'm a long haul?"

"No, I mean, I'm committed to bringing you back, whatever it takes."

"You better. You're lucky to have a hot young thing like me."

"That's very true," he said. He leaned over and kissed her nipples.

"Look, you're coming back." She touched him there, stroking him.

"Amazing, really. It's your body, just so perfect."

"Maybe next time, we can get really naughty. I've got a few tricks up my sleeve."

"Naughty sounds nice." He kissed her forehead.

"What are you doing tomorrow, for Thanksgiving? Can you come over?"

"'m supposed to drive the girls and Suzanne to see relatives near Birmingham."

"Oh no, really? I thought you would be around."

"I kind of have to go. My dad is expecting me and wants to see the girls."

"Can I come? Maybe they wouldn't even know I was there."

"Wow, that would be interesting. I don't know. I'd have to ask Suzanne. She thinks this whole thing is a big . . . circus of some sort."

"Ask her. You have to. I mean you are divorced. She can't be jealous."

"Maybe so. Okay, well I'll ask her. I'll call and let you know."

She stood, stretching her hands over her head. "Just keep this body in mind. Maybe you could call her now." She walked to the bathroom. "Be right back."

He stood and dressed, looking for his cell phone.

Thirteen

S uzanne had declared him insane when he'd called and asked if Anna could come with them. He'd been persistent, and she'd relented, but only because she knew Anna wasn't real. Claire and Yancy were excited and couldn't wait to see what would happen. "Dad . . . is so interesting," Claire had said.

Michael drove Suzanne's Honda Pilot. They were to arrive at his dad's place at ten-thirty. With the time zone change that meant they needed to leave at nine. He'd had to wrangle with Mandy to let Anna go, since it was a holiday. Anna had been able to eat dinner with them, and Tom had seen with his own eyes. Michael pulled up in front of the house.

"Oh Lord," said Suzanne. "This is gonna be good. I can't believe we're doing this. Are you absolutely sure you're taking your meds?"

Michael squinted. "Ugh, just wait and see." He ran up to the porch and knocked on the door. It was Tom, and he looked shaken, tired, and naked without his ballcap.

"Yeah, come on in," said Tom. He stood with his hands behind his back as if digesting a whole ham.

"Hey, Michael," said Mandy. "We're so excited about last night. I couldn't see her, but her fork and glass moved. Her pork chop and potatoes went bite by bite, and I could barely hear her voice."

Michael looked at Tom.

He cleared his throat. "I can't explain it. I couldn't stop staring. I thought about calling the news or a priest or something."

"He's joking," said Mandy. "Is she here?"

He was watching the hallway at the end of the living room. Anna walked in, wearing tight jeans and a red sweater with a black print of a smiley face.

"Yeah, here she is." A lump formed in his throat. She was gorgeous.

Mandy turned. "Anna, have a great time, Honey. We'll miss you. I want to hear all about it when you come back. Where are you?"

"I'm here, Mom." She touched Mandy's shoulder.

"Oh, my God."

"Hey, you look great," said Michael. "She's wearing jeans and a smiley-face red sweater. Lots of curves!" He laughed.

Mandy laughed with him as Tom looked on, kind of sick.

"Thanks," said Anna. "And you're looking spiffy in your plaid shirt."

"Spiffy. I like that, almost as much as *unique*." He put his arm around her. "The ladies are waiting in the car. We should go. We should be back around five or six. We're not staying too long."

"So, your dad is newly married?" said Mandy.

"My mom died, and the very next weekend he was out dancing with this lady. She's eighty, and he's seventy-nine. It took them all of two months to get married. I wasn't too happy about it, but what can you do?"

"If he's happy that's all that matters, right?" said Mandy.

"I suppose," said Michael. "Okay, we're off!"

"Bye, Anna. Have fun."

"I will, Mom."

"Uh, goodbye," said Tom.

"Bye, Tom."

"It looks like you'll be sitting between Claire and Yancy. The dog is in the back in his crate."

"That's fine." She held onto his arm. "Can you give me a quick kiss?"

"Ha." He leaned down and kissed her soft lips.

"Ooh."

Claire was getting out. "Dad, is she here?"

"Yep, she's getting in now."

"Okay. Should I buckle her in?"

"I don't know, let's watch."

Yancy was pressed against the door on her side, a look of doubt.

"Can you buckle?" said Michael.

"Let me try," said Anna. "Almost but not quite." She was between Claire and Yancy.

"Okay, Claire, buckle her in."

Suzanne was gaping at them.

He closed Claire's door and hopped in. "Everybody set?"

"Yes, Father," said Yancy. "So, she's really here, right?"

"Yes, Dummy," said Claire.

"I'm sorry, Queen," said Yancy.

"Girls, no fighting. Got it?" said Suzanne. She was wearing makeup, which was unusual. "I don't see anything."

"Maybe as time passes you will," said Michael.

"What are you, the Energizer bunny?" She laughed.

"You could say that. Right, Anna?"

Anna laughed. "Exactly!"

"Whoa, I heard her," said Claire. "Did you?"

Yancy looked a little afraid, but laughed. "Yeah."

"God, you've got the girls totally believing this," said Suzanne. She tossed her graying hair back and forth when she spoke.

"Yep," he said. He glanced in the rearview.

They hit the interstate, heading south, and pulled off to buy gas. The girls knew that he would buy himself a Doubleshot Espresso, the Starbucks drink in a can, and he did. It was a driving ritual. Everyone got something to drink, including Anna, who was feeling stronger by the minute.

Gassed up, they continued, the radio playing the Charlie Daniels Band. All eyes were on the bottle of green tea that Claire was holding. Anna reached for it, but it slipped through her fingers.

"Damn," she said.

"Should I just keep holding it?"

"She's not ready," he said. Just put it in the cup holder. He sang along with "The Devil Went Down to Georgia."

"Not very convincing," said Suzanne.

He frowned. "Hey, you have to believe. That's part of it. Don't be a party pooper."

"You're impossible." Suzanne opened up a crossword puzzle. Before the divorce, on their long drives to Florida, she would do crosswords, reading him the clues "A dog jumps into the fire. Six letters."

"Hot dog," he said.

"Really?" she said. "It fits." She penciled it in. "Okay, difficult to understand, eight letters. Obscure? No."

"Um, conundrum?"

"Too many letters."

"Abstruse, right?"

"Hmm, possibly."

He glanced in the back and winked at Anna. She winked back, and they drove, traffic not nearly as bad as he had anticipated. They soon crossed the Tennessee state line into Georgia and then into Alabama.

"Anybody got to pee?" he said. "I do." He pulled into the welcome center, shaded with tall pines. "Anna?"

"Sure," she said.

They piled out, stretching. Suzanne leashed up Mr. Spritely to take him for a short walk.

"Girls, you stay with Anna. Just walk slow. Okay?"

"Yeah, Dad," said Claire. "Maybe she can give us a sign."

Anna walked beside him. "I'll yell if I need help." She took his hand.

"She'll yell if she needs help. Just listen, pay attention. I'd hate to lose her at a rest stop, kidnapped by a trucker."

They entered the building that smelled of disinfectant. An attendant in a brown uniform sat behind a waist-high desk, nodding as people passed. Michael watched the girls and Anna enter the restroom and went to take care of business.

Anna and Yancy had to wait for a stall to open and when one did, they looked at each other.

"Uh, Anna? You go first," said Claire.

"Thanks," said Anna. She entered the stall.

They watched the door close slowly.

"Oh my God," said Yancy.

"Told you," said Claire.

They each took a stall and soon re-emerged, unsure of what to do.

"Hey guys, I'm here," said Anna. She touched Claire on the arm. "Claire?"

"She touched me," said Claire. "She's with us."

Yancy looked on wide eyed, and they walked out. Michael was there waiting on them.

"Hey, you made it," he said.

Anna walked up to him. "I need a hug, and kiss me. I need your energy, bunny with a drum."

"Here?" he said. Motorists came and went. An old man with a walker was struggling by them.

"Yeah. Show them I'm real."

He embraced her, his hands on the small of her back. She leaned up, and they kissed.

"Dad!" said Yancy. "You look crazy."

"Just leave them alone," said Claire.

"Nice," said Anna. "Just hold me tight for a minute."

Michael held her. A woman with a headscarf passed, watching him, grinning.

"If only they could see," he said. He squeezed her and briefly grabbed her butt.

"Frisky," she said. "I like that."

"Ha, we better go. Get on the road. Ready?"

"Okay." She took his hand.

Back inside the Pilot, all eyes again were on the seat buckle. Suzanne gasped, watching the buckle click. Claire and Yancy applauded.

She turned and stared out the front window. "How did that happen?"

Michael was laughing. "The unbelievers among us. You saw it. She buckled herself. She's coming around."

He pulled out and onto the interstate. Suzanne still had a look of disbelief.

"Michael, I don't know if this is good for the girls. I mean, really? What about their friends? You know they're telling their friends, and then they're telling their parents."

"You worry too much, right, Anna?"

Anna shrugged her shoulders.

"Somebody has to worry. What is your dad going to think, and his new wife? What's her name?"

"Shirley."

"Yeah, Shirley."

"They'll freak," said Yancy.

"They'll be like, Dad is insane," said Claire. "I'm already posting." Her thumbs whizzed over her cell phone. "I wish I could see her . . . you. Sorry, Anna."

"That's okay," said Anna. "I know it's hard to understand."

"Am I hearing things?" said Suzanne. She turned down the radio.

"Yes," he said. "You are."

They settled in, the long straight highway rolling across gentle hills. The day was cool but warming, the sky clear with a mustard yellow sun. Within an hour they exited, taking the back way toward Pell City, finishing one crossword and starting another. They were back on the interstate briefly and exited. The house was the first on the left across the bridge, an old rancher that his dad and his new wife had bought and fixed up. Several cars were parked in the driveway, on the grass.

First they had to take care of Mr. Spritely, leashing him to a post on the side of the house, and then they headed to the front door. Michael's dad hadn't seen Suzanne since the divorce, and it had been a few months since he'd seen Claire and Yancy.

"Ready?" said Michael. He held Anna's hand.

"This is exciting," she said.

The door opened. "Hey girls!" and there were hugs all around. They walked inside and a dozen set of eyes looked them over.

"Just stay with me," said Michael.

"What's that?" said his dad. His name was Derrick, and he was tall and skinny with big ears. His false teeth seemed too big for his mouth.

"Nothing," he said. "Good to see you."

"Y'all come on in," said Derrick. "Here's Shirley."

Suzanne introduced herself and gave her a quick hug.

"Y'all just make yourselves at home," said Shirley. "We'll eat in an hour or so."

Everyone stood around, hesitant to speak. Michael had yet to meet most of Shirley's extensive family. He nodded at various faces.

"Y'all come in the living room. Plenty of chairs," said Derrick. He wore his jeans high on his waist secured with a tattered belt.

Suzanne stopped to introduce herself. She was the social one of the group, and got into a conversation with Shirley's daughter Isabel.

Michael and the girls followed Derrick, taking seats. Anna sat beside Michael on the couch, and he put his arm around her, which looked strange.

Derrick oofed into his recliner. The room was paneled, the ceiling made of plywood with trim. A sixty-inch TV on the wall. The room used to be a carport.

"Your arm hurting?" said Derrick.

Michael looked surprised. "No, uh . . ." Anna pinched him. "Ow."

"Well you girls look healthy," said Derrick. "You been exercising?" He laughed.

Yancy and Claire looked at each other.

"Not me," said Yancy.

"Not really," said Claire.

"I been gaining me some weight," said Derrick. "Had my chemo last Thursday. My back and shoulders ache, but I take a pain pill. I probably told you that."

"You look good," said Michael.

"Yeah, Shirley feeds me good. We went dancing last night up in Munford at the high school. Just seniors." He wiped a bit of drool with a handkerchief.

"That's good for you," said Michael.

Suzanne joined them. "This is just lovely, Derrick. Thanks for inviting us down." She moved to sit beside Michael.

"Oops, other side," and he pointed. "Anna."

"Right." She looked annoyed and sat. "You look good, Derrick."

"Yeah, I was just telling them that we went dancing last night. I can really dance." Michael's mother had never once danced, viewing it as sinful.

"That's wonderful," said Suzanne.

They made small talk, and Michael excused himself to check on the dog. Anna followed him outside.

"That's a houseful," she said. "So, your dad has cancer? He doesn't seem to let it get him down."

Mr. Spritely groveled at his shoes, whimpering. He scratched his head.

"Yeah, I know. It's spread to his bones from his prostate."

"That's sad, though." She moved in for a hug. "I need the physical contact."

Michael looked around and hugged her. "Your hair smells nice."

"I actually showered, turned the water on and everything. I locked the door so Mom wouldn't barge in."

"That's amazing."

"It really is."

Claire and Yancy came around the corner.

"Little puppy," said Yancy.

"Is Anna with you?" said Claire.

"Right here." He put his arm around her.

"Dad, that looks strange."

"It's fine," said Anna. She put her arm around his waist.

"Mom's schmoozing it up with everybody," said Yancy. "Think they'll have anything I can eat?" She was the gluten-free one.

"I think I saw some sweet potatoes. You'll just have to pick and choose."

"Want to walk around?" said Anna.

"Hey, we're gonna take a stroll," said Michael.

"We don't know anyone, and there's no kids," said Claire.

A train was coming down the tracks behind an overgrown swatch of land. On the other side of the tracks was a lake slough. The ground vibrated.

"That's mighty loud," said Yancy. "I can't believe he lives so close to the tracks. That would drive me crazy. Are you hugging her? It looks like you're hugging her. Oh my God, Dad. Really?" She laughed.

"Oh let them hug," said Claire. "Want us to leave you two alone."

"Well us lovebirds do need some space." He grinned.

"That's just gross," said Yancy.

"No, come on. Let's go, leave them alone," said Claire.

"Thanks, Claire," said Anna. She buried her head in his chest. "I don't mind them coming with us."

"It's fine." He let go of her and kissed her hair. "Come on."

They moved to a wooden fence on the far side of the yard and followed it to an old outbuilding. There was a commode in the tall grass, a roll of barbed-wire fencing, old boards. They were basically hidden from sight.

"Are you thinking, what I'm thinking?"

He smiled. "What are you thinking?"

"We could go behind this building and do it. Maybe then people could see me."

"Wow, that would be risky, maybe." He was aroused nonetheless.

"Come on. You've never done it outside?"

"Once, in a park at midnight."

"You'll have to tell me about that some time." She laughed and pulled him by the hand. "Got a stiffie?" She put her hand there.

"Yikes. Oh."

He let her lead the way through a patch of junk trees and vines. There was a three-foot space between the fence and the building. It looked as if it would fall on them. She was lifting her red sweater. He was unbuttoning his jeans.

"This is crazy," he said.

"It'll feel so good, though. I'll leave my bra on, okay?" She worked her tight jeans down to her shoes. "Don't make me fall." She pushed down her panties, a tuft of brown hair.

He gazed at her, already throbbing, his hand going to her breast. Down went the jeans and underwear, his member halfway there.

"Do I need to, you know, help you out?" She fondled him.

"Gosh, I don't think so." He waddled closer to her, embraced her, pushed her body to his, kissed her, moved his hands to her soft cheeks and massaged them.

"Feels good." She was touching herself, making herself wet.

Unsteady, he reached and braced himself against the building to keep from falling. He wanted to squat down, but he couldn't with his pants around his ankles.

They stood there wobbly, groping, moaning. The sun was out, feeling warm on their skin.

Back at the house, Suzanne wanted to know where Michael was.

"On a walk with Anna," said Claire. She sat on the seat of an old organ that no one knew how to play.

"Go find him and tell him to come inside and chat. These people want to meet him."

"I'm going with you," said Yancy, looking bored.

"Whatever, you ho," said Claire.

Outside, they looked around but didn't see anything. They walked toward the back where the train tracks were, examining little piles of junk here and there.

"What's that noise?" said Claire. "Shh."

They listened. It was moaning. Yancy held up her hand and pointed to the dilapidated building, her eyes wide.

"Oh my God," said Claire in a whisper. "What if it's not them?"

"Who cares? Let's look."

They took slow careful steps past the commode. Claire hung back, but Yancy moved forward until she peeked behind the building then withdrew like she'd been burned.

"Dad!"

"Shit!" Michael reached for his underwear and fell, scraping his butt on blackberry briars.

"It's them," said Yancy. She looked away.

Claire looked just in time to see Michael standing, pulling up his pants, and there was Anna doing the same.

OMG!" said Claire. "I see her."

Anna was blushing. "We surprised you, huh? Sorry. Don't want to scare you." She tried to laugh.

"Jesus," said Michael. "You can't tell Suzanne. Okay? God, I guess I think I'm eighteen. My apologies, girls."

"Okay, Dad. Gross, but Mom wants you to come inside. Anna, you're so pretty, and young." Claire gawked.

"Anna, I'm sorry I didn't believe you were real," said Yancy. "But, you're real."

They emerged from behind the building, brushing off leaves.

"I'm glad you can see me finally. It's your dad. He does it. It's like magic."

"I like your sweater," said Claire. "Is it on backwards?"

Anna looked and laughed. "Jesus, it is." She pulled her arms inside and rotated it. "Thanks. I feel silly."

"This day just gets more and more interesting," said Yancy.

"For sure," said Michael. "Just forget what you saw."

"I'll try, but I doubt that I will," said Yancy. She laughed and stared at Anna.

"Hold my hand tight," said Anna. "I need you to keep me here."

"Right," and he did that.

They entered through the side door, everyone turning to look. Shirley spied them from the kitchen. "Y'all come on, we're getting ready to eat." She stepped to the end of the island that opened into the dining room. "Who's your friend? She just get here? Sure is a pretty thing. We were gonna fix you up with a lady friend, but I guess you already got one."

Derrick came in from the living room *cum* carport. "Where you been hiding, boy?" He took a hard look at Anna.

"Everyone, this is Anna, my friend. She came with us."

Others peeked in at them, and then there was Suzanne.

"Holy fu . . . fudge! Where? How?" said Suzanne.

Derrick looked confused. Claire and Yancy laughed.

"It's Anna. She rode down with us. You know that."

"Yeah. She must have. I mean she did. Hi, I'm Suzanne. Nice to meet you finally." She extended her hand and Anna shook it, holding tight to Michael with her other one.

"Hey, I guess it just seems like we've never met." She looked around the room happily.

"This your girlfriend?" said Derrick.

"You bet it is," said Yancy.

"Yancy!" said Claire.

Anna looked up and nodded.

"Yep, my new girlfriend, Anna."

Derrick came over and shook her hand. He looked confused.

Shirley put hands to hips. "Alright y'all, dinner's about ready. Y'all come on, and Derrick will say the blessing."

The scattered bodies assembled in the kitchen, flowing into the dining room toward the living room. Derrick said a simple prayer, thanking everybody for coming.

Michael held back, letting others go first.

"You have to keep holding my hand," said Anna. "And kiss me every now and then. Like about now." She tilted her head, and he kissed her.

Michael smiled and introduced himself to a daughter and son of Shirley. He squeezed Anna's hand. After the crowd in the kitchen thinned, he led Anna there. Dishes covered the counter and island. There were two crockpots, one with green beans and another with a pork roast.

He leaned toward Anna. "We'll have to let go to get our plates."

Anna looked afraid. "Kiss me, like every minute or so, just kiss me."

"Okay." He kissed her.

"He likes her," said Shirley, showing off her dentures.

They filled their sturdy paper plates with turkey, macaroni and cheese, stuffing, deviled eggs, green beans, and then turnip greens for Michael. His dad had saved them a place at the dining room table, but it was one chair short.

"We'll share a chair," said Anna. "You'll be right up against me."

"Okay," and they sat.

"Let's get you a chair," said Derrick. He was at the head of the table sitting next to Suzanne. Claire and Yancy were across from her. Shirley would come soon for the last seat.

"No bother. We're fine. We like it this way," said Michael. He tried a vague laugh and pecked at a green bean.

They ate and talked, and thankfully nothing political came up. His dad was a staunch conservative. He had a bumper sticker on his car: marriage = one man + one woman.

"This sure is good, Shirley," said Michael. "These greens are yummy."

Suzanne gave a firm second, as did Claire and Yancy.

"Thanks. It's a little bit of everybody here, although I made the greens."

"It's delicious," said Anna. "Kiss me," she whispered.

He leaned and kissed her on the mouth. Her tongue darted into his mouth, and he looked surprised.

"Couple of love birds," said Derrick. He chewed with his mouth open, grinning from ear to ear. "So, y'all are divorced? Is that right?"

Suzanne answered. "Yep, I know it looks a little funny, but we are. Sometimes I forget."

"Yeah, just a little strange," said Derrick. "She sure is a pretty girl. What's your name again?"

"It's Anna. Thank you."

"Yeah, we've been dating about two weeks now," said Michael.

"Got'cha a newbie, cowboy," said Derrick. He licked his spoon of peach cobbler. Shirley reached and dabbed the corner of his mouth with a napkin. "She takes care of me." He grinned.

The plan was to leave an hour or so after dinner. Michael just didn't have it in him to forge new ties with Shirley's family, and really only cared about seeing his dad, and quick visits seemed best. Growing up with his parents had been hell, but that was water under the bridge.

They wound up outside in the sun, standing and sitting on the small front porch. Isabel took the stage, telling one-liners about the antics of her four kids. She was thin, had wiry black hair, and wore jeans and a red-striped shirt. Apparently the twelve-year-old was on birth control. Isabel gestured and postured, settling into what seemed a stand-up routine. Michael held tight to Anna, draping his arm over her shoulders, and all seemed relatively well, until he had to go to the bathroom. His meds often kept his stomach upset, that and he had eaten too much. Tears squeezed from his eyes.

Anna stood, fidgeting, folding and unfolding her arms, waiting for Michael to return from the bathroom. Shirley's son Jarvis was giving her approving looks. Isabel was on a rant now about her oldest daughter who had a kid, not picking her up from school when she was sick. Isabel had had "to haul ass down there" and take poor little Pumpkin home, where she found her daughter passed out on the couch topless.

Claire and Yancy milled about, catching snatches of the solo show, checking their phones, asking Suzanne if it was time to go. She seemed enthralled by Isabel's performance.

It was Jarvis who noticed first, that Anna seemed to be fading. He adjusted his ballcap to block the sun and took a good long look. And then Claire noticed, able to see right through her. She grabbed Anna by the hand, but it slipped through.

"Hurry," she whispered. "You're fading."

Anna said "Uh oh" and followed Claire around to the side of the house where stood Mr. Spritely, wagging his tail. Yancy followed. "I need Michael. Can you check on him?"

Jarvis had followed and was pretending to walk to the road, craning his neck at them. Yancy figured it out and stood in front of Anna, getting fainter and fainter.

"That guy's staring," said Anna. "He knows."

"Just stay there," said Yancy. She was a head taller than Anna. "This is crazy, crazy."

"You're telling me," said Anna. "I wish he would hurry. Am I still here?"

Yancy swallowed her gum and coughed. "Oh my God, just barely."

Jarvis had had enough, whiskey or no whiskey. He hitched his pants and walked that way. He was blonde, about six feet, and lived in an underground house on some property Shirley owned. He lit another cigarette. Anna was gone.

Yancy turned. "Hey."

"That girl, where did she go?" said Jarvis.

"I'm still here," said Anna.

"What the . . ." Jarvis scratched his belly and looked up into the maple tree. "I saw plumb through her and now she's gone."

"Huh?" said Yancy. "Who's gone?"

"That girl that your daddy brought."

"Uh, that's Suzanne, my mom."

"No, not her, that young girl with the brown hair. His girlfriend." He had his hands on his hips as if serving a warrant. "Something's going on."

Michael came jogging out of the house with Claire on his heels. He stopped and surveyed the situation. Anna was behind Claire.

"Hey," he said to Jarvis. "I never introduced myself. I'm Michael, Derrick's son."

"Right. Name's Jarvis. Shirley's oldest." His t-shirt was too small, his arms tan.

Anna drifted toward Michael and took his hand. "Kiss me, stranger."

"Oh," said Michael. He kissed her.

"What the hell?" said Jarvis. He watched as the faint outline of Anna reappeared. "I'm seeing things. No, I'm not. But maybe I am."

"It's the sunlight," said Michael. "I guess you noticed. All's well, right?"

Jarvis put his hands in his pockets and left, returning to the porch where Isabel had moved on to a parody of a cashier at the grocery store. He held his tongue, waiting for a chance to speak, but that took another minute and by that time, Michael had reappeared with Anna fully intact. Jarvis mumbled to himself and lit another cigarette.

Fourteen

The drive back was lively, talk turning to Jarvis and the look on his face. They arrived at Suzanne's house and parted ways, Michael taking Anna home in his Corolla. She had faded but with Michael's hand on her knee, there was a faint image.

"Want to grab a bite to eat?" said Michael.

"Goodness no. I'm still stuffed. The food was good."

"Yeah, me too, I guess. Were those turnip greens a bit gritty to you?"

"I didn't have any, just the turkey and sweet potatoes and some stuffing. Maybe we should swing by your place? Flesh me out for Mom and Tom?"

"Hmm, I guess I need to grade some assignments."

"You're on break, silly. It's a holiday. You don't have class tomorrow do you?"

"No, forgot about that."

"So?"

"Sure. Let's do it. I guess we need to finish what we started behind that damn barn or whatever it was." He laughed and squeezed her thigh.

"Right on, Soldier. I wish I could sit right next to you."

"If I still had my old Monte Carlo, you could."

"There's still a lot I don't know about you, Soldier." She had faded completely, although he could still see her.

"Soldier."

"Soldier."

They arrived at his place and said hey to all the animals and took Arty on a short walk. He peed and pooped like a champion. Michael was seriously worried about being able to perform twice in one day and tried to pump himself up.

"Carry me, Soldier."

He scooped her into his arms, her legs hitting the floor lamp. "Where to, my princess?"

"Do you have to ask?" and she was kissing his neck.

He turned sideways to go down the hall. "My bed's a wreck."

"Let's wreck it some more." She fell on the bed and pulled him on top.

They settled into a long embrace, kissing deeply, clothes coming off one piece at a time until they were naked. He was limp as he had feared but she went to work, bringing him to full attention.

"Me on top," and she mounted him. "Get ready, Soldier." She moaned as they became one, and she gently lifted up and down, gazing into his eyes.

"It's gonna be a long ride, princess. But I'm ready."

And they moved with each other, ground into each other, pausing for long slow kisses. He was still holding his own, and she had climaxed twice, sweating.

"Slap my behind," and he did, and they rolled in the sheets, twice pushing Leonard from the bed.

"Soldier, I want you to come. God, you make me horny." She slid away from him and went to her stomach, raising up on her knees. "In all my glory," and she guided him inside.

He gazed at what he had and considered himself a lucky man, but could feel his inertia waning. He concentrated on her beautiful behind and made his most valiant effort, their skin slapping. It took several minutes, but soon they were both just right there, and then that explosion of sex. Panting, he slowed, gripping her thighs, going for as long as his body would allow, and then falling onto the bed.

"Jesus," he said.

"Tthat was super, my strong soldier. God, I could do it again."

"I'm afraid, I'm spent. Have to walk around the block, smoke a cigarette." He caressed her back.

She turned toward him, her breasts falling to the bed. He circled her nipple, sighing.

"I'm done," he said. "I can pleasure you in other ways, if you need it."

"I guess I can't be greedy. Let's hurry back so Mom can see me."

And they dressed in a hurry, Michael donning a ballcap. They had one last embrace and were out the door.

"Drive a little faster. I'm excited. Here, hold my hand."

He drove with one hand, coming to partial stops at stop signs. It took him twenty minutes, but she was still there, beaming and ready. Before he could fully stop, her door was open, and she was running for the house. She tripped and fell, scuffing her palms.

"Mom!" She knocked on the door and pushed inside. "Mom!"

Mandy emerged from the kitchen, shocked. "Baby!" She nearly went to her knees.

They embraced and began crying. Tom had left to meet some friends at a bar.

"Baby Girl. How? What? You look so . . . natural." They hugged again, but she was already fading.

"Hello?" said Michael.

"Group hug!" said Anna.

The three stood there hugging, laughing. Michael worried that they smelled of sex.

"I just can't believe my eyes," said Mandy. "It's too good to be true. Thank you, Michael. This is the best gift, and on Thanksgiving."

"My pleasure," said Michael.

"Hurry, let's sit down and talk," said Mandy. "What did you do today?"

"So," said Anna. "We had sex behind a barn. And we ate some really good food. How's that?"

Mandy paused. "Really? I mean, you did? Okay. I guess you can do that. Whatever it takes." She gave Michael an uncomfortable look.

"Mom, it's all good. I'm alive and well. Michael is my soldier. That's his new nickname. He's fighting for me."

Michael blushed. "All in the call of duty, ma'am." He laughed.

"You're slipping away," said Mandy. She reached to hold Anna's hand, but it passed through.

"Don't worry, Mom. I'll still be here. Michael come beside me."

Michael sat beside her, his arm around her, kissing her, and the fading halted.

"Honey, you're just a shadow, but that's a miracle in itself. I wish Tom was here."

"I think as time passes, I'll get stronger, as long as I have my soldier boy," said Anna.

"Michael, promise to stay with us on this, okay?" said Mandy. "You're my only hope."

"I couldn't do otherwise." He squeezed Anna hard, kissed her cheek.

They talked, Mandy bringing wine, as Anna slowly, slowly faded away, but her voice remained.

"Hallo!" and it was Tom. He'd had a few.

"Tom! She's here. I could see her. We hugged. They had a great time today, she and Michael."

"Where is she?" He kicked off his tennis shoes.

"Between us, on the couch."

"Hey, Tom," said Anna.

Tom stared at the couch. "Okay, that's the second time. Anna? Why can't I see you?" He took the armchair across from them.

"It's Michael. You just can't see her. Like now, but you heard her?" said Mandy

"Tom, it's really me."

Tom scratched his head. "I really don't know what to do. Maybe I need a glass of wine. Anna . . . I love you." He went to the kitchen and returned with a new bottle. "You guys need a pour?"

"Yes," said Mandy. "Michael?"

"Oh just half a glass is fine. Thank you."

Tom poured, staring at the empty spot between them. "This is really hard. I want to shout hallelujah, but I can't. I don't know why. How is this possible even? Michael?"

"It's just a matter of desire. I wanted to go out with Anna before, before she went away, but I blew my chance, and now she's back. But I think it took you guys as well, your longing for her. Anna is strong, despite what she may have thought before. She can do anything. We just have to believe is all."

"Michael, kiss me when you say that," said Anna.

He kissed her cheek.

"So you just kissed her?" said Tom. He finished off the glass and poured more.

"I did."

Mandy winked. "And that's not all from what I hear."

Tom frowned. "This is over my head. Anna, just tell me how you are. What we can do."

"Like Michael says, just believe. Like right now, I can feel myself getting stronger. I feel you, Mandy, and Michael." The vaguest shadow was forming.

"Tom, look now. She's back."

Tom stared, his lips parting. "I see it, Anna, dear." He sank back in the chair. "I'm just at a loss."

They sat and talked, all eyes on Anna's dim image, finishing the wine and opening another bottle. Tom had excused himself to go smoke, and Mandy had her arm around Anna.

"I should be going," said Michael. "Work to do."

Anna tried to pinch his leg. "You need to stay, just a while longer. You still have wine."

"I'll finish and then go. You and Mandy and Tom need some alone time. I'll call tomorrow. I promise. I might have to take one of the girls shopping. Ugh, I hate Black Friday. I do all of my shopping online." He tousled her hair. "Goodnight, my beautiful." He took his last gulp of wine.

Mandy stood and hugged him. "Thank you, Michael. This is so special. You're a godsend."

"My pleasure," said Michael. He stood and helped Anna to stand. They gave each other a good squeeze. "Alright, good night y'all." He picked up his cap and headed out, passing Tom on the porch.

"You leaving?"

"Yeah. I'll call tomorrow."

"I hope you're in this for the long haul, good buddy. There's really no choice. None of this can be undone." He blew smoke.

"Yeah, I get it. I can't let Mandy, or Anna, down. You've got my word." He shrugged his shoulders in the chill air.

"Right," said Tom. "Good night." He turned to go inside.

"Night."

Despite the cold air, Michael drove with the windows down, considering his position in the affair. He was getting anxious at how deep he was in the situation. He had an appointment with his therapist, a nurse practitioner, on Saturday at ten, and wondered what she would make of the story. Maybe he should just keep quiet about it, but now he was feeling vulnerable, as if he was holding a very heavy weight over his head in a room full of babies. He desperately needed to get back to his writing, his novel, and made up his mind to do so.

Back home, he greeted the animals and took his meds. One was an antipsychotic that held the thoughts of death and self-harm at bay. The thoughts overpowered him, reducing him to gelatin, but the pills worked wonders. He briefly wondered if Anna was just a figment of his imagination, but that wasn't possible. She was real. He had sex with her.

After cleaning the litterbox and feeding the cats, he put on his ratty fleece jacket, grabbed a fat cigar, a beer, and his laptop, and settled into the cold plastic chair on the patio. He tried to clear his mind, but he could only think of Anna, her body, her smile. He shook his head, as if fending off cobwebs and concentrated, reading the last page he had written. The novel was based on his own history of mental illness. In the book, the protagonist was a young boy of four. His mom had put him in a daycare, which was a cover for a whorehouse. Slowly the words came, the keys tapping when hit, the backlit keyboard and screen the only light. And he managed three pages before hitting a dead end. What happens next? It was always about what happens next.

He got cold pretty quick and decided to call it a night, puffing on the robusto. As usual he turned on the TV to decompress. Writing made his brain crave mundane things like hoarders or couples looking to buy a villa in Mexico. Leonard jumped in his lap, soon followed by Tweezer, both purring and licking their fur. Before he knew it, an hour had passed, and he picked up the book he was reading for his research paper, little sticky notes protruding like fins. Images of Anna. Of Mandy weeping. Of Tom scratching his head. He couldn't read and decided to call it a night, bringing Arty to bed and pulling the blanket over his head.

The next day, his phone woke him at six-thirty. He usually slept to seven-thirty, getting ready, and then taking the girls to school, but it was a holiday. It was Anna.

"Hello?"

"Michael? Did I wake you? I'm sorry. You sound so sleepy."

"No worries."

"Michael?"

"Yes?"

"Mom and Tom can see me this morning, just faintly, but they can see me. Wow, I'm getting real."

"Wow is right. Did you do anything different?"

"No. But I was able to pick up the phone and dial, too."

"Huh, that's great. I wish I could see the look on Mandy's face. Is she excited?"

"Oh yeah, and Tom, too. He said that maybe I wouldn't need you anymore, but I set him straight. I kind of feel bad now."

"I'm here for you as long as you need me." He wondered if that was the right thing to say.

"I know, and I love you for that. Did I just say that I love you? I guess I did."

Michael thought. "Uh oh, the L word." He felt like hiding.

"Michael, what do you mean?"

"I mean that's a serious word, right? I love being with you. You're becoming a part of my life."

"But you can't say it?"

"Gee, I do love you, that's true . . . but."

"But what?"

"Nothing. I'm just waking up."

"Okay, sleepyhead. I forgive you for now. Are you going shopping today? With Claire and Yancy?"

"I almost forgot about that. Haven't talked with them yet. Would you want to go? It would be weird if you were just a shadow, though. We would cause a scene."

"You don't want me to go?"

"No, no. What the hell. Let people gawk. Maybe you'll flesh out when I get there. Claire and Yancy would love for you to go. They're fascinated, although Yancy is skeptical."

"Yeah, I could tell. Call me back, okay? Maybe by nine?"

"Sure, okay. They should be up by then." He scratched Arty's neck. Leonard was playing with a loose feather in the hallway, Tweezer looking on with wide eyes.

"And I may have a surprise for you," said Anna.

"Really? What?" He yawned and scratched his belly.

"Can't say. It's a secret. You'll find out."

He was fully awake now, his mind racing. "Okay. Surprise me."

"I will. I'll let you doze some more. I'm going to see if I can eat a bagel with cream cheese. I'm starving."

"Sounds good. Okay, I'll call you back."

"Bye, Soldier." She laughed.

"Bye."

He laid on his back, wondering if she wanted to move in with him. How would that work? And soon he was asleep again, dreaming, dreaming.

Fifteen

He awoke again right at nine and sat up, thinking he'd missed taking Yancy and Claire to school. He wondered what Anna's surprise could be. He realized it was a holiday and relaxed then remembered he needed to call. When Suzanne answered, she was already out with Claire shopping. They'd been at it since seven that morning, but Yancy was home and might be interested. He called her, and she was reluctant until she heard that Anna was going.

It took until eleven, but he and Yancy picked up Anna. As promised, she was visible, but ghostly to Yancy, although vivid to Michael. Mandy didn't want Anna to leave, but relented with Michael's promise to have her back by the afternoon.

"Okay, bye, Baby. Love you bunches," said Mandy. "Michael, take my credit card, in case she wants to buy some presents."

"Love you too, Mom."

Michael took the credit card.

"It was a great Thanksgiving, and it's going to be a great Christmas too," said Mandy, beaming.

Michael opened the door for Anna, and Yancy got in the back. The day was cool and dry, the drought continuing, although most of the fires had been quenched. Yancy wanted to go the mall, which Michael thought was a bad idea, but he relented. He hated shopping, especially at malls, and on Black Friday to boot. Traffic was slow on the interstate and parking at the mall was like looking for a business card in a cornfield.

They entered through Barnes and Noble, and it was packed. Yancy wanted something from the Starbucks and that was the first line of the day. Anna kept her vague shape, showing stronger when Michael held her hand. They had gotten a few looks, but nothing serious.

"Want something?" said Michael.

"No, I'm fine," said Anna.

The blenders were grinding amid the names of customers being called. "Phil! Iced chai latte!" The line crept forward.

Yancy was quiet, shouldering her bag. Anna was in jeans and a light wool sweater of purples and reds and browns. Michael wore jeans as well with a long-sleeve t-shirt. He folded his arms, slightly chilled.

Soon they ordered and with their drinks walked into the mall proper. Michael held his black coffee with one hand and Anna's hand with the other, steering her clear of clumps of shoppers. Yancy wanted to look at makeup, and they headed to Sephora. The sales clerks were heavily made up, one like a cat. Yancy showed Anna items on her gift list, an Urban Decay palette, a makeup brush, eyebrow tweezers.

"She's a makeup junkie, just like me," said Anna.

"I love it," said Yancy. "But I keep it simple."

They talked foundation and highlighting, Cupid's bows, and T zones.

"This is my face of the day," said Yancy, swatching a nude blush.

Michael just followed, steering Anna through the crowded aisles.

"Can I help?" said a young clerk. Her makeup was thick and bold. She looked just this side of evil. She had noticed Anna. "How do you do that?"

Michael was confused, but then got it. "It's like full body makeup, made to fade."

Anna laughed. "It's true."

Yancy smiled. "I think we're good. Dad, maybe we should go."

"Don't you want to buy something? But don't get the Kat Von D product. I'll order it online.

"Maybe the lip gloss," said Yancy. She worked her way back to another aisle. There was only one left, and she grabbed it.

The clerk had followed them and was whispering to another young lady, nodding their way.

"Anna, you want to buy something?" said Michael.

"Nothing here."

They entered the long checkout line.

"What about that surprise you were talking about?" said Michael.

"It's coming. We have to go to a drugstore first."

"A drugstore? There's not one in the mall."

"Yeah, just any drugstore will do."

"Okay."

Yancy paid, and they left, moving back into the swirls of humanity pounding the mall beat. They strolled and browsed, winding up in the food court. They each ordered chicken teriyaki, piled with stir-fried cabbage. There was nowhere to sit, and they waited until a table opened up. It was so busy that no one noticed the shade of Anna, the fork lifting to her mouth. Back in the bookstore, Michael couldn't resist and bought a book each for the girls and Suzanne before heading back to the car.

"So, to the drugstore?" Michael backed out of the space.

"Sure, you pick," said Anna.

"Go to Walgreen's, near the house," said Yancy.

"To look at more makeup, right?" said Michael.

"Father, you know me so well."

The fifteen-minute drive took them thirty, but soon they pulled into the parking lot.

"Anna, can I show you some product?" said Yancy.

"Sure," said Anna. "But first, a little whisper for your dad." She leaned toward him, cupped her hand, and told him what she needed.

"God, are you sure?" He stepped out and opened the door for her, his face drained. "It can't be possible."

"Are you afraid?" Anna smiled.

"Yeah, I guess I am."

They walked in and Yancy headed to the makeup with Anna in tow, leaving Michael. He wasn't sure where to look and walked up and down the aisles until he found it, a pregnancy test kit that cost $8.97. He decided to get two, just to be sure, and held the boxes like baby chickens.

A man was looking at the condoms. "Big day, huh?" He had a long beard.

"Yeah, I guess. Could be a real shocker."

The man laughed. "Guess you should have bought some of these."

"Yeah, right." Michael moved on, his pulse quickened. The man had broken some cardinal rule, commenting on his goods, like talking to a stranger at the urinals. He felt a bit dizzy and found Anna and Yancy examining lipstick.

"You got it. Two?" said Anna.

"What?" said Yancy.

Michael held the boxes behind his back. "Got it."

"There's no bathroom here. Can we go by your place?" said Anna.

"What's going on?" said Yancy.

"Nothing. Here I'll go pay, while you guys look." He hurried off to the register.

The cashier looked at him without smiling and rang him up. He swiped his card and took the bag, his hand shaking.

"It'll be just fine," said the cashier, an older woman with graying hair.

"Thanks." He went and stood near the exit beside a display of soft drinks. Soon, Anna and Yancy joined him.

"Dad, you look pale. You okay?"

"Yeah, fine."

Anna poked him in the ribs. "He'll be fine. I'm sure of it. Let's go."

He drove to the house, dropping off Yancy. "Love you, Honey."

"Bye, Dad. Love you too. See you, Anna."

He waited until she was in the house and then headed for his apartment, his hand on Anna's knee.

"I'm so excited," said Anna. "What if it's true? What will you do?"

"Jeez, I don't know. It just doesn't seem possible, but maybe it is."

They arrived and Anna tugged him down the stairs to the door.

"I've got to pee really bad," she said.

Inside it smelled faintly of cigar smoke. His new heavy-duty air filter did a pretty good job of keeping the odor down. Arty was on the couch wagging his tail, the cats sleeping, probably in the spare bedroom. She took the bag from him and hurried into the bathroom.

"Come on!"

"You want me to watch?"

"Yeah, just be with me."

She dropped her jeans and panties and sat on the commode, opening the box. If she was pregnant, there would be two pink lines. She peed, stopped, and then held the stick between her legs and resumed. She handed the stick to him, like handing off a baton and finished, standing and zipping up.

"Come on!" She walked to the living room and sat on the couch, patting the cushion next to her. "Sit. Cover it with your hand for three minutes. I'm about to lose it."

He did as he was told, staring at the sliding glass door. Arty was snuffling his legs, smelling where they'd been. Leonard appeared and walked through with tail erect. One minute, two, three.

"I think it's ready," said Anna. She clapped her hands.

"Dear God, Jesus Christ," said Michael. "I can't believe this. Ready?"

"Yeah, ready."

"God." He removed his hand. Two pink lines.

"Oh!" said Anna. "I knew it. That's why I'm more visible. I've got you growing inside me." She snuggled into him.

"Jesus, Mary, Mother of God." He put his arm around her. "I guess this changes everything."

"What do you mean? This is great. You love me, right? I mean we did have sex without a condom."

"I just . . . never expected this. I don't know what to say."

"Don't say anything. Just kiss me."

He kissed her. She moved in closer and kissed him back harder. He placed the plastic stick on the coffee table, moving as if in a dream. He responded as she kissed his neck, his hand moving to caress her shoulder. Soon, they were making out on the couch, clothes coming off. She went to her knees, giving him a blowjob, coaching his limp member into action.

"What's wrong, Soldier?"

"Maybe I'm in shock. Maybe my meds. It just may take a while."

She went back to work, going this way and that, taking him deep. He moaned and squirmed, unable to sit still. She managed to coax him into an erection, and they moved onto the rug, taking a pillow with them. It only took a couple of minutes for her to come, but he was struggling, his stomach muscles tiring. But on he went, kissing her, whispering into her ear until he collapsed in complete exhaustion, his belly to hers, sweating.

"You okay?" she said.

"Yeah. I'm sorry I ran out of steam." He caressed her breast, pushed back her hair.

"You're fine. I'm just so horny. I feel so alive. Thank you for being so sweet. I love you." She touched his face.

He coughed. "That word again. Don't be angry. I mean I do love you, but it's so soon to be saying so, right?"

She pouted just a bit, standing, her sleek body enveloped in the light from a single lamp. "Either you do or you don't. Life is short. Life is dangerous. Maybe it's time for me to go home."

"Don't be mad at me."

"I'm not mad. Just disappointed is all." She found her panties then slid on her jeans. "You going to get dressed?"

"Yeah." He stood with a groan, his knees popping.

She headed to the bathroom while he dressed and reemerged, her hair combed back. "I'm sorry for being snippy. I mean I'm pregnant for God's sake, with your child. I couldn't be happier."

"Maybe it will be a boy. Haven't had a son yet." He tried to smile.

"But I want a cute little girl. I've always wanted a girl. But, whatever it is will be just fine."

"I guess we're assuming that you can actually give birth. It would be a major miracle, right?"

"At least we're past step one. I swear I can feel it inside me, growing, growing. It makes me more real."

"It certainly seems to have had some effect. Do you think Mandy will be happy? And what about Tom? Will you tell them today?"

"Of course I will. She might be puzzled. Tom is a different story. We'll just have to see." She moved in for a hug. "Squeeze me, Michael. Hard. Harder."

He held onto her tightly, kissing the top of her head. "What an adventure. How will we ever explain this to like our friends and other relatives? They'll think we're crazy, that it must be some kind of hoax."

"Who cares? Let's just be happy. You ready?"

"Yeah, let me find my keys."

They soon arrived at Anna's, her face flush with excitement. Mandy was in the yard, pouring water into the birdbath. She waved, a big smile on her face.

"Mom!" and Anna ran to her. There was a neighbor in the yard next door, looking on with curiosity.

Michael walked up.

"Anna, you're, like, fully visible! Oh my God. I was getting worried. Did you get some shopping done?"

"Not really, mostly just looking," said Michael.

"Mom. I have some news. Maybe we should go inside and sit down."

"What? Oh my, what is it? You're not moving out are you? You can't do that."

"That has occurred to me." Anna took Michael's hand. "Come on."

Inside they met Tom who had a glass of wine. He'd been watching football. He looked shocked to see Anna.

"Holy smokes, you guys. What's different? Anna?" He moved close and hugged her, his face drained of blood. "Gosh, I can feel you. I can see you. Jesus, this just gets stranger."

"It's Michael. He's my soldier. You guys sit down."

"She has some kind of news," said Mandy. "I hope it's good news."

Michael and Anna sat on the couch, Tom and Mandy in chairs. Anna gazed around at the faces. "First, Michael has to kiss me."

"Oh? Okay." He kissed her on the lips, and she lingered there.

Mandy coughed. "Anna, tell us. You're making me crazy here. Do I need to get a drink first?"

"No, you can have a glass of wine after I tell you," said Anna. "Ready?"

"We're ready," said Tom. He leaned forward.

"Mom, Tom . . . I'm . . ." She looked at Michael. "Pregnant." She grinned.

Tom sat back straight. Mandy's eyes grew, as if watching her daughter give birth in the living room. Michael just looked at his feet, clearing his throat.

"What?" said Mandy. "How can that be possible? I mean I know how it happens, but with you . . ." She looked to Tom for help.

"Oh my God, how do you know?" said Tom.

"I took a pregnancy test." She fumbled in her purse and brought out the plastic stick. Two pink lines."

"Wow," said Mandy.

Tom stood. "This is just too much. I feel like I'm dreaming, maybe having a nightmare. Michael, you've gone too far. This can't possibly be good." He walked through the dining room to the kitchen.

"Baby," said Mandy. "I'm happy. If this is what's best, then I'm happy. But it is hard to grasp, right?"

"Maybe I should go," said Michael.

"No, stay," said Anna. "Tom will cool down. He just needs more wine."

"Speaking of wine. Tom! Bring the wine and glasses. We have to celebrate, right?"

They sat there looking at each other. Anna's old cat sauntered in and walked past as if nothing had happened. Tom returned with a bottle and glasses. He placed them on the coffee table, shaking his head.

"Going outside for a smoke," he said. "Need to think."

Mandy took charge and poured three glasses, glancing at the label.

"We'll have to think of names. Is that too soon?" said Mandy.

"That's right," said Anna, and she punched Michael in the ribs. "Boy names and girl names. I want to be surprised."

"You know we'll have to find you a doctor. And you don't have health insurance anymore," said Mandy. "But, don't worry, we'll take care of the bills. This has to go as smoothly as possible. You just seem so vivid and alive, almost like before . . . before it happened." Tears welled in Mandy's eyes.

"Maybe I should go out and talk with Tom," said Michael. He stood.

"That might be good," said Mandy. "So what's your favorite boy name?"

Michael opened the door to the cool air. Tom saw him and stubbed his cigarette in a glass ashtray.

"This takes the cake," said Tom. "Not that I actually believe it. Are you a magician, a wise man, an alien imposter? What are you?" He lit another cigarette, holding the pack out to Michael.

"Thanks. I'm just a guy who saw an opportunity. To help, to bring her back. It just occurred to me that it was possible, and I acted."

"All that we see or seem is but a dream within a dream," said Tom.

"Edgar Allen Poe," said Michael. "The world is my will and my representation."

Tom smirked. "Who said that? Hitler?"

Michael laughed. "Schopenhauer."

"Deep," said Tom. He spit off the porch and sipped his wine.

"Are you able to believe, just a little bit? It's important that you believe, for Anna's sake. For Mandy."

"What am I going to tell people at work? That my Anna who committed suicide is back and pregnant?" He choked back a sob. "Jesus Christ."

"I'm sorry," said Michael. "I know it makes things complicated, but think about Mandy. How happy she is."

"Yeah, and you must be happy. Banging a girl that's half your age. I just feel a little crazy about this. I'm beginning to doubt that even you are real, that you're just part of some conspiracy to drive me insane."

"Hell no. I'm not trying to hurt anybody. And she is an adult. But that's why I never approached her when . . . before . . . the age thing. But that went out the window."

"I've seen it all through the yellow windows of the evening train . . . I can honestly say that's true now."

"Who said that?" said Michael.

"Tom Waites."

"Cool. I like that. Look, maybe I should go now. Let you guys talk. I'd like to offer to not see Anna again, for your sake, but that's impossible, especially now."

"Yeah, maybe you should go for now. Finish your wine, though." He flicked his cigarette onto the lawn.

"Might start a fire," said Michael. "Hasn't rained in sixty days."

Tom glared at him and went to the grass stomping on the butt.

Back inside, Michael sat beside Anna and took his glass.

"I'm leaving after I finish this. I think Tom needs me to be gone for a while."

"Whatever," said Mandy. "Anna likes the name Jon Thomas for a boy. I think it's nice."

"It's a great name," said Anna.

"Hmm," said Michael. "I could work with that." He gulped his wine and placed the glass on the table.

"So, you're leaving?" said Anna. She stood with him.

"Yeah, lots to do anyway." He embraced her and kissed her. "Take care, okay? I'll call you tomorrow, or you can call me. Probably sleep in late."

"I have to see you tomorrow, right? I mean, think of something we can do. Okay?" She followed him to the door.

"Okay, sure. We'll do something."

He passed Tom, nodded, and was soon headed to his apartment but stopped to buy ice cream.

Sixteen

It was eight or so and Michael watched TV with Leonard and Tweezer curled in his lap. He'd eaten a whole pint of Ben and Jerry's chocolate fudge brownie. He wanted to call someone, to tell them the news, but that seemed foolish. He'd recently ordered his medical records from the psychiatric hospital. He was planning to write about his experiences of the lowest point in his life. Over the course of four months, he'd been admitted four times. His diagnosis had been bipolar disorder with a mixed personality disorder. He wondered now if that was still true. But how could it be? He held a full-time job teaching. For years after the hospitalizations he'd felt wounded, had felt that others could see through the façade and see his insanity. But he was taking his meds, miracle pills. The depression was still with him, but it no longer crippled him. He flipped the channel to *House Hunters International.* A husband and wife were looking to buy a home in Granada. He wanted to someday buy a house in the south of France or Italy. And now he was going to be a father again. Or was he? He lifted the cats from his lap to make himself a glass of bourbon. He felt strange, as if he had violated some fundamental law of physics. What did it all mean?

The next day was Saturday, waking at eleven. The phone. It was Anna wanting to go somewhere. Hearing her voice energized him, but he needed some space. He felt crowded, as if caring for a patient versus dating a beautiful woman. They agreed to go walking along the river as it was a bright sunshiny day, not a cloud in the sky.

He hadn't heard from the girls or Suzanne and wondered if he should tell them about the latest development.

He and Anna took their time, walking and talking, discussing baby names. They passed people on bikes, kids on skateboards, other walkers and joggers. The world seemed somehow so perfect yet ripe for tragedy. They walked across the bridge and had ice cream. He ordered pecan praline and she had the pistachio. It was obvious that she was visible, alive and well. She had barely faded from the night before and he felt that was why she didn't ask to go back to his place. She called him Soldier.

After three hours, he took her home. She was going grocery shopping with Mandy. Mandy couldn't wait to be out again with Anna. She'd had Tom do most of the shopping after Anna died and couldn't stand to go places that she'd been to with her. Tom had mellowed a bit but was still in no mood to have him around, so he cut the visit short and headed home, stopping to buy even more ice cream.

He spent two hours on his little patio reading and smoking, Arty on his tether. He'd called Suzanne, and she'd invited him over for dinner. She had chicken to grill. Should he tell them?

He pulled into the driveway still wearing his baggy hiking shorts and tennis shoes. Yancy was on the deck in a patch of sunshine with Mr. Spritely on his leash.

"Hey, Dad!" She was watching *The Office* on her laptop.

"Hey!" he said, bringing Arty out of the car.

Mr. Spritely perked up and barked. Arty strained at his leash.

He wrangled Arty inside. "Hello!"

"Hey," said Suzanne. She went straight for Arty and rubbed his head, telling him that she loved him.

"Hey, Dad!" Claire was upstairs doing laundry.

"Hey!" He plopped onto the couch.

"What's wrong?" said Suzanne. "You doing okay? You look worried." She had her hands on her hips, her face sympathetic.

"Nothing. Just tired is all."

"It's that time of the year for you."

"True, but the Adderall really helps. Boosts me. I needed that a long time ago."

"We're getting the tree tomorrow. You have to help me put it up. Right?"

"Brother, the damn tree." He ruffled his thinning hair.

"So, how's it going with, you know, Anna, and Mandy? Is she still real? God I can't believe I said that. I told my sister about it. She thinks we're loony."

Michael laughed. "She's loony. We're loony. Everybody's loony, especially this time of year."

"So, you didn't answer my question. Want a beer?"

"Yeah, that would be great. None of that porter, though." He stood, a little dizzy.

"Help yourself."

He ambled to the fridge, sidestepping boxes. "Gifts?"

"Oh yeah, already got 'em coming in. Don't be looking. Anna?"

He found the beer, found the opener. "There's been a development."

"Oh."

"Yeah, complicated." He had her attention.

"How could it be more complicated?"

He fell back onto the sofa. "Maybe I should wait."

"Wait for what? Tell me. Now you've got me worried. The chicken is in the fridge."

"I'll marinate it in just a second. Just feel bushwhacked."

"Damn you. So tell me. Don't make me beg."

"Okay, um. So here it is. She's pregnant." He sipped the beer.

"What? You've got to be out of your mind." She sat on the loveseat.

"We did the pregnancy test. It was positive."

"You mean you've been having sex with her, with Anna? Good grief. You should have thought this through."

"Should have, should have," he said. "What am I going to do?"

"First, it just seems impossible. And . . . well I don't know." She reached and touched his knee. "Are you sure? Did you dream this? Are you hearing voices?"

"No, it's true. I swear. Maybe I thought she wasn't really alive, that she was just a ghost, but she's very real. I feel bad, feel guilty, feel that I was using her . . . or maybe . . ."

"That she's using you?"

"She made a mistake, taking her life. She wants another chance. I get it. I mean, I survived my attempts. She didn't. Plus, there's Mandy and Tom."

"You can't have the whole world on your shoulders. What will this baby be like? Invisible? Please, don't tell the girls this, okay. It's too complicated already." She toyed with a coaster.

"Right. Okay, the chicken."

He took the chicken and pounded it between two layers of plastic wrap then dunked it in a bag with soy sauce, rice wine vinegar, and garlic salt. Claire emerged, watching him. She had picked up on his cooking habits, and was a great cook. Some of his fond memories of her as a toddler involved cooking, baking cakes. He stretched out on the couch for a while. "I'm resting my eyes." After a little nap, he was up, wondering what to cook with chicken and decided that rice would be fine. He put the rice on and went outside to fire up the grill.

It only took a few minutes to grill the chicken, and he bellowed that dinner would be ready in ten minutes. He pondered his situation. Was it a mess? Was it a dream come true? Would he marry Anna? Would she move in with him? His mind swirled, an electric storm of possibilities. Jon Thomas. If it was a boy. He laughed to himself.

"What's so funny?" said Claire, cutting her chicken.

"What? Nothing. Nothing." He caught the cautious look of Suzanne, her eyes saying no.

"So, Dad, how did your little date with Anna go today? Is she still visible? I mean to other people." Yancy was only eating the rice.

"Yeah, how was it?" said Claire.

"Um, it was great. And yes, Mandy and Tom can see her now. I think others can see her as well. Not sure why." He sipped his Heineken, coughed. He needed to tell someone else, to hear the words coming from his mouth.

"When's she gonna come back over? My friends want to meet her," said Yancy. "They don't believe me. But, I did see her."

"I haven't told my friends," said Claire. "There's no way, at least not yet."

"That's probably best," said Suzanne. "No need to tell everything, right, Michael?"

"Ha. I suppose."

"What is it?" said Claire. "Mom is trying to shut you up. I can tell." Her eyes twinkled.

"Yeah, Dad," said Yancy.

"Michael," said Suzanne. "You promised."

"I knew it," said Claire. "Tell us, please."

Michael fumbled his fork onto the floor, and Arty was right there licking it.

"Damn, need a new fork." He stood. "I promised your mom I wouldn't tell you." He was nearly bursting with the news. He sat back down, feeling Suzanne's stare. "Just a queer little something that's happened."

"Dad!" they said in unison.

"It won't hurt to tell them. Look. It's this way."

"Michael?" said Suzanne.

There was a moment of silence. The oh so quiet hum of the refrigerator. The nails of the dogs on the hardwood floors. The blips from Yancy's cell phone, the texts never-ending.

"Okay, so she's pregnant. There."

"What?" they said in unison.

"She's pregnant. She took a test. It was positive."

Suzanne just shook her head, chewing slowly.

"But how can that be? She's not like a real person," said Yancy.

"She can't be a ghost," said Claire. "We saw her. But how could she be pregnant? My God, Dad?"

"Jesus, I'm so confused," said Yancy.

"So am I," said Michael. "But, you have to keep this a secret, okay? It could just be some weird phenomenon. Maybe I am dreaming some of this. Anything can happen it seems."

They grilled him for details, but he refrained, citing adult privilege, and dinner lasted longer than usual, everyone with a look of wonderment, even Suzanne.

After helping with the dishes and taking out the trash, he bid them goodbye and headed home. He'd barely returned when his cell rang. It was Anna.

"Hey!" she said. "Where are you?" She was in the living room, Mandy and Tom still eating at the table.

"Back home." He sat in his recliner. Leonard jumped into his lap, purring. "Just had dinner with the girls."

"Huh. You don't still have feelings for Suzanne do you?"

"We're divorced. It's over. We're still just good friends. I go over mainly to see the girls and help out here and there. It's good to see Suzanne too." He rubbed Leonard's head.

"Okay, just checking. You're the father of my baby, right? I have to keep tabs on you." She laughed.

"Yeah, I guess so."

"And you're not dating anyone else, right? You said I was the first since the divorce."

"Yep, that's true. I swear."

"That's sweet. I was your desire?"

"You could say that."

"And wishes come true?"

"More than we'll ever know. I mean, I still find it hard to believe. That I imagined you back into existence. If that's what it was."

"I think you really did. I have no idea where I was before I came back. It's just a blank. This is much better, though. Mom is so happy. Tom is too, but he's still doubtful for some reason."

"That's reasonable, I think. Have any of the neighbors noticed you yet?"

"I'm not sure. There's a lawyer who comes over and jaws with Tom, but he couldn't see me at the time. Now, it's different. I've got you right inside me to light me up. Can you handle that?"

"I have to. I'm the dad, right? I was reading up on ultrasounds. We should be able to see something at six weeks. Have you found a doctor yet?"

"Not yet. Mom wants to find someone we don't know. It could get tricky otherwise. But I should have an appointment soon, maybe a couple of weeks. I enjoyed our walk today. I even feel a little sore, my feet. I guess I have to get used to gravity again."

"Yeah, gravity. Look, what's up otherwise? I need to get some writing in. Get my ten pages down or maybe seven. Class starts back tomorrow, and I have some prep work to do."

"Oh God, that's what Tom says. I can't believe you guys work together. I mean, I would have never met you otherwise."

"Do you think someone else could have had this effect? I mean if it's just a matter of desire, I'm sure there are plenty of guys out there who could've done the same thing."

"No way. You're the one, Soldier. You did it. You pulled me back, from somewhere."

"I know this is a creepy question. But . . ."

"You want to know if my ashes are still in the jar, right?"

"Ha, yeah. I mean would it have been different if you had been buried?"

"I don't know, but I did look in the jar. Mom keeps it beside her bed on a little lamp table. There were definitely ashes in there. I was looking at myself. It was kind of gross."

"Huh. I don't know what it all means. You have a new body. Not like a resurrection, the same body."

"I'm still me. I look the same. I've been reincarnated, I suppose."

"I wonder what Hinduism has to say about that, reincarnated back into what looks to be the same body?"

"Gosh, I have no idea. That can be your next research project. I mean, I suppose I should join a freak show."

"Don't talk like that. It's just a miracle. I guess I have to leave it that."

"I think it's the work of you and Mom. It took effort, versus being a miracle. You had to have faith. I think you still have to have faith, otherwise I might fade away. I'm depending on you. I really am. But, I'm so happy about being pregnant. I had an abortion when I was sixteen. Maybe this is a second chance in some strange way."

"I didn't know that. I'm actually afraid now to think about other people . . . who have died. I mean, you know."

"You mean that one resurrection is enough? Yeah, you better believe it, Soldier. I'm not sharing you with any other undead. Hey, we should watch *The Walking Dead* together. Maybe I'm a zombie, a nice zombie, a pregnant zombie."

"Sure, but I haven't really gotten into the whole zombie thing. Suzanne watches with friends every Sunday night."

"Watch it with me, and not her, okay?"

"I promise. So, I should probably go."

"You're not tired of me, are you?"

"No, no. Just a lot of work to do. I get anxious if I haven't prepped for class. I always have to do the readings again. I guess I'm a little OCD in that regard. That's also one of my newer diagnoses."

"Well it takes crazy to love crazy, right? Okay, I'll let you go. Maybe I could come to your class one day. You could say I was an interested student. I'd like to see you in action."

"Hmm, anything is possible. You might see people you know, though. I feel like you should put an ad in the paper to let people know you're back."

"What if the news did a story on me? That would be freaky. They would have to interview you, though."

"Hmm, I could lose my job. They would think that I was unstable in some way, which I guess I am anyway."

"Yeah, maybe not a good idea. I'm just planning to tell people that I went to Mexico, that I had amnesia, that I'm back now." She laughed.

"That's actually not a bad idea. I'll keep that in mind. We should all have the same story, though. Where in Mexico?"

"Mom and Tom took me to Puerto Vallarta once when I was in high school. How about there?"

"Okay, sounds good. And how did you get back here?"

"Hmm, maybe I freaked out there and was locked up in a mental hospital. Mom and Tom found out and Mom came to get me. And that's why they've been so secretive. They didn't want people to know I was crazy."

"Sounds pretty convincing. You'll need to let them in on the story too."

"This is all so exciting. I feel like I'm part of a movie. I'll let them know. Mom's clearing the table now. Okay, I'll let you go for now. Can you come over tomorrow, maybe after your class? I'll make some cookies."

"Sure. I have about two hours between class and picking up the girls. Sleep well, and get them in on the story. It could save a lot of explaining."

"I will. And you know I'm gonna say it. Do you want to say it first?"

Michael sighed. "Love you."

"Did you just sigh?"

"No."

"Okay, Soldier, I love you too. Good night."

"Night."

Michael put his phone in his lap, exhausted.

Seventeen

Nine weeks passed, the holidays flew by, and it was the New Year, time for an ultrasound. Anna was seeing Dr. McCormick for her prenatal visits. Thus far everything seemed normal, no spotting, and then there was the nausea, the true sign. Not a day had passed without Michael seeing Anna, and the phone calls were frequent. As the days went, she became more visible, but still not quite all there, which startled people, unless she was with him. They'd begun talking about her moving in with Michael

Michael knocked on the door, a cold sleet falling from a palled sky. He wore his green wool coat and jeans. His legs were cold. It was a Tuesday, and he had no classes that day.

"Come in out of the cold, Michael," said Mandy. She was still wearing her Christmas sweater with the reindeer on it. Tom was at work.

"Cold definitely, and thank you."

"So today's the big day," she said. "I'd like to go, but this should be between the two of you. Make sure you get the pictures and a video, too. They do videos now."

"I will. Where's Anna?"

"In the bathroom doing her girly things. You know girls." She walked into the dining room and straightened the tablecloth.

Michael took a seat, facing the window behind the couch. He noticed the old Persian rug, threadbare in places and tapped his foot. He'd gotten so behind in his writing, but had caught up over the holidays, but now classes were in full swing again. He wished for more hours in the day.

"So, don't go out for a drink to celebrate, okay? You come straight back here and give me a full report, except for the gender, right?"

"Too early for that, and she wants to keep that as a surprise. We did that with my two girls." He wrapped his coat around tighter.

The bathroom door opened. "Michael!" and she ran to him, giving him a big hug.

"Hey. About ready? You look really good."

"Thanks. So do you." She was wearing stretch jeans, having already gained ten pounds, and a gray wool sweater. "Let me get my purse."

"Okay, we'll be back when we're back," he said.

Anna returned. "Bye, Mom. Love you. Wish us luck."

"Everything will be fine, I'm sure. Just good to check, right?" She beamed.

"Doing our duty," he said. "See you in a bit."

Outside their breath streamed. He opened the door for her and lent her his hand. It took ten minutes to reach the hospital and another ten to find a space in the parking deck and walk inside hand in hand.

"I think we're in the right place." He examined a windowed board with names and numbers. "Third floor."

The elevator door opened, and an elderly man pushed a large woman in a wheelchair. Her arms were purple with bruises. The doors closed.

"You excited to see your baby?" she said.

"Of course, should be a breeze. I've done this twice before. How's your belly? No kicking yet, right?"

The doors opened.

"Oh not yet, but I know it's there. It's just a sensation, very real. I can't wait to hear the heartbeat. Can they even hear it now?"

"Yeah, I think they can."

He led her to Dr. McCormick's suite, shared with three other OB/GYNs.

"Here we are," he said. He felt like his spine was an icicle. He looked around at the cushioned blue chairs, the tables with magazines. The receptionist was behind a tall counter with a little bell. They checked in and took seats.

"I was going to wear that green sweater you bought me, but this is my favorite one, brings good luck. I feel like I'm squeezing the baby when I sit down."

She picked up a magazine and flipped through it. Across the way, a very pregnant woman was coughing without covering her mouth. She looked miserable as she stood, holding her belly with both hands. Michael pressed his feet into the tiled floor as if he could move it. He checked his watch, cleared his throat. Just waiting.

"You know for your spring break we should go somewhere, maybe to the mountains. You ever been to Gatlinburg?" she said.

He laughed. "Like a hundred times. My grandparents used to take me in the summer camping. Haven't been in a few years, though. It's mostly just shops selling stuff. The Smokies are great, though. I'll have to see what Suzanne and the girls are up to."

"Right. I forget. Do you think they really like me?"

"Why do you keep asking that? Of course they like you. How could they not?"

"Well maybe we could all go together? Or maybe just with Claire and Yancy." She smiled.

"That would be wild. I guess they would like that, but there is Suzanne. I have to check."

"Right. You guys are just still so close. It makes me nervous. What if you decide to go back to her?"

"We're finished. She doesn't want me back. We just have a good arrangement is all. It's good for the girls."

"I like how much you care for them. You're sweet."

"Am I your sweet little apple dumpling?"

"Don't mock me. That's not nice."

"I was just kidding. I like apple dumplings."

A woman in scrubs appeared. "Anna Golding?"

"That's us."

She popped up. He stood slowly. He'd run the day before, and his legs were stiff.

"Wait for the old man," he said.

The woman was an ultrasound tech named Barbara. She was attractive with high cheekbones and dirty blonde hair, wearing blue scrubs.

"Right this way," said Barbara.

They entered a cold room with an exam table and the hulking ultrasound machine. Barbara washed her hands.

"So, we have you down for your first ultrasound today. You excited?" said Barbara.

"Yeah," they said.

"Gonna need you to hop on the table." She pulled down a fresh sheet of paper to cover the pad.

Anna did as she was told, Michael at her side.

Barbara explained the procedure and readied the gel. "Pull your pants down for me, Sweetie, and take off that top if you don't want goo on it."

Anna pulled off the sweater and pushed down her jeans. "Don't get excited, Michael."

Michael made a nervous laugh. It had been two weeks since they'd had sex, and she looked great on the table.

"First, we'll listen for the heartbeat, okay? I have this little gadget here called a Doppler. I'll put some gel on your belly and slide it around, okay? It'll be a little cold at first."

"Okay," said Anna.

Barbara turned on the Doppler, and it made loud radio sounds. She dipped the receiver in the gel and pressed it to Anna's belly. There was a steady swish and crackles as she moved it around. And then there it was, a rapid swoosh, 150 beats per minutes.

Anna stared at Michael.

"There it is," said Barbara. "That's a great sign." She let the swooshes go for a minute while Anna squeezed his hand.

"My god," said Anna. "It's just hard to believe that a baby is growing inside me. Kiss me." She drew Michael in closer, and they kissed.

"Okay, now for the real deal, the video." Barbara squirted a glop of gel on Anna's belly. "Should take us less than five minutes."

Anna held her breath.

Barbara turned on the video monitor and made sure that the DVD was in place. She applied the receiver and pressed it into Anna's belly. The screen lit up with color, but they couldn't make heads or tails of it.

Barbara finagled the receiver, pushing it from one side to the other. "Huh." She kept at it, trying to conjure the image of the fetus. "It must be hiding. The heartbeat was there. That wasn't your heartbeat, too rapid. Let me check your pulse."

Anna looked worried. Michael just gripped her hand.

"Your pulse is eighty-six, so that was definitely the baby, a nice strong heartbeat. Let me try again." She moved the receiver here and there, going up and down, side to side, but nothing appeared. "I can see the placenta." She tried again. "Well this is just weird. Let's do the Doppler again."

"Is something wrong?" said Anna.

"No, except that I can't find the baby. Hold on." She reapplied the Doppler and found the heartbeat again. "Yep, there it is. It's in there, but hiding."

Anna gripped Michael's hand tighter. Barbara did her best to locate the fetus, but she couldn't.

"Don't worry. You've got a healthy heartbeat but the fetus just won't show. Strange, but again, don't worry, okay?" She tried one more time and gave up.

"So, what do we do?" said Anna.

"Nothing. I say we reschedule for a couple of weeks from now and try again. I'll let Dr. McCormick know what we've done thus far. Definitely a little strange."

Michael wondered if the fetus was invisible, like Anna had been at first. Maybe they should have had sex before they came. Maybe the fetus fed off of his energy like Anna had before she was pregnant? He kept quiet.

"So, that's it?" said Anna. "Michael, are you worried?"

"No," he said. "Could just be too small to see yet. We'll come back in a couple of weeks like she suggested."

Anna pulled up her pants, and they left without a video, Barbara apologizing.

In the car, they sat, the air cold.

"Is it going to be okay? You think?" said Anna.

"Positive. The heartbeat was strong. I think maybe it's just faded, kind of like you were faded."

"But why? It doesn't make sense. I'm fully visible. She had no trouble seeing me. It's just creepy."

"Not creepy. The circumstances are unusual, right, so we have to be prepared for the unusual." He cranked the car. "Want to get some coffee or something, have an early lunch? No classes today."

"I guess. I just wanted to see it so badly."

"Yeah, me too. It's okay. Want to go to the deli near the bridge, have a muffuletta?" He pulled up to the gate and inserted his parking ticket then fed in a dollar bill.

"Okay, if you say so. Maybe we can walk across the bridge, get some exercise?"

"Sounds like a plan."

Near the deli, he had to pay to park, and the machine kept asking him to slide his card. Heavy white clouds filled the sky, a brisk breeze blowing. The area was crowded, the shops doing post-holiday business. The deli was beneath an ice cream store and faced away from the main street in front, making it nearly invisible. Inside there was a short line, the unfinished ceiling low, the interior dim. The giant muffuletta in the display case was cut in wedges.

"I brought some cash. Want me to pay?" said Anna.

"No, not at all. My pleasure." He said the *s* like a *z*.

They took a table against the yellow wall, waiting for their sandwiches to be heated.

"So, I'm a depressed person and you're a depressed person. What will the baby be like?" She sipped her Diet Coke.

"Gosh, I don't know. Let's just hope for the best. When did you first become depressed?"

"My dad shot himself. I told you that. He had lost his job and was depressed. I think it was around then. I tried to cut my wrists. But I had been depressed before that, maybe as early as twelve. I missed a lot of high school, spent some time in the hospital."

"How many times did you try?"

"Four, including the last one. I finally got it right. But here I am. I'll never do that again. I haven't really felt depressed since I've been back, just sad a little. Do you have a history in your family?"

"No one officially diagnosed. I'm convinced my mother was bipolar. She would go off the deep end at least once a month, screaming her head off that she wanted to die. I'd just go outside. I couldn't stand it. But, there was never any talk about illness, just that she was crazy."

"That's sad. Must have been hard."

"Yeah, about drove me insane, or maybe it did. Maybe we'll beat the odds. I think sometimes there has to be a trigger to make the walls come tumbling down, like your dad killing himself."

"Yeah. Depression is the absolute worst. I was anxious, bulimic, and OCD too, but it was the depression that really got to me. I would just give up, barely able to breathe."

"Twenty-two!"

Michael went to get the sandwiches, which were six inches high.

"Lord, that's a sandwich," said Anna.

He sat. "I know that nag of hopelessness. I get these racing thoughts of killing myself. Without the meds, I can't get rid of them, and they drag me down like I'm suffocating. You have to squash it down, the sandwich I mean."

"Right. I think I need a bigger mouth. Jesus." She took a sideways bite. "So your meds really help? Mine didn't work, but I did stop taking them. That's what I used to, well, you know."

"Yep, weird. Works like a charm. It took me about five meds to find the right antipsychotic, but it knocked out the racing thoughts like magic. That and the antidepressant help with the anxiety and OCD too. I'm pretty much on the max dosage for everything, except the Adderall. I take forty milligrams a day. Keeps me awake."

"Mandy wants me to go back to the psychiatrist. She's afraid I'll relapse. But, I'm so happy. I feel really good, except for the nausea. It's weird how it only comes in the morning."

"Gee, what if you went to your old shrink? What would she do?"

"I know, right? She'd probably accuse mom of making up the whole suicide thing or maybe she'd flip her wig. But I'm fine. It's like I've been cured for now."

He nodded and stretched his mouth to take a bite. He ate a bite of pickle. "Just let me know if you need someone to prescribe drugs for you. I go to a public mental health clinic. It's just a nurse practitioner, but it works. I even have my own social worker."

"You told me that. What, is it like for the poor?"

"Yeah, most are on Medicaid and Medicare, disability. I fit right in."

A very tall family walked in carrying a baby.

"Huh, I might like that. I'll let you know. Mom might not like the idea. I guess I don't have insurance. How could I?"

"Ha, I guess that will be tricky to navigate. I'd say you qualify for disability. Anyone who comes back from the pale should meet the criteria."

"Or they would have to rewrite the rules. Mom's thinking about Obamacare. She doesn't want me to see any of my old doctors, for good reason. Like you said, they would probably freak." She was making good progress on her muffuletta wedge.

"Yeah, you break all of the rules. I wonder if there's anyone else like you. I mean there has to be. You can't be the only one." He drank all of his soda and stood to get more. "Need more?"

"No, I'm good."

He returned. "So, I wish I was still in grad school. The stories I could write for workshop. What about the writing series party that's coming up? It's always at your house. Is Tom still holding it there?"

"I think so. The plan is just to keep a straight face, I think. Let people think what they will."

"Wow, I can't wait for that. Should be a hoot. I can just see the looks on faces, the questions, the doubting." He laughed. "Damn, I'm full." He still had half a sandwich to go.

"I'm working on mine. I'm just so hungry, the baby you know. Your baby. My baby."

"Yep, and add that to the mix and folks will really be talking. I'm kind of looking forward to it. That's a really tall family." He nodded to himself.

"They have a cute little baby," she said. "They are tall. You know we have to talk about living together."

"There's that."

"What, you don't want to?" She looked hurt.

"Not that, it's just that we'll have to work something out. I could save rent if I moved in with you."

"Yeah, but you have the animals. That would be a bit much, I think. I like your apartment. It seems quiet."

"Yeah, it'll work out. No need to do anything just yet."

"What, are you afraid the baby won't make it?"

"No, but nothing is for sure. It worries me a little, the ultrasound I mean."

"But that strong heartbeat. It wants to live. I just know it. I can feel it."

"What if it's born invisible?" He sucked his cup dry and chewed on ice.

"That would be crazy. But, everything about this is crazy."

"I can truly say that I lead an interesting life. Thanks to you."

"What am I? Just some curiosity? I'm real, in the flesh. If you want me to prove it, we can go back to your apartment after this. We haven't done it in a while." She nudged his leg under the table. "I had a girlfriend who had sex when she was eight months pregnant."

"Yeah, I've been thinking about that. I think maybe it's good for the baby, especially in our case. Maybe it needs me like you do."

"I like to think that I'm cured, that I'm here to stay."

"What, that you don't need me anymore?"

"I need you, but maybe not to stay visible. That would be good, right? I mean, what if something happened to you?"

"I've wondered about that. I was kind of down yesterday, having bad thoughts."

"Michael, really? To hurt yourself? That's just not an option."

"I know. I can't control the thoughts. At least they go away. Without the meds, I would spiral out of control. It would be great if you were good to go on your own. But we do see each other every day."

"What, you don't want to see me every day?" She ate the last bite.

"No, not that. I just wonder what the effect would be, say if we didn't see each other for a week. I have a couple of school trips that I'm taking this summer. It could be that you couldn't go. I'd hate for you to just fade away."

"We'll see. I would love to go with you. For now, just promise that you'll see me every day. I mean, you have to. Get me some more Diet Coke?"

"Right, yeah, no problem." He went to refill her drink, glancing at the tall family. The guy looked like a ladder. For the first time he noticed that music was playing, very soft, Van Morrison.

"Thank you," she said. "Can we get ice cream after this? I'm craving something sweet."

"Okay, just have to get Yancy at four and then Claire at four-thirty. Still have about four hours." He poked his finger into the bread.

"So, how are they? I haven't seen them in a few days."

"Okay. We found out that Yancy was cutting again. Her therapist didn't tell us, though, at first. Suzanne found out."

"I'm sorry. I used to do that in high school. Where does she cut?"

"I hate to think about it. On her inner thighs. She'd been cutting for a year before we first found out." She has some pretty serious scars, part of her OCD."

"I wonder why she started again?"

"She says its stress." He shook the ice in his cup. "She can't control it, she says. But things have been pretty weird."

"You don't think it has anything to do with me do you? Can I have your sandwich?"

He pushed his sandwich to her. "I just wonder. It seems she first started cutting when I moved out, so I felt responsible. Maybe she needs more attention from me and this is . . . taking away from time she needs."

"Michael, that's awful. Now I feel bad. Look, we can do things together with her. I don't want her to feel that I'm taking you away."

"Yeah, I'll work it out. I'm trying to spend more time at the house." He sighed.

"Gosh, everyone needs you."

"It's good to be needed. I don't think I would be here if it wasn't for them. We're good for each other. I hope. You ever watch that show about people who hoard, *Hoarders?* There's always a trigger that sends them over the edge and usually it's the loss of parent. That keeps me honest."

"That's a depressing show. I can't watch it."

"It's fascinating. Anyway, ice cream?"

She chewed the last bite. "Definitely."

He took one last look at the tall family, and they left, back into the crisp air. The sun was peeking through the clouds. He zipped his coat and put on his knit cap, pulling her close to him.

Eighteen

Wednesday proved a bit icy, his windshield still frozen. He had class and turned the defroster up high, sitting on his hands, waiting. It took a good ten minutes before he could see to drive. He had graded assignments that morning for his online classes, scientific writing. In his creative writing class that day they were workshopping short stories, including "Popular Mechanics" by Raymond Carver, a story about a couple fighting over a baby. *In this manner, the issue was decided.* The last line of the story.

He had his route to school down to a science. The only variable was the tricky intersection onto Fourth. He parked with two minutes to spare before his four-minute walk to class. He knew he would arrive exactly five minutes early, and he arrived five minutes early.

"Hello," he said to the early birds. Heads nodded. He logged onto the computer to kill time. He wouldn't be using it today, just the overhead projector. If the ultrasound DVD had worked out, he had planned to show it to the class, just for kicks. "Cold enough for everyone?"

The weather always generated a smile or two. Everyone had an opinion on the weather. The seconds marched by as he perused his hardcopies of three stories, all very short. Carver, when he wrote, it was said, unplugged his telephone, wrapped it in a blanket, and stuffed it in a drawer. Michael checked roll quickly.

"So, today we have three short stories we'll look at. This is a workshop, so I need your full participation." He went through the spiel. The class of fourteen looked on with minor interest. He passed out hardcopies of the stories, flash fiction, and had them read the first, Carver's story. He needed to hook them, get them to swallow some bait, and run with it. He gave them five minutes to read.

"Jesus," said Ronesha.

"Okay," he said. "What's this story about?"

Jay raised his hand. "About a man and his wife fighting over a baby."

"Exactly. What kind of narrator do we have here? Is there any omniscience? Do we have access to the thoughts of anyone?"

"I'm not sure, but I would say no," said Riley.

Michael opened his hands. "It does seem so. There is just one line—'She would have it, the baby'—that could possibly be interpreted as her thought, but primarily this is a very objective piece, just like you would find in *Popular Mechanics,* the magazine. "Why else is this story called 'Popular Mechanics'? It was originally titled 'Mine'."

Jackie spoke. "I guess because *Popular Mechanics* means that you know how to fix things, and they obviously have a situation they can't fix."

"That's good," said Michael. "And also, when we think about mechanics, the way things work. When the flower pot falls, what happens? It breaks right? And when you pull an infant between two people what might the mechanics result in?"

"Ugh," said Ronesha. "A broken baby."

Michael felt his heart beating just a bit faster. "That's right. It's a bit of foreshadowing, the flower pot breaking." He walked to the other side of the classroom. "What's the inciting incident here? What kicks off the plot, the fight between these two?" He waited and called on Coco.

"Um, I would say when the woman sees the baby's picture on his bed. She realizes then that he will take the baby." She smiled.

"Exactly, and then we have this rising action, blow by blow, until we reach the climax, which is?"

"It's that last line," said Macy. "Something bad happens to the baby."

"Yeah, this is an angry story. We know something bad is going to happen, and probably to the baby. We have to talk about desire here. What do this man and woman want most, beside the baby?"

"Maybe the woman wants to have a happy marriage, wants to keep the family together," said Andres.

"Yeah, we think that's a possibility, except at the end. She's definitely not getting what she wants, it seems. What about the man?"

Sam spoke. "He just wants out. He's had it for some reason. And he'll definitely get what he wants."

"Yeah," said Michael, "they're done it seems. Let's take a look at the imagery. What about that first line, a great line: 'Early that day the weather turned and the snow was melting into dirty water.'"

"It's like the marriage is melting into something nasty. Something happened, like the weather turned," said Ashley.

Michael was full-on excited, barely able to contain himself. "Right. A Great image, very simple. Always go for strong and simple images that reflect the action."

There was a pounding on the door. The class cringed collectively. Michael was dumbfounded, his reverie broken. The door opened and in came Anna, tears streaming. She grabbed him and hugged him. Behind her was Mandy, holding a purse.

"Anna? What's wrong?" He looked at the class. "Hold on. Hey, come with me into the hall. I'll be right back y'all."

"Michael," said Anna.

"Hey, what's wrong?" He held her in the hall, passersby looking on. He glanced at Mandy who was shaken.

"She had a panic attack, just like before," said Mandy. "She had to see you. I was afraid she'd hurt herself. I'm sorry we barged in."

"Michael." Anna wept, clutching him. "I can't lose you."

"It's okay. It's all right. Just take some deep breaths." Tears wet his sweater.

"I'm . . . I'm sorry. I just panicked. I felt you weren't real. I had . . . to see you. I'm sorry I'm such a burden." She balled her fists to her face.

Anna Claire had come to the door, looking through the narrow window.

"No. You can always interrupt me. It's not a problem. You're going to be fine."

"What do I do?" said Mandy. "She's a wreck."

"She could stay here, sit in the back? I can bring her home after class. Anna, you want to do that?"

"And she was fading," said Mandy. "That's what scared me the most. Like she was leaving for good."

"Is she faded now?"

"No," said Mandy.

"Okay, great. Just come in. The class won't mind. We're just talking about stories. Could be interesting."

Anna's crying had subsided into just tears leaking from her eyes. "Okay. Mom, I'm okay now. He'll bring me home." She tried to smile.

"If that's okay, Michael. Again, I'm sorry," said Mandy. She was underdressed in a short-sleeve shirt.

"Yeah, not a problem. Okay, we'll go in now. Thanks, Mandy." He led Anna into the classroom and the buzz went silent. "Hey, everyone, this is Anna. She's going to join us." He led her to the back of the class next to Kia. "Okay?"

"Yeah, okay." Anna sat.

"Okay, just another half hour or so, and we can leave."

He went back to the front of the class and gathered his thoughts. "Okay, let's move onto the next story 'Stone Belly Girl' by Jamie Granger. This is another story with some of the same themes, perhaps, of 'Popular Mechanics.'"

He gave them five minutes to read the story, and gave Anna a copy. He watched her read, her hair mussed.

"So what happens in the story?"

No one spoke.

"Kia, what happens?"

She spoke very softly, and he strained to hear her words.

"It talks about a girl. Her father takes her to the carnival and breaks stones on her belly with a hammer."

"God, what do you think of this father?" said Michael.

No one spoke.

"Sara?"

"It says he's a drunk. He's just using her to make money. He's pretty gross."

"Yeah, he is that," said Michael. "What's his desire here?"

Someone said, "To make money."

"Absolutely. Is there a mother anywhere?"

"Probably not," said Riley. "No mother would allow that."

"So, like the broken stone, maybe a very broken family." He watched Anna. She was gazing at him. "What about the narrator? Any omniscience?"

"Umm," said Coco, "the narrator knows about past events, knows about the Aunt explaining to the girl about her period."

"So, yeah, limited omniscience, I think. We don't get into the heads of the characters, though. What about figurative language? Any examples? Ashley?"

"It says the stone broke like an egg on her belly."

"Why an egg?"

"Because an egg is fragile, like the girl's life," said Sam.

"I like that."

They talked for a few minutes more, and he dismissed the class early. Anna sat at the desk, unmoving, looking sad. He walked toward her.

"Hey, you okay?" he said.

"Yeah, thank you." She stood and smoothed down her jeans, zipped her down vest. "I'm cold."

"Let's get in the car and turn up the heat. I have an excellent heater." He laughed, put his arm around her.

Together they walked through the building and to the parking lot. A light mist fell, the ground damp like a sponge. They rode in relative silence, the heater blasting. At the house, Mandy met them at the door, warm air greeting them.

"I was so worried," said Mandy. "Come in, can I make some hot tea?"

"Sure," said Michael.

"Thanks, Mom. For not being mad at me." Anna went to the couch, sat down heavy. Michael followed. "My stuff is coming back. It feels horrible. I thought I was going to die."

"Did you take meds before, for panic attacks, anxiety?" he said.

"Yeah, and it generally worked. Maybe I need to see the shrink. But I would want to see my old doctor. She knows me." Anna was trembling.

"Maybe that's what we'll have to do. There'll be some explaining to do, though. Do you think she'd be able to take it all in?" said Michael.

"She has to, everyone does. I'm here, right?" said Anna.

"You are definitely here. It could be expensive, without insurance, but whatever is best. That's what I want," said Michael.

"Kiss me when you say that," said Anna.

They kissed.

Soon, Mandy came from the kitchen with a pot of hot tea and served them. Anna explained that she wanted to see her psychiatrist again.

"That could be awkward, but if you need to. I'll call her office," said Mandy.

"I can tell that I'm getting depressed. I felt kind of lifeless yesterday and the day before that." Anna snuggled up to Michael.

"You know, what, Anna? I'm just going to go ahead and give Dr. Lane a call right now. No need to wait. I've learned that." She dialed her cell and put her finger to her lips. She punched 2 for scheduling. "Yes, hey. I need to set up an appointment for my daughter with Dr. Lane. She was a patient of hers about five months ago, but wants to see her again."

"We're not taking new patients. I'm sorry," said the secretary.

"She's not new. Dr. Lane has treated her for years. She just hasn't been in five months, that's all." She paced as she talked.

"The patient's name and date of birth?"

"Yes. Her name is Anna Golding. Her birthday is April 23, 1987."

There was silence, the sound of fingers tapping a keyboard. A throat clearing.

"And who am I speaking with?"

"This is her mother, Mandy Golding." She made a hand gesture in the air.

"Mrs. Golding, are you sure about this appointment? I mean we have the patient as deceased. Are you wanting to see Dr. Lane? Maybe we can work you in, even though she's not taking new patients."

"Lord, it's just hard to explain. So, yes, just put my name down, and we'll both come. If that makes it easier. Her symptoms are coming back. It's never a good idea to wait." Mandy ruffled her neat silvering hair.

"Okay, right. We have an opening on Friday at ten-fifteen. Will that work? Otherwise it will be three weeks."

"Yes, that works," said Mandy.

"Okay, I have you down. Be sure to bring your insurance card, okay? Take care."

Mandy looked relieved. "There, I did it. Friday at ten-fifteen. We just have to keep an eye on you until then. You know I still have some of your meds. Do you want to take some of those? I think it's the trazodone, the duloxetine, and the Lamictal."

"Gosh, I hate the idea. I was hoping that I was cured, but I guess not. Sure, I'll take them. Just put them in my room."

Michael stood and stretched. "Should you just give her the dose versus the whole bottle?"

"Michael?" said Anna. "She can trust me. I'll never try to hurt myself again." She threw a pillow at him.

"Maybe he's right. You won't be tempted. When you're sick, you're really sick. You make bad decisions. I've seen it over and over. Remember when you went off your meds and started shoplifting at Walmart? I never in a million years would have thought you'd do something like that."

"You two are ganging up on me." She sprawled on the couch, laying her head back.

"See," said Mandy. "You're doing it. You used to lay like that when you were depressed, just lay there all day."

"You do seem to be down," said Michael. He poured some more tea.

"Okay, whatever you want," said Anna. "But I want to take them now. Get you guys off my back. Geez." She sat up. "I'm sorry." She put her face in her hands and cried.

"Aww," said Michael. "It's because we love you." He put his arm around her. "I just thought of something. I wonder if the meds are safe with the baby?"

"That's right," said Mandy. "Good call. Anna, we should wait until Friday. Think you can make it?"

"The little baby," said Anna, still crying. Mandy sat beside her. "I'm just so selfish."

"No, no. We have to take care of you *and* the baby." Mandy rubbed her back.

Anna sniffled. "I'm such a damn problem. Will I be a good mother? How can that be, though?"

"You'll be a great mother," said Michael. "No worries. Best mommy in the world. Look, I need to be going, to get the girls." He kissed Anna's cheek. "Salty."

Anna nodded, but didn't stand. "Bye, Soldier."

"Okay, you take care," said Mandy. "Thanks for letting us interrupt your class today."

"That's fine. Not a problem. It'll give them something to write about, maybe." He said goodbye and left.

Within twenty minutes, he had pulled into Yancy's school parking lot. He turned on the radio, listening to NPR. They were talking about Donald Trump building a wall on the Mexican border. He changed the channel to music. Eurhythmics, "Sweet Dreams." It took about ten minutes, but there she was shouldering her backpack bursting at the seams.

"Hey."

"Hey, Dad." She dumped her pack in the backseat. She hopped in and turned off the radio, turning on her iTunes. Twenty One Pilots. Michael found the music strange, kind of like rapping.

"How was your day?"

"Fine. My geometry teacher lost my test, and I have to retake it. That bitch."

"Whoa, really? Shouldn't she just give you an A?"

"You'd think." She turned the music up louder. "How was your day, Father?" she said in a mock tone.

"Interesting. Mandy brought Anna to my class. She was having a panic attack."

"My God, really? Did you have to leave?"

"No, she settled down and sat in the back. I took her home."

"So, she just freaked out and had to see you? That's weird."

"Yeah, one of her diagnoses is anxiety disorder, panic attacks."

"We all know someone else who has that as well. Right, Father?"

"Ha, well we both do. It runs in the family."

"Just like diarrhea," said Yancy.

"If you say so."

They arrived at the house, and he let her out, made sure she made it through the back door, and headed to pick up Claire. It was still drizzling and cold, the sky a wash of white and gray. Coming off a ramp, he muscled the car through two lanes of traffic and into a turn lane. It was the most dangerous part of his day. He remembered driving around as a teenager, trying to get up the nerve to plow the car into a tree. He shook his head.

He was two minutes early and backed into a space. He needed to pee, and he thought about walking into the woods, but saw Claire coming across the lawn, through the large oaks. She was wearing her prized rain boots.

"Hey, Daddy-O." She shoved her backpack into the floorboard.

"Hey, how was school?" He pulled out.

"I left my lunch at home, so I'm starved."

"I'm sorry. Want to get something to eat?"

Claire laughed. "Sure."

He drove and pulled into a McDonald's drive-thru. "Guess what I'm going to get."

"A chocolate milkshake."

"How did you guess! What do you want?"

"Chicken sandwich, no fries or a drink."

"You sure. I don't want you to choke."

"I've been drinking water all day, trying to keep my stomach from rumbling."

The guy who took his credit card was unusually cheerful. Michael had seen him before at the YMCA, during one of Claire's volleyball games. With their order, he pulled back onto the crowded four-lane. He drank his milkshake as he drove, all 630 calories, and told Claire about Anna's panic attack. He pulled up to the house and went inside for a few minutes. Usually he fed the cats and let Mr. Spritely outside to pee. Yancy was at the table watching *The Office* and eating tortilla chips.

"When's Mom coming home?" he said.

Mr. Spritely had grabbed his chew toy and was growling, shaking his tail, shaking his whole back end.

"Not sure," said Yancy.

Michael gazed around the open room. It was a bit messy, boxes on the coffee table, dishes in the sink. He checked the recycling and took it out front to the blue bin, bringing Mr. Spritely along. He sniffed and sniffed finding the perfect spot to pee.

"Come on, boy," he said. "Oh, shit."

It was the black-and-white stray cat. Mr. Spritely took off with Michael yelling for him to stop. Michael ran down the rutted road, and the dog took off into the woods yelping like a madman. There was nothing he could do but yell some more and wait. It took about five minutes, but soon Mr. Spritely was within reach, and he grabbed him.

"Bad boy!"

He carried the dog up the stairs into the house, holding the recycling container. He fed the cats and announced that he was leaving, going home to walk Arty. Both Claire and Yancy hugged him, said they loved him.

"Love you too." In the car his cell phone rang. It was Suzanne.

"Hey, you at the house?"

"Just leaving."

"Did you walk the dog?"

"Sort of. He ran off again."

"I had burgers thawing out. I was hoping you would grill."

"Need to get home and take care of the pets."

"Did you feed the cats?"

"Yes, I fed the cats." He drove, talking on the car's speakerphone.

"Thanks. I'll be home at five-thirty. Just had a shitty day."

"Sorry about that."

"Nothing new. Okay, talk to you later. You can stay with the girls tomorrow night, right? I have a dinner with students and Ted."

"Yes," he said. "Maybe leave the burgers for tomorrow. You still have that barley soup."

"Right, maybe I'll do that. Okay, bye."

"Bye."

The phone rang again. It was Anna.

"Hey!" He turned down the steep hill. The heater was on high.

"Hi . . . Michael? I thought I was having another panic attack. I just need to hear your voice."

Michael sighed. "I'm here. You okay?"

"Yeah, I guess. Can you come over?"

"I have to take care of the pets, walk Arty, then make some dinner. Have some assignments to grade."

"But you don't have class tomorrow, right?" She sounded desperate.

"No, I can come a bit later. Is that okay?"

"Yeah, but hurry. You can have dinner with us, right, Mom?" Mandy was in the room and nodded. "She's roasting a leg of lamb, with garlic mashed potatoes."

"That sounds good. Sure, I promise I'll be there. Probably about seven. That work?"

"Could you come earlier? I was starting to lose my breath."

"I think it'll have to be seven. You'll be fine."

"Okay, seven then."

"Okay then."

"Michael?"

"Yes?"

"Do you love me?"

Michael turned right and then made a left up into the complex. "Yes, I love you."

"Okay. I love you too, Michael. I really do. I'll let you go, sounds like you're driving."

"Yeah, just pulling in." Someone was in his space. "Damn, somebody parked in my space again. Shit. Okay, bye, see you soon."

"Bye."

He had to drive around and find an unmarked space.
He got out, the chill enveloping him. He made a face as
he passed the car in his space, and he spit. He thought
about letting the air out of a tire, but hurried down the
steps.

Nineteen

Michael had class at noon, and Mandy wanted him to go with her and Anna to the appointment with Dr. Lane. Mandy drove them to the office that was near the airport.

"Hey, this is where I take Yancy to her therapist," said Michael. He was in the back seat with Anna. "Huh."

"Dr. Lane came here about a year ago," said Mandy. "She's been seeing Anna for the last five or six years." She pulled the emergency brake.

They walked in. Soothing piano music played. The room was warm and dim with seating on either side. A young woman that he recognized slid the glass window open. She looked startled. Michael hovered behind Mandy, holding Anna's hand.

"We have an ten-fifteen with Dr. Lane," said Mandy.

"Sure. Now, is this for a new patient?" She checked her screen. She had tattoos of squiggly lines on her fingers, her black hair plastered to her skull.

Mandy looked at Michael. "Not really. For Anna Golding."

"Oh." She looked at Anna and Michael. "Yes, okay. We'll need a new insurance card or will you be paying cash?"

"Probably cash today," said Mandy.

"Then that's one-twenty-five for the half hour."

Mandy fumbled her purse, set it on the narrow ledge, and pulled out her checkbook. Anna led Michael to the wooden chairs. A middle-aged couple sat stiffly, looking at their hands.

"It's just like I remember it," said Anna. "Even the awful music."

"Ha," said Michael. "Very therapeutic I suppose."

"Or not. Gosh, I'm so nervous. What will Dr. Lane think?"

Michael thought. "Did she . . . go to the memorial service for, you know . . ."

"The what? I don't know." She crossed her legs. She was wearing black jeans, a white men's shirt, and a black down vest.

Mandy sat beside them. "Now we wait. Keep your fingers crossed." She sighed. "I guess I didn't miss this place. But it's all good, right?"

"Yeah, need to keep her on track," said Michael.

"You too," said Anna. "I'm not the only loony tune here."

Michael laughed. "True. Birds of a feather . . ." He checked his phone and glanced at the sullen couple. The door opened to the back and a large man emerged, his face flushed, and he hurried out. A bearded man motioned for the couple, and they stood, stumbling over each other. In came a young woman with blonde hair. She looked tough, like a brick layer.

They waited, mostly in silence. And then Dr. Lane was at the door. She opened it and stood there, her gaze fixed on them. Mandy stood.

"Come on," she said. "Hey, Dr. Lane. Are we next?"

"Yes, you are. But . . ." She held the door open as the three passed her into the spacious back area.

They stood there in a little circle facing one another.

"I . . ." said Dr. Lane. She wore a sleek pantsuit with a ruffled long-sleeve blouse and heels. "Follow me." She led them to her large office with a window. There was a desk with a computer, a love seat, and two stuffed chairs. On the bookshelf were the letters PEACE.

"Hi, Dr. Lane," said Anna. "It's me, Anna."

"Well . . ." said Dr. Lane. She was tall with long blonde hair held back with barrettes, distinctly highlighting her thin face. "Have a seat, please."

Michael and Anna took the leather loveseat. Mandy sat near them, holding her purse in her lap like a picnic basket.

"You'll have to excuse me, but I'm completely dumbfounded," said Dr. Lane. She was still standing, as if about to go into the wrong restroom. "Anna, I was informed that you had . . . had passed. What's going on?"

"She's back," said Mandy. "Michael brought her back. She's pregnant, can you believe that?"

"She's back? But how?"

Anna spoke. "Just believe that I'm here. That's all. I know it's weird. Maybe I never left. I've just been in hiding, if that makes it easier."

"Okay. So who am I seeing today?" She remembered to sit and adjusted a pink coffee mug on her desk. She took the empty stuffed chair. "You'll have to excuse me. I'm just very confused."

Michael couldn't help smiling.

"It's for her, for Anna. She had a panic attack like you've never seen, on Wednesday. And her depression is coming back," said Mandy.

"Okay, well let me just get used to the idea that Anna is back." She looked from one face to another. "And, this is Michael?"

"Yes," said Michael. "We're like dating, I guess you could say, since last November."

"Hmm, last November. Right. Okay, I guess we can just get into this. There was a panic attack? Anna?"

"It was scary. It was about Michael. I had to see him. I was afraid he'd somehow . . . disappeared. Just like I used to do. And my depression, like Mom said, is coming back. It's hard to get up in the morning."

Dr. Lane took notes. "And you're pregnant? How far along?"

"About ten weeks."

"And Michael is the father?"

"Yep," said Anna. She squeezed his thigh.

"I see," said Dr. Lane. "I'll have to get your chart out of storage. What meds were you taking, for the panic attacks?"

"Oh," said Mandy. "She was on duloxetine, trazodone, and the Lamictal."

"Thank you. I suppose we'll just send in new prescriptions. I think we'll move you from the duloxetine to Paxil. Should help more with the panic attacks and the depression." She scribbled notes. "Are you having thoughts of hurting yourself?"

"Who me?" said Anna. She looked down then at Michael. "Yes."

"Honey," said Mandy. "Really? That can't be."

"Mom, I'm just telling the truth. The thoughts just come to me."

"Okay. Do you think about specific ways to hurt yourself? I need to know," said Dr. Lane.

Anna folded her hands. "Just the usual, pills, but I think about using a rope. It just plays in my mind."

"That's concerning, you know. Is there a rope in the house, or anything that you could use?"

"Not that I know of. I haven't looked for a rope, just think about it."

"What about pills? Do you have access to any?"

"Mom has them."

"We'll need for her to keep them under lock and key. Just to keep you safe. But we need to figure out how to keep those thoughts under control."

Mandy spoke. "We'll do whatever you suggest. We just got lax, you know, before."

"Before, meaning?" said Dr. Lane.

"Before she overdosed this last time. I found her, in bed."

"And she survived this overdose, which is not what I was told. You have to excuse my confusion here."

"No, she didn't. But she's back. Revived, whatever you want to call it."

Dr. Lane shook her head. "I'm still not clear. She's sitting here in front of me. Was there a service?"

"Yes," said Mandy. "She was, um, cremated." Her eyes were wide with possibilities.

"Okay," said Dr. Lane. "Gosh, I have to be honest, again, and ask you, Mandy. Do you have a history of any mental disorder? Should I be focusing on you? I feel that somehow I should be concerned."

"Not me. I'm fine," said Mandy.

"Okay. And Michael. Have you known Anna for long? Did you know her before . . . the overdose?"

"Um, I had met her twice, at parties at their house. I really wanted to ask her out then, but was too shy and afraid of the age difference. I wanted a second chance for me, for Anna. I wanted to help Mandy too. I started from there, and now we're here."

"You have to understand that I can't help but think that there is something terribly wrong here. I mean, I want to treat . . . Anna . . . but this somehow involves the three of you. You know that this sounds rather, um, unbelievable."

"But, I'm here," said Anna. "You remember me, right?"

"Yes, I do. And that is making my head spin. Do others know that you're back, that you've survived somehow?"

"Not everyone. Just the ones who can handle it," said Anna. "The neighbors freaked out."

"Gosh, I can imagine," said Dr. Lane.

"It's been tricky," said Mandy. "We were afraid of what you would think, but she needs help. Right?"

Dr. Lane put down her pen. "I guess I just have to accept what I am seeing. It's difficult. So, back to you, Anna. I want you to tell your mom and Michael when you are thinking of hurting yourself. Hopefully the meds will help. But, you can't carry the burden alone. Can you promise that you'll be honest with them? It's very important." She checked her watch.

"I promise. I just hate to worry anyone."

"Even if it worries them, you need to talk about this with people you can trust. They are there to support you, okay? I want to see you in a week. Are you still using the same pharmacy? I'll send those scripts in."

"Yes, the CVS," said Mandy. "We like the pharmacist there, Tom. My husband's name is Tom too."

"Okay, great. Can I do anything else for you today?"

"Thank you, Dr. Lane. I'm sorry to be troublesome," said Anna.

"No, no. You're fine. I'm the one with the problem getting my head around this. Okay, it's nice seeing you again, regardless, and call if you have any concerns okay? Just check with the receptionist to make the appointment. I'm thinking that I may want you to undergo some testing, just written tests, to gain more insight. We'll talk about that next time. Okay?" She stood.

Michael helped Anna stand. "Thank you," he said.

"Thank you so much, Dr. Lane," said Mandy.

"Yes, thank you," said Anna.

Back at the house, Michael had half an hour before leaving for class, and Mandy made them chicken noodle soup and cheese sandwiches.

"I feel so much better," said Mandy, seeing Michael to the door. "Thank you for going."

"Yeah, thanks, Soldier," said Anna. She leaned up, and they kissed.

"Okay, I'm off. I'll check in later this evening."

Michael walked into class with five minutes to spare. He said his usual hello and logged onto the computer. He soon checked roll, and five were absent, which he attributed to it being Friday. The day had become progressively grayer, as if it would snow. The low that night was supposed to be in the twenties.

They were still talking about flash fiction, and he had handouts. Since they were such a small group he had them gather their desks in a circle for an old-fashioned workshop, as he called it. Desks scuffled and screeched, and he took a seat beside Kia. He passed the first story around, "Reading the Paper" by Ron Carlson.

"So, let's take a few minutes here, five to be exact, and read this. This is a tight story. Pay attention to the rising action and the absurdity of what you're reading."

Five minutes passed.

"All I want to do is read the paper . . . but I've got to do the wash first." He read the first line. "What does this story sound like it's going to be?" The circle was quiet, eyes cast down.

"Coco, what do you expect after that first line?"

Coco scanned the single page. "It sounds like this woman is going to read the paper, but maybe she has a few chores to do. She's kind of annoyed."

"And then what do we learn? Riley?"

"Um, the family was killed in a car wreck last night, all except for her and Timmy. She's washing the blood out of the clothes. Kind of bizarre."

"Yeah," said Michael. "She just wants to read the paper, though, as if the deaths were a normal part of things. She just wants to get back into a routine. Is she crazy or just in denial?"

"She must be crazy," said Ronesha.

Michael laughed. "Perhaps. And then what happens next? What do we learn? By the way, this story is being told in the present tense, narrated from a first-person perspective, which brings us in close to the woman. What's next?"

"Timmy goes outside to walk to school and he's abducted," said Sam.

"What's the detail we are given here that helps to make this real? Sara?"

"The abductors are in a late model Datsun, light brown."

"Yeah, always use concrete details. That's a great detail, the Datsun. And what is the narrator's reaction?"

"It seems that she still just wants to read the paper," said Ronesha. "She *is* crazy."

"It seems that way," he said. "I used to work on a lock-up psych unit when I was younger. I was an orderly. We had this lady come in who had thrown a butcher knife at her mother. You know what she said when asked why she had done it?"

He had their attention, eyes glancing.

"She said, 'I just threw it like a banana,' as if that was the explanation. She was schizophrenic."

A few laughs.

"So, this is not so unrealistic, maybe? How we process information can sometimes be totally out of context with what is happening. And then what happens? The story moves quickly." He felt that race of excitement that discussing literature gave him. "Ashley?"

"A guy who's escaped from prison comes to the back door and asks if he can come in and rape her and cut her up a little. Jesus," said Ashley.

"That's right, and she lets him. Are we still in the story? Do we have some confidence that this lady is telling it straight?"

"I don't think so," said Andre. "She's just too far from reality."

"And maybe we don't like that," said Michael. "It makes us uncomfortable. We're feeling really uncomfortable right now, but we have to be concerned, right? She's telling the story, talking directly to us. What's a detail we get here?"

"Her coffee gets cold," said Andre. "Like that matters."

"Exactly," he said. "The coffee, the cold coffee keeps us grounded. We stay with the story based on that simple detail. What happens next?"

Coco spoke. "Her brother Douglas comes by, and he's got this growth on his shoulder. There's a John Deere cap over the growth."

"Ha," he said. "Right. And then two greasers steal his T-bird from the driveway, and she's worried they'll hit the mailbox but they don't. She doesn't even mention her family being killed the night before. How does the story end?"

"She stirs Cremora into her coffee," said Sara.

"And the last line." He reads: "'You know, as much I stir and stir this Cremora, there's always a little left floating on top.'" He looks up with a grin. "Does that ring true, the bit about the Cremora?"

"It happens," said Ronesha. "But why is that the end?"

"Yeah, why?" he said.

Sara spoke. "It's the concrete detail. Like you said, to keep us grounded, to keep us believing."

"I think you're right. The details. The genius is always in the details. A strange but satisfying little story." He paused then moved on to the next story, passing around the handout. The story was just as strange, "The Witch" by Shirley Jackson.

He finished up, without a minute to spare, and he reminded everyone to replace their desks. "Have a great weekend," he said, and the class emptied. He was high, excited, and remembered Anna and their baby. There was a party that night at her house that Tom was throwing. He wondered how it would go, what the details would be, how the story would progress, how it would end.

Twenty

The party started early at four-thirty, and Michael arrived at six. He was supposed to bring a dish, but just brought two bottles of wine instead. Tom met him at the door and glanced at the bottles. Zinfandel, Old Vine. He nodded his approval. The room was full, perhaps ten souls milling about, clustered in small groups, mostly folks from the creative writing department and their significant others. He paused and spoke with Edwin, an African-American poet whose poetry often resonated with the taboo N-word. When he read his work aloud it was like slow jazz.

Michael moved on, nodding to others and walked into the kitchen to deposit the wine. Anna was there, talking with a new hire, a tall guy with a permanent three-day beard and piercing blue eyes. She didn't seem to notice Michael. He placed the bottles on the counter and spoke.

"Hey, Jim." He touched Jim's shoulder.

Jim turned. "Hey, Michael. I was just talking with Anna. She was telling me about the baby. Congrats. I had no idea." He was drinking a Newcastle.

Michael hesitated. He moved closer to Anna. "Yeah, about three months along. You doing okay?"

Anna looked shy. "I'm fine. Thanks for going with us today, to the doctor." She let him hug her.

"No problem," he said. "Guess I'll get a glass of wine. You good?"

"Sure. One would be okay. I've heard that one glass is fine."

He poured the last of a bottle into his glass and opened a new one. He poured for Anna and handed her the glass.

"Last glass," said Anna.

"Okay, well I'll go mingle," he said.

"Okay," said Anna. She launched back into a conversation with Jim. She was wearing a short dress that highlighted her figure, cut low in the front.

Michael lingered for a moment, listening to Jim explain about his last job at the Naval Academy, and then moved on, back into the dining room. He gazed at the table filled with bowls of hummus, plates of carrots, little rounds of quiche, and a plate of carved ham among other delicacies. He spotted Mandy, and she walked his way.

"Hello, stranger," said Mandy. "It's been awhile."

Michael laughed. "Yeah, like six hours." He took a deep drink of wine and reached for a bite of quiche.

"I'm just so glad that we got her back in treatment. She can spiral out of control in a heartbeat. Been like that since she was teenager, since her dad died really. That's what triggered it. I'm pretty sure."

"There's always something," he said. He saw Florence and waved. She was a new hire as well, an essayist married to a guy from Italy. She wore beads and what he would call a hippy dress.

Mandy pulled him close. "Now don't let these other guys get too friendly with Anna. She's awfully impressionable." She squeezed his arm. "You're the best, though. You're the magic man."

Michael glanced toward the kitchen. "She's fine. What do people think? I mean, has anyone been freaked out that she's here?"

Mandy whispered, "Everyone seems to be taking it pretty well. They're all surprised that she's pregnant and that you're the father. But nothing can shock these people, you know, they're writers." She laughed.

Tom passed by, headed for more wine.

"Right," said Michael. "Maybe this will inspire some poems."

"That was the timer. Got some sausages in the oven." She moved past him.

He peeked into the kitchen and Anna was still in deep with Jim, a look of awe on her face. He waved but she didn't see it. Back in the living room, a chair had opened up, and he sat next to Sandra, a novelist, although she was writing mostly creative nonfiction lately. She wore a gray skirt with a maroon sweater. She was talking with Edwin's wife, Katia, an engineer originally from Germany. Michael listened in, the talk surrounding a recent school bus crash that had killed six children. He winced at the thought.

Sandra grabbed his arm. "Hey, Michael." She gave him a long look.

"Hey." He waved at Katia.

"Michael," said Sandra, "what do you know about Anna? Is everything I'm hearing true? How could it be?" Her eyes begged him.

Katia scooted her chair closer. "Yes, you must tell us."

Michael smiled. "She's back. I had wanted to ask her out before she, you know, and decided to see if she would appear again. At first no one else could see her, but she's become more solid, especially since getting pregnant." He felt that he was explaining a visit inside a black hole.

"That's just crazy," said Sandy. "You mean you basically imagined her back into existence? I mean, she's here. I see her with my own eyes. But I still can't believe it."

"It's hard to believe, but it's true. I just had to try, for Mandy's sake too, and Tom's. I suppose I was just the vehicle and now she's on her own. We've been dating since last November."

"But, she is pregnant, no?" said Katia. She had wavy red hair and creamy skin.

"Yes, it's true. We did an ultrasound and heard the heartbeat, but couldn't see the fetus just yet. We're going back in a couple of weeks." Michael crossed his legs as if settling in to tell a long story. He noticed others looking his way, eyes filled with questions. He realized that the three across from them on the couch were listening. Soft blues played in the background.

"God, this really is stranger than fiction," said Sandy. Her short brown hair was parted in the middle and bounced when she talked. Two graduate students were coming in the front door.

Michael spoke a bit louder. "Speaking of fiction, I've really been having trouble writing since Anna returned. It's like all of my creative energy goes into her. But, I guess that's okay. I'm really happy that she's back, that we connected. I just have this nagging feeling that if I had asked her out before she attempted, and succeeded, that maybe things would have been different. I don't mean to sound pompous."

Heads were nodding. It seemed the whole room was listening or trying to. He downed his wine. "Be right back."

He sauntered to the kitchen, his head down, hoping that Anna would be free, but she was still talking to Jim. He kind of looked like a football quarterback with his square jaw and broad shoulders. Michael opened one of the bottles he had brought and poured. He hesitated but then decided to join them, moving around Jim and facing him.

"So, what's up?" he said.

"Gosh, I don't mean to monopolize her," said Jim. "It's just such a fascinating story, you and her."

"Oh?" said Michael. "How so?" He turned to Anna. "You doing okay? You look good. Love that dress."

"Thanks," said Anna. "I thought that maybe with the baby I wouldn't be able to wear it, but my bump is not really a bump yet." She laughed and rubbed her belly.

"I hate to ask," said Jim. "But has there been, like, any media interest in this? I mean, it's just miraculous, right? I'm trying my best to imagine how this could be. I mean, this is the first time that I've met Anna, so maybe that makes it easier."

Michael shifted to one leg. "No, I've wanted to avoid that. It could be dangerous. I think this all depends on how well everyone believes. Most people would just think it was a hoax or something, right?"

"But, they can't. I'm here," said Anna. "There's no doubting allowed."

"But people can be pretty mean about something like this," said Michael. "Not everyone wishes us well." Others were gathering around, cramping the small kitchen.

"But no one here, right?" said Anna. "I mean, Jim believes."

"Totally," said Jim. He gazed around at the others, all listening but trying to seem inconspicuous.

Mandy squeezed in. "So this is where everyone went. Anna, you okay, Sweetie?"

Anna rolled her eyes. "Yes, Mom."

"Good. Come out and eat, mingle instead of staying holed up in the kitchen." She moved some paper plates to the trash and began rinsing silverware.

There was a general silence in the room.

"I guess I'll step out and puff on a stogie. Want to join me?" said Michael to Anna.

"No, they're bad for you. You can't smoke when the baby comes." Anna looked defiant, her arms folded.

"I'll come with you," said Jim.

"Aww," said Anna. "We weren't through talking. Don't stay long. It's cold outside."

"We won't," said Michael. "Just a quick one."

Michael made his way through the small crowd and Jim followed. Just off the dining room was a screened-in porch with chairs and ashtrays. He pulled out a tin of Partagas 1845 minis and offered one to Jim. Florence and her spouse, Orlando, had joined them. He pulled a pack of Camel Lights from his jacket pocket. Michael lit up and passed the lighter to Jim.

"Not really a smoker, so this should be interesting," said Jim. He took a seat on the padded glider.

"I usually smoke when I write," said Michael.

"I wish I could quit," said Florence. She had shoulder-length graying hair. "My vape helps, but I still bum off of Orlando."

Orlando smiled and shuffled his feet, taking a chair. Florence joined him, and then Michael felt that he should sit as well. He waited for the questions.

"So, we hear that you're going to be a dad?" said Florence. Orlando put his arm around her. He was tall with long curly blonde hair.

Michael laughed. "Yep, again."

"I hope you weren't trying to keep it a secret," said Jim. He puffed on the little cigar.

"I wasn't trying to broadcast it, but it's fine. As long as everyone believes. That's what's important. It's like you have to keep turning the page." He inhaled the smoke, which he didn't usually do and coughed. "Oh . . . sorry."

"What's not to believe?" said Florence. "She's here in the flesh. I met her once last semester, right after we moved here, at another party here. I was shocked when I heard about what had happened. And I guess I was shocked to see her now. I have to be honest."

Edwin walked out with Tom, and they took the last two chairs.

"Want a smoke?" said Michael.

"Sure," said Edwin.

"I'm out," said Tom. "I'll just inhale your breathy exhalations." He laughed and placed an open bottle of red on the small table.

Michael handed the lighter and a cigarillo to Edwin.

"So, Tom, I'm eager to hear what your reaction has been . . . to Anna returning," said Florence. "And here she is."

Anna stepped down onto the porch, wearing an oversized leather coat, Tom's. Immediately, Jim stood, and offered her his chair.

"Sit, silly. I'll sit in Michael's lap. He is the father of my baby after all." She flipped her hair from inside the coat.

"My pleasure," said Michael, brightening.

"So, Anna, we were just talking about you," said Florence. Orlando glanced around nervously.

"My ears were burning," said Anna. She leaned back into Michael, wrapping the coat around her. He dropped his cigarillo in the ashtray.

"She's a miracle," said Tom. His cheeks were red from the wine and his breath made smoke in the cold air.

"Michael," said Anna. "Stop shaking your leg. You're jostling the baby."

Florence seemed desperate to speak. "So, how? I mean, how? Tom, you must be as mystified as I am. Sorry to be so direct."

"Yeah, how?" said Edwin.

Tom glanced at Michael. "It's Michael's doing. He wished her back. He came over one day and said that he wanted to take Anna out for coffee. When Mandy told me, I was furious. At that point I couldn't see her, but gradually she began to appear, to eat at the table. The more time she spent with Michael, the better she got. That's all I have."

"Gosh, Tom," said Anna. "I'm not a science experiment." She laughed and snuggled with Michael.

"He doesn't mean like that," said Michael. "At first I was afraid, but then I just had to do it. Like writing a story that I'm driven to write. There was no chance for failure after that."

"Hmm," said Florence. "Fascinating."

The silence.

"So, Jim was telling me about his love life. He's doing the website dating thing," said Anna. "Have you been on more than one date with anyone?"

Jim cleared his throat. His cigarillo was down to the nub. "Once, because she wanted to. I didn't really want to, though." He looked embarrassed. "It's just hard, meeting new people in a new place. Um, so, Florence, how did you and Orlando meet?"

Florence looked at Orlando. He was shy, but spoke. "She was my teacher." He laughed and batted his eyes.

"Really?" said Tom. "Interesting."

"Yeah, my ex was my teacher too," said Michael.

"You still have feelings for her," said Anna. "He's always at her house." She play-slapped his face then kissed his forehead.

"We're just good friends still. I go over mostly to see the girls. It's important. You know how it is. I hate to say it, but my leg's going to sleep, Honey Pie. I'll get another chair."

"No, no," said Jim. "Here take mine. I'll get another one."

"I'm cold anyway, Soldier. I think I'll head back inside. You smokers can smoke."

"Really?" said Michael. "Okay."

Both she and Jim went inside.

There was that silence again, and Edwin stood and left them, but out came Sandra and Katia, taking the empty chairs.

Talk meandered around a recent luncheon that had been billed as being sponsored by the "people of color" faculty at the college. Someone had objected to the terminology accusing the organizer, who was African American, of being racist, which had everyone stymied. But talk soon returned to Michael and Anna.

Katia spoke. "So, Michael, will you get married?" A little film of ice seemed to glaze over the group.

"I've been wanting to ask the same thing," said Sandra.

"We've discussed it, possibly moving in together. You know, one thing at a time. We're not sure that it will be necessary, marriage that is. Not that I'm against it, with the baby, of course." Michael reached for the glass left by Edwin and poured himself wine.

"You definitely have to live together before you get married," said Florence. "Otherwise, how will you know that you'll be compatible? Right, Orlando?"

Orlando nodded. "Of course. To be sure."

The talk meandered, Michael repeating himself. He suddenly felt the cold and excused himself, hoping to not find Anna with Jim. He pushed the door open with its glass doorknob and stepped up into the warm house. He grazed for a moment at the table, eating some ham and a cookie. He peered into the kitchen. He walked into the living room where there were half a dozen gathered, including the graduate students. Mandy motioned for him to come and sit by her. He glanced into the hall. He then could see the outline of two bodies on the front porch, Jim and Anna. He felt a sinking feeling and sat beside Mandy who patted him on the leg.

Twenty-One

The next day, a glum Saturday, Michael awoke around noon. He'd promised to take Yancy to the coffee shop and worried that he'd missed his chance. He enjoyed hanging out with the girls and was worried that he was spending too much time with Anna. He had not missed a day without calling or seeing her and decided to see if she would call him. He pulled on his wrinkled jeans and an old green sweater. Arty was thumping his tail, impatient to go for a walk.

"Hold on, boy." He scrubbed Arty's ears, looking for his phone. He found it charging in the living room and texted Yancy. She responded right away, had a friend over and could she go too?

He took Arty for a short walk, seeing two squirrels, which sent Arty into a frenzy. He fed the cats and cleaned the litter box then headed over to Suzanne's wearing his Trinity College ballcap that Claire had brought him from Ireland the previous summer.

Inside was Claire, her hair wrapped in a towel.

"Daddy!" She coiled herself around him.

"Daughter!"

Suzanne came out from her bedroom. "Gosh, you're looking pretty homeless. You okay?"

"Just slept late."

"Hey, Dad!" said Yancy from upstairs. Soon, she and her friend Emma came bounding down the stairs.

"Hey!" he said. "Ready to go? Claire, you want to go?"

Claire made a face. She didn't necessarily enjoy hanging out with Yancy. "No, got chores and a school video I'm doing for history. I might need you to take me to a cemetery, though, maybe later or tomorrow."

"Sure, what's the topic?" He sat on the battered mauve couch. Suzanne was threatening to replace it any day now, which was fine with him.

"You know Ed Johnson, the guy that was hung on the bridge?" She folded her arms, assuming an academic pose.

"Yeah, that was horrible. What year was that?"

"1906. I found out where his grave is."

"Cool, yeah we'll go."

Suzanne stood, listening. "It's a great project. So how is Anna? I'm surprised she's not with you."

"At home I guess. I saw her at the party last night." He pulled his cap over his eyes.

"Something wrong?" said Suzanne.

"Dad, let's go," said Yancy. "I'm eager. Emma's eager."

"Okay, hold on. Contain your eagerness. I guess I'm jealous. She was talking with this suave new guy from the department. I like him, but she talked to him the entire evening it seemed."

"I'm sorry. I'm sure she just needs a little breathing room, that's all. You're the dad in the picture. When's the next ultrasound?"

"Next week."

"Don't worry, Dad. She has panic attacks over you," said Claire.

"Dad's worried, aww," said Yancy.

Michael stood. "Okay, coffee and an espresso pour moi." He jingled his car keys, and they were out the door.

He parked on the street and saw the homeless man with the shield of hair. His afro was solid, like a piece of wood that he peered around. He never spoke, never begged, but people gave him money and cigarettes anyway. Michael started to cross the street.

"No, Dad! Go to the crosswalk. You'll get hit."

He turned and followed them, crossed the street. There was a long line inside.

"So, Emma, what've you been up to?" he said.

"Just dance is all, dance, dance, and more dance."

"She's a dancer, Dad, in case you missed that."

"Ha. A dancer. Why you must dance?" He wiggled his eyebrows.

The line moved and soon they ordered, both Yancy and Emma getting the frozen chai lattes, even though it was forty degrees outside. He ordered coffee with a doubleshot of espresso on the side. He needed it, still feeling groggy.

They took a table and had to borrow a chair from another. Emma eyed him curiously and whispered to Yancy.

"Dad, like this is a surprise, but Emma wants to hear more about Anna."

"Okay. What do you want to know?" he said.

Emma sipped. "Is it true that she . . . committed suicide?"

"That's a harsh one," said Yancy. "A real digger, this one."

Michael sighed. "I wish it wasn't true, but it is. She overdosed."

"Well," said Emma. "Yancy's explained this to me before, but how in the world did she come back? I mean like a resurrection? My mom keeps asking me about it and my sister too."

"Yeah, Dad, all of my friends ask me about her, about you, whether or not you're crazy, which you are."

Michael laughed. "Think of it this way. I'm writing a story and I needed her for the story. She wanted to be a part of the story, and voilà you have Anna. There's no magic, just a lot of faith."

"Wow, that's just so cool. Are you guys like in love?" said Emma.

"I think so. We've said the L word. She's a beautiful person. She deserved a second chance." His eyes misted.

"Aww, Dad, don't cry," said Yancy.

"Sorry. Maybe I still can't believe it's real myself."

"She's real, for sure," said Yancy. "And so are you, Pops. A swell guy." She punched him in the arm.

"Ow, thanks."

Within seconds Anna was forgotten as Yancy showed Emma her latest Minecraft creation, a mansion complete with swimming pool and indoor garden.

Michael gazed around the busy room. The coffee shop had been a Subway before. A skinny girl with long dreads was doing some kind of math homework it seemed. He glanced at the young cashier behind the counter. She always wore really tight tops that outlined her breasts. Her nipples were poking out like ice cubes. He marveled that it had been at least a month since he'd had sex with Anna. At first it was every day, but since she became pregnant, she seemed uninterested. He wondered if the meds would give her libido a kickstart, but it would probably be the opposite.

The girls finished their drinks and were ready to move on, so up they went and out the door onto the gray sidewalk, a plastic beer bottle in the gutter. At the crosswalk, he pulled out his cellphone and started to dial Anna, but put it away. The dress shop on the corner was having a sale. The Mexican place was busy as always, and the art store empty.

Back at the house it was decided that he would grill steaks and have dinner with them, for which he was grateful. Until then, he left and did a little grocery shopping—Diet Coke, beer, orange juice, coffee, yogurt, and a frozen pizza. He had a few hours to kill and once again started to dial Anna, but didn't. He wondered if she'd given her number to Jim. Surely, she wouldn't do that. Right? He remembered some grading he needed to do and donned his jacket, his knit hat, grabbed a cigar and his computer, and headed onto his little patio. Arty was happy to be on his leash and promptly began barking at a passerby.

"Arty, no!" he said. Arty toned it down, but still barked. Michael opened his laptop and got to work, a cold breeze blowing.

Anna was flush, combing her hair in the bathroom mirror. She brushed her teeth, flossed, and applied makeup, taking special care with her eyes. She'd not told Mandy and hoped to slip out without much of a fuss. In her robe, she hurried to her bedroom, petting her old cat on the head. She slipped into some loose jeans, worried about squeezing the baby, and tried on a couple of shirts, before settling on an old flannel shirt from the thrift store. Her breasts were getting larger and larger. She tucked it in and tightened her belt. Mandy had bought her a new pair of hiking boots and that rounded out her outfit. She planted her hands on the dresser and checked her teeth.

She encountered Mandy in the hall.

"You're going out? When's Michael coming?" She rubbed Anna's belly. "Keep that baby warm. Wear your wool coat."

"He'll be here soon. Going to the art museum."

"Really? That's new. Should be fun."

"And maybe we'll have dinner after that, not sure. Okay, Mom, move, I need a glass of water."

"Geez, settle down," said Mandy. "I'm still your dear sweet mother."

"I love you."

Anna filled a glass and drank it down, checking the clock on the stove, three p.m. Now she had to pee and hurried to the restroom. Before she could flush, the doorbell rang.

"Shit," she said. She could hear the front door open, voices.

Mandy's eyes grew wide at the sight of Jim. He was wearing slacks with a tailored shirt with thin pink stripes and a corduroy blazer.

"Hey, wasn't expecting you. Are you going with Anna and Michael to the museum?" She put her hands on her hips as Jim passed.

Anna emerged. "Jim, hey, right on time." She walked up to him and touched his arm. "Ready?"

"I thought Michael was coming. Is he meeting us there?" said Jim. His teeth were perfect and bright white.

"Yeah, he'll meet us there. Thanks for the ride by the way."

Mandy looked puzzled.

"Okay, Mom, we'll be back. Jim's a big boy." Anna laughed.

"If you say so. Don't be too late, though. Don't want to tire the baby."

Jim fidgeted. "Okay, see you soon."

Anna rushed out to his car—a Subaru Forester—opened the door and got in. He slipped into the driver's seat. The car smelled of something tropical.

"That was close," said Anna. "And, no, Michael's not meeting us. I just had to say that to keep her from worrying."

"Wait, so just you and me?" said Jim. "Are you sure? I mean is Michael okay with it? I mean your company is desired, but . . ."

"Of course he is. He's not the jealous type. I need to get out. We need some space. I realized that at the party. You look good."

He drove. "Thanks, and you as well. Looks like you're going on a hike. Nice boots."

"I'll take that as a compliment. She brushed back her shiny hair. She had to direct him to the museum, and they had some difficulty finding a space on the street.

The exterior of the museum was swank and curved with glass and steel. Inside was dead quiet, and Jim paid their admission getting a university discount. The visiting exhibit was a collection of photos by Frank Paulin, street scenes.

"So do you like art?" said Anna. She walked very close to him.

"Yeah, I do. This is a treat. More of a modern art person, but they're supposed to have a nice permanent collection here."

They passed a line of charcoal sketches, pained faces.

"So, was Michael busy today?" said Jim.

"Probably busy with his girls. He needs to spend time with them, and I understand that. Want to go see the photos first?" A gallery of paintings and sculpture opened to their left.

"Yeah sure. I just don't want to get in the middle of anything is all."

"You're fine. I'm just getting to know you, to know new people. It's my new life, right? I can't just spend it with Michael."

They took the stairs. A guard sat outside the large exhibition room divided into two spaces by a short wall.

"Will you sign the register, please?" said the guard.

"Sure," said Jim. He signed and gave the pen to Anna.

Anna began to write, but nothing came. "Pen's out of ink."

"Really?" said the guard. She fumbled in a small drawer for another pen.

Anna tried again, but nothing. "That's weird."

"Go on ahead," said the guard. She wore a white shirt and gray trousers with big black shoes.

"Yeah, okay, thanks," said Anna.

"Odd," said Jim.

"Pens," said Anna.

They began to their left, viewing a large horizontal photo of a man carrying what looked to be flowers. He had dark shades and a black leather jacket. Behind him were blurry people.

"Times Square, 1956," said Jim.

Anna was already at the next photo, an image taken through an upside-down triangle of glass into a diner. A waitress framed there.

"Interesting," said Anna.

"Yeah, the contrast of the black and white is pretty vivid. Must have been taken at night." Jim took a few steps back for a better look.

"Oh Lord, we'll be here all day," said Anna, laughing.

They perused the exhibit more at Anna's speed and then headed downstairs to the permanent collection, passing very few people. Jim was drawn to a vivid painting, "Pomegranates with Murano Vase" by Daud Akhriev. The vase and pomegranates oozed a rich carmine. Anna stood slightly behind him and held onto his jacket like a little girl peering from behind her father.

Jim looked down at her and smiled, but noticed something odd. "Hey, are my eyes playing tricks on me?" He stepped away, gazing at her.

"What? What is it? I'm not fading am I?"

"It seems that maybe you are. Should I do something?" said Jim.

"Maybe I need to see Michael. He keeps me solid. I haven't talked to him today. I think maybe he's angry with me."

"Because of me? That's not good. I really thought that he was coming with us."

"Maybe I told a little lie," said Anna. "But I don't want to leave just yet. Let's just keep looking. Maybe the art will inspire me."

Jim looked troubled. "If you say so. This is just so strange."

"Come on, how about this next one? Tell me what you think."

March by the Sea by Milton Avery. A lone sunbather in red and black reading on a beach.

"It's so simple," said Jim. "Look at how plain the sky is and no features on the face. Kind of disturbing in a way. Like the person is not really . . ."

"I like her hat, kind of like a sombrero," said Anna.

"This was created in 1945, but looks like it was painted yesterday. The end of the war. I wonder if that plays into this, the anonymity, the general blankness of war."

"Now you're getting too deep. Keep it simple. She's enjoying herself, reading. It's a bright day. No clouds, and it must be warm. She's wearing a short skirt it looks like."

Jim was looking at her. "Yeah, that's a good observation."

They meandered through the rooms, Anna dimming just ever so slightly. No one else seemed to notice. They paused in front of a dark painting. *Landscape with Moon* by Ralph Albert Blakelock. Greenish moonlight played through thin clouds reflected off a pond, a dark, dark wood.

"Reminds me of Halloween," said Anna.

"Yeah, very eerie but beautiful," said Jim. "I hate to say this, but maybe we should go. Maybe you should call Michael. I'm worried about you."

"But you and I were going to have an early dinner, but I'm not hungry. Let's get coffee. The shop is just a block away. We can walk there." She tugged on his sleeve, a pleading on her fading face.

"Okay, but I feel like we need to hurry."

They glanced at a few sculptures on the way out, back into the brisk air. The sun was smeared on the clouds. Across the way, land had been cleared and graded for a new hotel. They walked, Jim keeping his eyes on her. By the time they reached the coffee shop, he could see through her hands.

Inside was crowded, mothers with kids, dads looking helpless at the chaos. By the time they had their coffee, no tables were open and they stood against the wall.

"Want to sit outside?" said Anna.

"Hmm, it's fairly cold. Want to just walk to the car?"

"No, but maybe we should. Let's finish our coffee at least. We didn't get it to go."

"Right," said Jim. "So do you have to see Michael everyday somehow, to keep going . . . to stay visible?"

"Not every day lately. It's the baby. It's like he's inside me. Maybe he knows I'm with you, and he . . . he's making me disappear." She took a deep swallow of hot coffee. "Ooh."

"That can't be good. It would be great if we could all be friends, right?"

"I guess, but I should be able to date other people if I want to. It can't just be him."

"Date? So is this a date?"

Two chairs at a counter opened, and they moved into them.

"I don't know. I was hoping it would be. I had such a great time talking with you last night. You're my age, right? Michael is older, kind of like my father."

"I suppose," said Jim. He shifted on the stool. "This is not so comfortable."

"Okay then. Let's just go. I can tell you're creeped out."

"I'm sorry. I'm just worried is all. Yeah, let's go." He took a last sip.

On the walk to the car, she faded even more, her legs, her face, her hair. Jim walked at a clip. They piled into the car and were off.

"Gosh, don't drive so fast," said Anna.

"Mandy's going to be upset, and Tom too, when I bring you home like this. Which way?"

"Left and then right. Maybe I'm being selfish. I don't know."

With her directions, he had her home within fifteen minutes, and she was a shadow of herself, except around her belly, which seemed to be floating. He jumped out and opened her door.

"God. Hurry," he said.

"It's okay. It's okay. I'll come back. I can't even feel it."

Jim followed her up the sidewalk. She opened the door and warm air whooshed out.

"Anna, is that you?" said Mandy from the kitchen. Tom was at the dining room table doing email.

"Yeah, we're back," said Anna.

"Anna?" said Tom. "What's happening? Jim? Where's Michael?"

"Hey, Tom," said Jim. "I tried to get her back as quickly as possible. I had no idea."

Mandy emerged from the kitchen, wiping her hands on a dishtowel with a trefoil pattern. "What's wrong?" She stared at Anna. "Anna? Oh no, you're going away. What happened?" She hurried into the living room.

"I'm sorry," said Jim. "Maybe it's my fault."

"Mom, I'm okay. Maybe I just need to call Michael. Maybe he can come over. I feel fine."

"This is just not good," said Mandy. "How will this affect the baby?"

"The baby's fine," said Anna. "I feel just fine."

"Here, sit down," said Mandy. "Take your coat off. I can see right through you." She reached to touch her hand but nothing was there. "Where's my cell phone?"

Jim cleared his throat. "Maybe I should be going. Thanks, Anna, for showing me the museum."

"Yeah, that was fun. Promise me we'll do it again. You have my number."

"Okay, will do. Okay, bye ,Tom. Bye, Mandy." Jim let himself out, as if escaping a burning building.

Tom had stood but looked unsure of what to do.

Mandy was back with her cell phone, dialing. It rang. Anna sat on the couch, a leg folded under.

"Hello? Michael? It's Mandy. You have to come over right away."

"What? Is everything okay?" said Michael.

"It's Anna. She's disappearing. Can you hurry over? She needs to see you."

Michael was in the middle of grading short essays. "Sure, no problem. Can I talk to her?"

Mandy handed the phone to Anna. "Talk."

"Hey, Michael. I'm fine, just getting misty is all. You don't have to come over."

"Yes, he does," said Mandy.

"What happened? You sure you're okay?" said Michael.

"I went to the museum with Jim. It started there." She looked like she might cry.

"Really? Huh, with Jim. You guys really hit it off last night. Is there something I should know?"

"No. We're fine. I just wanted to get out of the house. He called me."

"Okay, well I'm coming over. Mandy is upset. I'm a little confused about Jim, though. Was it a date?"

"Look, Michael, I need to go out with other people, not just you. I feel so isolated."

"I see. I guess I have to be okay with that, but I still feel concerned. Is he still there?"

"No, he freaked out and left."

"Anna, give me the phone," said Mandy. "Michael, she won't do that again. You're the reason why she's back and not Jim. We're sorry about what happened."

"Nothing happened," said Anna.

"Yeah," said Michael. "It's kind of like I could feel it, her fading. Let me go, and I'll be right over."

"Thank you, Michael. Be safe."

"Will do."

Mandy sat beside Anna. "You can't do that again, going out with other men. It's like negative energy. You never told Michael you were going to the museum in the first place, right? How could you?"

"Mom, I'm a grown woman. I feel trapped sometimes. I need friends."

"You haven't made any effort to reconnect with some of your girlfriends. Why is that?"

"I don't know. They just wouldn't understand is all."

Tom sat beside the couch. "It's clear that going out like that is not good for you. It's still a miracle. You have to respect that."

"Ugh," said Anna. "I'll be in my room." She stood and drifted toward the hallway.

"It just gets stranger," said Tom.

Mandy nodded in agreement.

Twenty-Two

Classes were over and July was hot and dry. Michael had the summer off, except for one online class, which he managed easily. Anna had progressed nicely, now at nearly eight months, the baby growing and her bump enlarging into a significant bulge, but to the consternation of everyone, the baby did not show up on the ultrasound, just the rapid heartbeat. Michael had helped start up a website of undergraduate research and creative activity for honors students and was scheduled to fly to Utah, where the group would meet in Bryce Canyon for a three-day workshop. At first Anna had said she didn't want to go but changed her mind. Mandy bought her a sleeping bag and a rugged outdoor gear bag. The day before they left was filled with last-minute packing, buying travel toothbrushes, and sorting out the logistics of the four students that would be accompanying them.

Michael picked up Anna at six a.m., and they rode to the airport in relative silence, the radio playing Jim Croce. He parked, and he carted both of their bags to the terminal. Three of the students were there, already checked in. They would be meeting in Utah with six students from two other colleges, Southern Utah University and Graceland University, each school sending a faculty mentor as well. Bobby Freyer from SUU had made all of the arrangements for camping and a space where they could meet as a group. Morton Ayers from Graceland University was a good friend of Bobby and a camping buddy.

After checking in, Michael gathered the students— Grayson, Ted, John, and Monica—and gave them their per diem travel money, $180 for each. They were all in awe of Anna, asking her questions.

"So is it safe to fly when you're pregnant?" said Grayson. She had red hair, was peppy, and always looking for the bright side.

"I think so," said Anna. "My doctor's okay with it. I just worry about sitting down for so long. My feet are already swollen." She wore tennis shoes tied loosely.

"Just want a happy baby," said Grayson.

Michael laughed. "And a happy Anna."

Passing through screening, Anna was selected for a full body scan. The only thing visible on the screen was a pen in her pocket. This caused some confusion among the screeners, but they let her through after a discussion with the supervisor who was dumbfounded. John was the first to suggest coffee, and everyone except Grayson got in line at a deli, the only thing open at the hour.

"So, did you hear the supervisor say that she'd only seen a case like yours once before, at a training institute in Maryland?" said Michael.

"Yeah, but that would mean there's more like me out there," said Anna. She wore a pair of gray stretchy maternal pants and a loose long-sleeve shirt with a heavy scarf.

"Exactly, and they know to make exceptions. Like they know what's going on without saying it."

"Sounds like it."

With coffee the group gathered loosely at the terminal, speculating about what the weather would be like in Bryce Canyon, how cold it would get at night. It looked like it would range from the forties to the high seventies. Michael had brought his zero-degree sleeping bag, knowing how miserable it was to spend a night cold and on the ground.

Flying Delta, their first stop was in Atlanta and then the longer ride to Salt Lake City. The students were scattered throughout the plane but Michael and Anna had adjoining seats. Anna pulled out her plastic knitting needles and yarn. She was working on a small sweater for the baby. Michael dozed at first, but then tinkered with his novel, using his laptop. The novel was about a shady character named Chevron who rented mobile homes on his property, which was a junkyard. One home was an old converted school bus. At night Chevron would lock everybody in by closing a gate to the fenced property and put padlocks on the trailer doors to keep the people inside.

"So, how's Chevron?" said Anna.

"He's got one lady pregnant who's married. The husband thinks it's his own baby, but the baby is going to be born with red hair, just like Chevron's. I expect there will at least be a fist fight."

"Will the lady deliver in a hospital?"

"Are you kidding? The baby's going to be born at night, so the gate will be locked. Home birth with the big revelation."

"That's sad. You have to be nice to your characters."

"I am. I have to push them into corners, though, to see how they react. That's part of the fun. Here's a typo. I spelled clam instead of calm." He laughed.

"The nitty gritty details," she said. "I need to use the restroom. The baby is sitting on top of my bladder." The stewardess passed, picking up cups and trash.

"Yeah, right. Sorry about that." He stood and let her pass. He waved at Monica, headphones on.

Anna wobbled down the aisle, holding her belly. She passed an Indian woman holding a little baby girl, and she stared as she passed. Anna's stomach was queasy. She pushed into the tiny lavatory. There were pee drops on the toilet seat, and she cringed. She used a paper towel to clean it and sat, and the pad in her panties caught her eye. There was some spotting of bright red blood. She panicked, thinking the worst. She finished and washed her hands, racing back to her seat. Before he could stand, she crawled over him.

"What's wrong?"

"There's some blood." She stared out the window, vast stretches of green and brown, a single road like a thread.

"Really? A lot?" He touched her thigh.

"Just some spotting."

"I think some can be normal, right? You're not having contractions are you?"

"No, but Dr. McCormick said to let him know. There could be some problem. Now I'm worried. Maybe this wasn't the best idea. Maybe we shouldn't have had sex."

"Maybe. But, you needed to get out of the house, get some fresh air," said Michael. "Maybe you shouldn't do the hike, though. We're supposed to go on a canyon hike in a couple of days. Bobby's leading it."

"I was looking forward to that. Would you stay with me, though, if I can't go?"

"Of course. I wouldn't leave you."

"Good." She picked up her knitting needles. "Mom was so against this, you know. I'd hate for her to be right."

"It'll be fine. You're not having any cramps are you?" He put his hand on her belly. "I can feel it moving."

"No cramps. Yeah, he, or she, is really doing some somersaults in there. I hope there's enough oxygen in this plane."

The air whooshed, the wings of the plane slicing through wisps of cloud with a small shudder. Behind them a few rows back the Indian woman's baby had begun to cry. They sat in silence, Anna knitting, and he returned to his novel.

On the descent to Salt Lake City, the sinus over his right eye wouldn't clear, and he winced in pain. Just as they landed the pressure released with a squeal inside his head. They walked slower than normal, letting the group go ahead of them.

"Need some food?" he said. "We have an hour."

"Yeah, I'm starved."

There was a TGI Fridays with a short line and soon they were seated. She ordered a steak with baked potato, and he took a giant hamburger with fries and a tall glass of cold beer.

"Near beer," he said. "Probably 3.2 percent alcohol. The Mormons, you know."

"Should you be drinking so early in the day?" She tackled her steak with gusto.

"It's the privilege of traveling. No rules, right?"

"I suppose. Don't get drunk."

"Ha, not on this. They have all sorts of rules about alcohol in Utah. You know you can't sit at a table in a restaurant if you only order alcohol? You have to sit at the bar."

"Huh."

"Yeah, but what you do is tell the waiter that you're thinking about what food you'll order, take the table, and then you just keep telling him that you haven't decided yet. It's a game the people play here."

"Weird."

"And you can only order one drink at a time. But you can order a sidecar, which is legal."

"What's a sidecar?" She put more butter on her potato.

"If you order, say a shot of bourbon on ice, you can order another shot to sit beside it called a sidecar. So it's considered ordering one drink. Kind of silly."

"Yeah, seems so."

The time slipped away, and they hurried to the gate, meeting up with the students. The next flight to Cedar City was on a CRJ900, relatively large considering the tiny airport at Cedar City. The flight took just a little over an hour. Anna had to use the restroom twice, the baby crushing her bladder.

Bobby met them at the airport, his truck already packed with gear. Michael rented another SUV, a Buick, and soon everyone was at the hotel for their first night in Utah. Michael lugged their bags down the long hallway, and Anna pushed into the clean room, the AC running full blast.

"Cold," said Anna. "I need to change my pad and check." She stepped into the bathroom and closed the door.

Michael arranged their things. It was closing in on three and he was hungry and sleepy. Back home it was five, so he slipped out his meds and downed them with a bottle of water. He sprawled on the bed, tempted to sleep.

"You okay in there!"

There was no response, but Anna emerged after a few minutes. "Not good," she said. "There's even more spotting. Bright red."

"Maybe it is because we had sex. No cramping, though?"

"No. But I don't feel right. It could just be the traveling." She climbed onto the bed next to him. "We may need to call Dr. McCormick. See what he says."

"If it seems right. We should call now, before we head out to eat."

"Yeah, I suppose. This is just making me nervous. What if he says I have to drive home and not fly?"

"I doubt that. That would be just as stressful. That's a long haul." He tousled her hair. "I'll take good care of you. You have the number?"

"Yeah." She sat on the edge of the bed and dialed her cell. "Hello?" She explained the situation to the nurse, and the nurse said that she would tell the doctor and have him call her. "Thank you," and she hung up. "That makes me feel better."

"Good, let's make this a fun trip. What did you think of Bobby?" Bobby was medium height with sun-weathered skin, a geologist at SUU. He always had a tiny sparkle in his eye, as if he was about to discover something new.

"He's nice. Is he married?" she said.

"Lord, do you think he's cute? He's a manly man."

"Stop. He is cute. I felt like he was flirting with me."

"Ha, he's newly married, less than a year I think, but his wife lives in another state. Maybe he's lonely."

"He'll have all of those young college girls to look at. And they're not pregnant. Am I still pretty this way?" She rolled into him.

He put his arm around her. "Of course, even more so. You have that pregnant glow about you."

"Yeah, you've said that before. It's not like gross to you, that I've gained some weight? I feel like an aircraft carrier."

Michael laughed. "That's an image. No, you're totally fine. You look great. That's why Bobby was giving you the business. I'll keep my eye on him, though. He might be another Jim."

Anna slapped his hand. "Stop. You just won't let that go will you?"

"Why should I? You had the hots for him, maybe still do. He is a handsome fella. He's dating someone, though."

"Good for him."

Her phone chirped.

"Hello? Hey. Thanks for calling."

She explained again about the spotting, about the trip, that they would be camping for two nights in Bryce Canyon. Dr. McCormick expressed some concern, said that the altitude could play a role, to take it easy, not to lift anything, and definitely not to go on any strenuous hikes. He added that she should stay well hydrated, being a dryer climate, as well. And that was that. He said to call if there were any new developments. She put the phone down.

"Did you hear that?" she said.

"Yep. I'm on it. No lifting for you, not even a toothpick. No hiking and drink lots of water. Here." He handed her his water bottle. "Drink."

"I can't drink after anyone. You know that. I'll use a glass from the bathroom." She went that way, and he pushed the remote, turning on the TV. It was Trump and Hillary, a very strange election indeed.

Dinner was pizza, and they drove there, very near the hotel. Talk with the ten students revolved around the website. Morton had arrived from Iowa and took over the conversation, proposing a strategy to get everyone on the same page regarding how the pieces would be edited.

Morton was thin, casual, and full of humor. The others chimed in but were mostly in agreement. Michael had ordered what he thought was beer, but it turned out to be a very strong ginger soda, and he struggled to drink it. They ordered six pizzas, and Anna nearly ate an entire pizza herself, feeding the baby as she said. The pizza was oven-fired with a thin bubbly crust.

"This chicken mole pizza is the best," said Monica. Her father was Muslim and her mother Catholic. She had been working with the website for two semesters. There was content on the site, but it hadn't officially gone live just yet. The goal of the Bryce Canyon retreat was to meet with other student editors and formulate an editorial plan and moves to engage viewers with the site.

Anna belched and held her belly. "Whoops," she said. "Excuse me." She stood, dropping her napkin and lurched toward the restroom.

Michael stood and followed, his heart in his throat. He stopped at the door and could hear her retching, the pizza coming up in waves. He waited a few seconds and knocked. "You okay?" And there was no response. He turned the knob and opened the door, hit by the smell of vomit. Anna was on her knees. He saw where she had partially thrown up in the sink and gagged.

"I, I think I'm cramping," she said. And then it came again, her face in the toilet bowl.

Michael held his breath and stepped in, letting the door close. He flushed the toilet once and then again. "You through? You okay?"

"God, I'm not okay. I've never thrown up dinner before, with the baby. I feel terrible." She held out her hand.

He turned on the sink water, trying to wash down the vomit, but it mostly stayed. "Here, try and rinse your mouth."

She cupped water and spit, gagging. "I've got it in my hair, dammit."

He wet a paper towel and tried to clean her hair. She took it from him.

"God, what a mess," she said.

"Let's get you back to the hotel. I'll run and get some Gatorade for you. Need to stay hydrated. Think you could hold that down?"

"Thank you, maybe so. God. I'm a little angry."

"Why is that?"

"You made me this way, right?" She wiped her face.

"Really? I mean it takes two, right?"

"You had sex with a ghost and got her pregnant. It just seems weird that you would do that."

"But, you're not a ghost. Right?"

"Right now I feel like one. My stomach is cramping." She took a deep breath. "Maybe it's a contraction."

"Let's get going. Do you need a minute? I'll go pay, okay?"

"Okay."

He left and walked to the table. They had already gotten a box and had the pizza packed.

"Is she okay?" said John. His cheeks were always flushed, as if about to reveal a dark secret.

"Is it just the baby?" said Grayson. "I mean, we're not sick."

"Yeah, morning sickness in the late afternoon." Michael went to the cash register and paid, leaving a big tip. He warned the cashier that the bathroom would need cleaning and apologized.

Anna stumbled out of the bathroom, looking down at the ground as if it was moving. "Michael?" She latched onto his arm.

The group murmured their condolences, and they hurried back to the hotel packed into two vans. Michael walked with Anna to the room and then left to buy some Gatorade, and she wanted Funyuns as well. He grimaced at the thought. He drove like a maniac and was soon back. He let himself into the room, and Anna was on the bed, taking deep breaths.

"You okay?" he said.

"I don't know. For now, I suppose. I brushed my teeth." Her eyes looked dark and rheumy. She took an open bottle of clear Gatorade and drank. "Thank you. That was the pits. I'm scared for the baby, though. Can't be good for it."

"We'll really take it easy with you. I'm serious. You're not even allowed to stir your coffee. Some better?"

"Yeah, just hold me a for a while. I'm really afraid." She drank, opened the bag of Funyuns, and put them aside. "Maybe a bad idea for now."

"Sure," and he nuzzled against her, smoothing back her hair that had gone a bit wacky.

"Do you still love me, after seeing me like that, like a chucking drunk? You're warm. It's still too cold in here."

"Of course. Ha, the body is designed to expel. Your system is a A-OK." He turned the AC off and gazed through the large window, an interstate in the distance. "Maybe that was practice for the baby."

"That's cruel," she said.

"Just kidding." He turned the TV on, and she guided him to *House Hunters*. "What about *Hoarders?*"

"That's an awful show."

"Maybe after the baby comes, we'll just let the trash pile up, throw dirty diapers in the corner, keep all of the baby gifts and boxes. One day we'll be squeezed between a pile of garbage and the ceiling."

"Lovely," she said. She focused on *House Hunters*. "Why is it that the couples always want a different type of house? She wants a bungalow and he wants something modern."

"That's the best. Real conflict. They'll have to duke it out. People love that sort of thing."

She sipped Gatorade and belched. "Oh Lord!" She slipped off the bed and ran to the bathroom with Michael right behind.

Twenty-Three

Anna made it through the night without further episodes, and the spotting seemed to have stopped. Michael drove to Southern Utah University's campus to meet up with Bobby and Morton, each with their own vehicles. It was just the second chance for all of the students to meet one another, and there was much smiling and glancing. Bobby split the groups up so that the students riding together were from different colleges, a first step toward team building. Michael and Anna wound up with John and his red cheeks, two students from Graceland, Amber and Studs, and one student from SUU, Marilyn. The back of the SUV was jammed full of sleeping bags and tents. Michael had not brought a tent, much to Anna's dismay, Michael saying that it was best to sleep under the stars. At one point, she threatened to shack up with Bobby if it started to rain, and she was serious.

The caravan headed up I-15 for roughly an hour, turning onto Route 20. The terrain rolled, passing by stands of pinyon pine and Arizona cypress, small lakes, and the occasional silo. The students hit it off, talking the whole way, while staying glued to their phones, although reception was spotty. Michael tended to drive in silence and enjoyed the scenery, glancing at Anna.

"How's the tummy? The baby? Moving?" he said.

"Yeah, kicking away. I'm okay for now. I only had that biscuit for breakfast, and I'm starving. I hope to God that the spotting has stopped. I feel like we're headed into no man's land."

Michael laughed. "Bobby and Morton bought a shit ton of food, so we can eat when we get there. Doesn't look like we're stopping."

"If I say stop, you need to stop, right?"

"Yeah, sure." The convoy was behind a log truck, but moving along.

Soon, they passed through the town of Bryce, an outpost with motels and an RV park. They would be staying in the North Campground and pressed on for another mile. The dusty orange canyon opened up to their right, a maze of building-sized, sedimentary hoodoos, towering rock spires eroded by wind, snow, and rain.

Once checked in they circled the campground, finding three adjacent camping sites, and everyone fell into line, unpacking and setting up tents.

"Gosh, we're just out in the open, except for these trees," said Anna. "At least put us near the bathroom."

"Okay, no problem." He located a flat piece of ground covered with pine straw and removed cones and small rocks. "Got you an inflatable pad. Just like a hotel."

"Yeah, right. I'll be back," and she headed to the bathroom.

Michael spread a tarp and arranged their bags and pads, leaning their bags against a downed tree that had fallen long ago, the bark calving with the weight of green lichen. He noticed Morton smoking near the road, trying to be inconspicuous, and he joined him, a small cigar in hand.

"Get set up?" said Morton.

"Yeah, we're roughing it. No tent." He lit up with his butane lighter.

"There's a fire ban, so no fires," said Morton. He flicked ash, a two-day stubble of beard on his face.

"We can use the camp stove, though?"

"Yeah, Bobby's in charge of that. He's the woodsy chef. He'll divide the kids into teams, let them each cook a meal at night, wash the dishes."

Michael glanced back and Bobby was already hard at work, setting up the stove, carrying portable bags of water for washing the plates and forks.

"Does he need help?"

"No. He's got a system." Morton laughed.

"I'm not really hungry, but I think Anna is."

"Is she going to be okay?"

"Yeah, I think so." He saw Anna and waved her over.

"Hey," she said. "I see the evil men have gathered to create clouds of smoke. Michael, really?"

"Hey, he started it," said Michael. "Just keeping him company." He noticed that Amber was staring at her tent. "Maybe I should help." He clenched his cigar in his teeth and walked that way. "Need help?"

Amber nodded, holding the end of a flexible rod. She was blonde and just a little hefty and seemed embarrassed that she needed help. Together, they arranged the poles, shoving them through the tent sleeves. He puzzled over how to attach the ends of the rods to the tent base.

"Here, like this," said Amber, and she showed him how.

"Right," and soon the half-dome tent was complete. Now he was embarrassed and retreated back to Anna who had drifted to talk with Bobby.

Dinner that night was burritos and Anna only ate one, although she wanted two. Her cramping was back, and she had spotted again. She told Michael that she needed to walk about, and he joined her, meandering along the dusty, rocky campground road.

After dinner and cleaning up, Bobby announced a short walk to the canyon rim where they would do a little team building exercise. It was getting dark, and they cut through some empty campsites to the main road. Stars riddled the fading sky. At the edge of things, Anna and Michael gazed out over the canyon below, holding hands.

"It's like a puzzle," said Anna.

Michael agreed. "It's like a red bathtub filled with toys."

Bobby corralled the group, instructing them to pair off with someone they didn't know well and to chat for five minutes. After that, he had each person tell the group three things that they'd learned about their new friend. It was a bit corny, but worked nonetheless, eliciting the group's curiosity about one another and a few laughs at the quirks discovered. Melissa, a beauty queen of sorts, enjoyed mowing her family's lawn with a small tractor. An hour passed and dark inched down, starlight casting shadows.

"I don't feel so good," said Anna. "Kind of dizzy, and I'm cramping."

The group had broken into clusters, heading back to camp, led by Bobby with the high-beam flashlight. The ground was littered with branches, stones, and spiky yucca.

"Hold on. Maybe the walk will do you good."

"God, I don't think so. Oh!" She doubled over.

"Jesus, you okay?"

"No!"

A group of students slowed. "She okay?" said Monica. The others looked on, concerned.

"Yeah, just need to get back to camp," he said. He put his arm around her, but she shrugged it off.

"We have to hurry. I'm feeling it, like the baby's coming." She stumbled forward. "I feel like I need to be sweeping the floor." She stopped again and groaned.

Gradually everyone passed them, all inquiring if she was okay. Michael guided her through the ground debris. She stopped every minute or so and grabbed her knees.

"I'm not going to make it, Michael. I feel so bad. It hurts so bad."

"God, we'll just have to get you to the hospital." He realized that he'd not thought to locate the nearest hospital beforehand and felt negligent. "Come on, not much farther."

To save time, Michael took them right through an occupied site. Two guys eyed them curiously. "Sorry, she's pregnant," said Michael. "No problem," they said. They hit the dirt road and then entered their site. Bobby and Morton were waiting for them.

"Do we need to get her out of here?" said Bobby. He adjusted his ballcap and scratched his chest.

"Maybe so," said Michael.

"I need to lay down," said Anna. "Now." She bent double and shrieked. Her water burst, liquid soaking her stretchy jeans, running into her shoes. "Oh, no! It's coming. Help me, Michael!"

They zigzagged to their sleeping bags. Michael wished he had set up a tent. She went to her hands and knees.

"Take deep breaths," said Michael. He'd watched his two daughters being born.

The students stood back, murmuring, straining to see through the darkness.

"Can you make it to the car?" said Michael.

"No, it's coming." She moaned and shrieked. "Oh no. Get my pants off. Now!"

Michael went to his knees and fumbled with her jeans, pulling them down. Her white skin seemed like the inside of an oyster shell. He felt the wetness.

"Can you lay down? Do you want to lay down? Can I get you some water?"

"I don't want any fucking water! Oh!" She squatted and lay back, her legs pulled up. "Take off my panties, hurry!"

At that Bobby and Morton retreated, Bobby searching for his cell phone. Michael pulled his sleeping bag over to cover her, but she kicked it off, lay back, and arched, groaning. He took his position at her feet, his heart racing, his hands cold. The night air was chill and dry.

The contractions seemed like laps at the Talladega Superspeedway, roaring passes with perfect timing. On his knees he coached her with deep breaths in and deep breaths out. She raised forward as if doing crunches, her face contorted. Only the starlight lit the scene, but soon Bobby cranked an SUV and beamed the lights toward them, like center circle at the circus.

"Fuck me!" said Anna. She pushed.

"Slow and easy," said Michael. "You're going to rupture a blood vessel."

"Fuck you!" said Anna, and her face contorted as if her feet were being sawn from her legs.

"I can see something. The baby's coming. Just keep pushing. Breathe deep."

"You okay!" said Morton from ten feet away. All around faces peered toward the scene.

"Yeah!" said Michael.

"Is it coming?" said Anna. She held her breath and pushed, her eyes bulging.

The headlights were blinding Michael. He squinted. "Coming. I see the head. Keep on!"

Anna grabbed her knees and pulled and pushed at the same time.

"It's face down," said Michael. "Doing good!"

Anna pushed, yelling at the top of her lungs.

"It's turning. I see the face. Oh my God! The shoulders!"

Anna grunted, panting, and pushed. The baby slid out face up. It was a boy.

"My God," said Michael. He held the baby in his arms, the umbilical cord dangling. He wasn't breathing. He turned him on his arm, held him upside down, and slapped his buttocks over and over.

The baby coughed and coughed and then let out a rebel yell. Sounds of clapping. A couple of the girls were crying.

Michael thought back to the birth of his two daughters. "Here, you need to breastfeed." He helped her pull up her shirt and bra. She gripped the baby, crying. The baby latched on, as if by magic, and Michael moved around behind her to support her torso, helping her to sort of sit up.

"Oh, God," she said. "Cover me up."

Michael reached for the sleeping bag and covered her. "You did it, you did it. You gave birth in the fucking woods. Jesus."

Anna gasped, looking down at the baby, holding it tight as it sucked, released, found the nipple, and sucked again.

Bobby approached from behind. "Hey, I've called 911. An ambulance is on the way, to take you to the hospital."

"Good," said Michael. "I guess that's good."

"Fucking yes!" said Anna. "I'm a mess. I'm still cramping."

"Lord, we have to cut the cord," said Michael. "Bobby! Get me a clean knife!"

Bobby hauled ass and retrieved a large knife. It was clean, and he handed it to Michael. Michael leaned over Anna and sawed at the glistening cord, severing it.

"The placenta is next," he said. "Do you feel like pushing? Anna?"

"Yeah, I think so," she said.

It took another five minutes. She bore down as if birthing Satan and out slid the huge organ, wet and bloody with the pearlescent cord attached. Michael sighed in relief. He sat back on his knees, his legs falling asleep. The baby on Anna's chest, seeming to smother her.

"Here," he said. "Let me sit behind you. Lean into me."

"Get me off the goddamn ground for Christ's sake. Get me one of those camp chairs and hold this baby while I try to dress. God, he's fucking cute! But, what a mess."

The students cheered her on from the sidelines. "Great job!" said Monica.

Morton dragged a chair over, averting his eyes as needed. "Should we call off the ambulance?"

Michael helped Anna stand, holding the crying baby with one arm.

"I don't know. Anna, do you want the ambulance to come?"

"Hell, yes! I need a warm bed to lay on, not pine needles. Jesus!" She lowered herself into the camp chair. "Give me the baby, sweet baby." She pulled up her sweatshirt to nurse him. He snuffed his crying, moaning and attacking her nipple like it was Fort Knox. "Ow, little bugger. Slow down."

Michael shielded his eyes from the SUV's headlights. "Bobby, what's the ETA on the ambulance?"

"They said forty minutes. The hospital is in Panguitch, a small one." He walked a little closer.

Michael dug a towel out of his pack and draped it over the baby, the baby sucking like a wild man, stopping every ten seconds or so to wail and hunt the nipple.

"You did great," said Michael.

"Yeah, but we should have been at home, not here. I must have been crazy to come." She rocked in the chair, wincing. "I need my shoes back on."

Michael eased them on. "There. You need something to drink?"

"Ha, I think you need something to drink," said Anna. "But sure, some water would be perfect. I feel dizzy."

All of the girls had gathered in a knot with the guys hanging back, murmuring. Monica heard Anna and drew off a plastic tumbler of water.

"Here," said Monica. "I've never seen anything quite like that." Her long black hair shined in the headlights.

"Thank you, but please turn those damn lights off. Maybe get a flashlight. I feel like I'm on *Star Search*."

Those nearest chuckled. Bobby cut the lights. He opened the rear hatch to keep the interior light on.

"Can I see?" said Michael. "My first son. I can't believe it. Born here. Maybe he'll be a park ranger." He squatted beside Anna, balancing on his toes.

"Oh God, I'm cold," said Anna. She pulled the towel back to show the shadowed pink face in the penumbra of the flashlight.

"Wow," said Michael. "Looks healthy. Has great lungs. That's good."

Another thirty minutes passed with Michael helping Anna struggle into sweat pants and vague sounds of a siren could be heard. The sound got louder and louder. Bobby had run out to the main road to flag it down. Soon, the ambulance pulled up and stopped, two paramedics piling out and rushing forward.

"Over here!" said Michael.

The female paramedic spoke. "Everyone okay? Ma'am, you okay?"

"I think so," said Anna. "Just really cold."

The male paramedic was checking her pulse. "Feels thready, rapid. Probably needs a liter of IV fluid. You did good, young lady."

"Yeah, that was fantastic," said Michael. "She gets an A-plus." He watched as the female checked Anna's blood pressure.

They returned to the ambulance and removed the stretcher. A crowd of onlookers had gathered. "Is anybody hurt?" said one. "Did I hear gunshots?" said another.

Anna crawled onto the stretcher, Michael holding the screaming baby wrapped in a towel. They lifted the stretcher like an ironing board and rolled her to the ambulance.

"Can I ride in the back?" said Michael. "No, I should drive. I have a rental." He fumbled in his pockets for keys and couldn't find them. "Shit."

The male paramedic started an IV and began a drip of normal saline. The female hooked up Anna to an ECG

monitor. About ten minutes passed, and they were ready
to go. Michael kissed her and then tried to kiss the baby,
but he was preoccupied beneath a warm blanket. Anna was
shivering, her teeth chattering, and off they went, lights
flashing but no siren.

Twenty-Four

Anna spent that night in the hospital and was released the next day around two. Everyone was healthy, the baby acting like he should, breastfeeding like a champion. Michael drove her back and booked a hotel room for her in Bryce. She had called home and given Mandy the news.

Michael made sure she had everything she needed, including lunch, and drove to the campground to check on things. He found the group gathered in an old cabin with a cathedral ceiling. Several folding tables had been set up. The students were deep into a conversation about how best to approach editing pieces for the website. They were going to do a trial run, reading and scoring an article and a story to try and reach some middle ground regarding scoring criteria. He was impressed with his students holding up against the others, taking leadership roles in the discussion, especially Ted who was always maneuvering to be at the head of the pack.

As five p.m. approached, he excused himself and drove back to the hotel to spend the evening and night with Anna and the baby. They had settled on Jon Thomas as the name on the birth certificate. He knocked on the door and swiped the key. The room was cool and smelled like a baby. He had bought diapers and baby powder at the drugstore.

"I'm home!" he said.

"Shh," said Anna. She was sitting up in bed, little Jon Thomas beside her covered with a towel.

Michael nodded and tiptoed over to take a peek. "Sleeping. How long?"

"About half an hour. Do you think we could leave early? I mean I hate for his first days to be spent in a hotel, plus Mom is about to go crazy."

Michael looked at her. She seemed paler than usual.

"I have to think about the students. I'm a driver. How would they get back?"

"Can't Bobby and Morton figure that out?"

He pulled the chair over to the bed. "Maybe, but one of them would have to drive us back to Cedar City. I don't know. It's just two more days."

"Can you just try? Call or get on the Internet and see about an early flight out?"

Jon Thomas stirred, his little fists trembling.

Michael nodded and watched in amazement. "Wow, we're so lucky, right? You feeling okay? Are you up for the flight? You look awfully pale."

"I lost some blood for sure," she said. "I'd just feel better at home."

"Yeah, I guess you're right. I'll check."

He pulled out his laptop from his carry-on backpack. He had to call the front desk for the Wi-Fi password.

"There's a noon flight tomorrow. Too late for today. How about that?"

Jon Thomas snuffled, his little mouth searching. His eyes opened, and he seemed to smile but then went into a minor wail. "Uh oh," said Anna, and she brought him to her chest. "Feels like a plunger on me."

"Ha, you're so beautiful right now." He reached and stroked Jon Thomas's head of damp brown hair.

"Thanks. I don't feel so pretty right now."

Jon Thomas sucked, his eyes closed.

"Okay. I'll call Bobby and see what we can work out."

He called and Bobby answered. "Hey, Bobby, it looks like Anna wants to leave early, tomorrow at noon. Can you give us a ride back to Cedar City?"

When Bobby arrived, he pulled Michael aside, saying that Anna looked "dim." Michael just passed it off as exhaustion and they drove directly to the airport with their bags, arriving an hour early. The small terminal was homey with what seemed to be too many persons working the small gate.

Anna clutched Jon Thomas to her chest, bobbing him as they made their way through the checkpoint. Michael showed the baby's birth certificate and had to fill out a boarding verification document. Since he was less than two weeks old, Jon Thomas also needed a letter of medical clearance to fly, but the clerk, listening to the story of the birth in Bryce Canyon, just winked and let them pass.

"Whoa, that was nerve wracking," said Anna. "I wish we had some baby clothes. People are staring." Jon Thomas was swaddled in a long-sleeve t-shirt and wrapped in a hotel towel.

"Nah, who cares? All he needs is us. Can I hold him?" He shifted his backpack between his legs. He gazed at her, her edges having become just a bit fuzzy. "Do you feel okay?"

He took Jon Thomas like a loaf of bread and cradled him, gazing at his tiny face, his tiny swollen eyes.

"I feel tired and damn sore. I need to stand." She stood and walked back and forth, her hand to her back.

Michael glanced from her to Jon Thomas. Jon Thomas yawned and popped a spit bubble. Michael moved him to his lap, cradling his head. Beside him sat a teenager with headphones on. Across the way in front of a large window, several people sat, including two young men, Mormon missionaries headed out to their assignments. The waiting room had been packed with family and well-wishers. They looked so young, wearing dark slacks and white shirts with ties. Anna went from one side of the room to the other.

"How's that precious baby?" said an older woman with long straight black hair.

"He's fine," said Anna.

"How old is he?" She had perfect little teeth.

"Just two days old." Anna sighed. "He was born in the canyon, Bryce Canyon, at the campground, in the middle of the night."

"Oh my," said the lady, her eyes widening just a bit. "How exciting. You must have been quite surprised. Was he early?"

"By about three weeks." She glanced back at Michael. "But we went to the hospital. He's got all his parts. Ha."

"Ha," said the lady. "You take good care of him. So young to be flying."

"Yeah, well nice to meet to you," said Anna, and she moved back to her seat. "Doing okay?"

"Yeah, he's a good baby. You're lucky he came out as fast as he did. I remember my youngest daughter. It took her forever to come out. She was facing up instead of down."

"Don't remind me. That hurt like hell, but he's worth it." She touched his warm cheek with her fingers.

"Better you than me. I can't imagine pushing out something that large, although he's so tiny. You forget how tiny they are."

At that, Jon Thomas opened his eyes and turned his head from side to side, his lips searching.

"He wants Mommy," said Anna. "Hand him over, big boy."

Michael whispered, "He likes mom's beautiful breasts."

"Shush," she said. "Give me the towel." She maneuvered as best she could and raised her sweater and unfastened the bra in front. Michael held the towel over her, and little Jon Thomas latched on like there was no tomorrow.

Michael gazed at the ceiling and then around the room. He could tell that people were trying not to stare. "We should charge them all a dollar to watch."

"Ugh," said Anna. "You're insane."

"Just kidding." He could smell her motherhood, the milk, the baby. "Mandy will lose her mind when she sees him."

"Yeah. She's been calling for the last half hour, but I'm just too tired to talk."

"She'll flip, and Tom will too, once he sees him. So, are you still going to live with me or do you want to go back home? I mean, I want you to stay. It's been nice having you around."

"I don't know. I feel like Mom needs to be around him, but all of my stuff is at your place. I mean, I'm not sure. Ow, he's biting me." She peeked at him beneath the towel. "Hey you. Be nice to mommy."

"Just like his daddy." He laughed.

"Okay, Soldier, enough of that. This is so totally *not sexual.* I mean I get this kind of thrill in my chest, but not like when we're having sex." A man with a long beard passed by, his eyes glued to the floor.

Within five minutes, Jon Thomas was satisfied and slid off the nipple, his eyes opening and closing. She burped him, and he fell asleep on her shoulder. They sat there for a few minutes and then came the boarding call. They were the first to board and walked onto tarmac, a stiff warm wind blowing. The stewardess, Ronette, oohed and aahed the baby, saying she had three teenage daughters. They found their seats, just even with the wing. Michael noticed that Anna seemed even dimmer and was alarmed but didn't say anything. He figured it was somehow connected to the baby.

Within twenty-five minutes, the cabin door closed. There was only the single plane at the airport and takeoff was quick. Anna bobbed Jon Thomas, but he opened his eyes, took it all in, and began to wail. She tried her best to soothe him, but on he cried.

"Here, hold him for a second."

Michael took Jon Thomas, whispering into his ear. Anna got herself ready and took him back, moving his mouth to her breast without bothering with the towel. "Hush, little baby." A woman across from them was smiling.

Soon, she had little Jon Thomas under control, distracting him with milk. He broke away twice, sputtering in complaint, but was soon going limp, called to slumber by a full tummy. She seemed to be having trouble holding him.

"You okay?" said Michael. His ears had not yet equalized, and he swallowed and pinched his nose, blowing out.

"Yeah, just weak is all. This is draining, and I should be hungry but I'm not. What's that about? I'm thirsty, though."

"Want me to get the stewardess to get you some water?"

"Yeah, and can you hold him for a while?"

"Sure." He took Jon Thomas from her like a tissue-wrapped crystal and cradled him next to his chest. He reached up and pushed the button.

Within seconds, Ronette was there. She nodded at his request and returned with a bottle of water for Anna. "Anything else?"

"No, thank you," said Anna. She struggled with the bottle cap. "I can't open it."

"Give it to me." He maneuvered the bottle to his lap and twisted the cap, all while holding the baby. "I'm like a Swiss Army knife."

"Thank you." She drank the water, and Michael imagined he could see it pouring down her throat.

In Salt Lake City, they had an hour, and killed some time walking but Anna said she was tired, bone tired, and that worried Michael. Jon Thomas had woken and spent a pleasant twenty minutes wobbling his head, eyes wide, mouth puckering. Michael held him like a banana in the crook of his arm.

They were first to board again, and this time the flight was full, and their seats were not together. Michael wound up next to a window near the back with Anna on the aisle a few seats forward. He helped her sit and adjust Jon Thomas before moving back to his seat. He suddenly felt very tired and with the large woman next to him reading a Dean Koontz novel, he closed his eyes and drowsed through takeoff. He woke an hour later to commotion in the aisle. He saw the stewardess holding a baby, his baby, looking about. An electric knife pierced his heart. He tried to stand, fell back from the seatbelt, and went to the stewardess, holding little Jon Thomas who was bawling like a scalded cow.

"My God," she said. "Do you know where she went, the mother?"

"That's my baby. I'm the father. She was sitting here. Our seats were separated." He reached out for Jon Thomas, but she held onto him, confused.

"Check the bathrooms, please. She can't just leave a baby lying in the seat like that. For God's sake."

Michael stared at the empty seat and bumbled his way to the back. One bathroom was open, and he opened the door. Nothing. He waited for someone to emerge from the other and hoped it would be Anna. But she wouldn't have left the baby like that. He could hear Jon Thomas screaming. After a minute, he knocked. He knocked again.

"Hold on!" came a voice, a lady's.

Michael turned and stepped on the shoe of a man wearing a tie. "Sorry."

The man examined his shoe and nodded. Finally the door opened, and it was a short older woman. Michael could see the part in her hair, the scalp just there.

"Shit." Anna was gone. He walked back to the stewardess. "Give me the baby please. She's not in the restroom."

"What? She can't just disappear." She made no motion to give him Jon Thomas.

"I can't explain it, but she has . . . disappeared. I'm the father. I have the birth certificate to prove it." The entire plane was watching.

"May I see that?" she said. "There, there, baby, it's okay. Shush, shush." The other stewardess was coming toward them with the drinks cart.

"Jesus Christ. Anna, please God." He rifled through his backpack, pulling out an envelope and carried it to her. "Here, there is my name, the father. I'm Michael."

"Okay, I need to see some identification from you. Shush, shush." She bobbed little Jon Thomas who was dressed in a humongous t-shirt and a diaper.

"God almighty," and he pulled out his wallet. "Here. Plain as day."

She examined his driver's license. "Okay, you're the dad after all, but where is the mother? Is she in another seat? You need to check every seat. I'll have Sandra go up front to first class." She handed over Jon Thomas.

Michael took him, instantly recognizing Anna's deep brown eyes, the way the eyebrows arched and bunched as he cried. He felt like he was standing alone on a tiny iceberg that was flipping over. He scanned the seats ahead, but saw nothing. He knew that she was truly gone and returned to his seat, finding it hard to breathe. He did his best with Jon Thomas, but nothing would console him. The woman next to him was horrified and had quit reading her novel, staring straight ahead. He didn't even have a pacifier, let alone milk or formula. It would be another three hours before the plane landed. Out of desperation he hugged Jon Thomas to his chest, tears streaming down his face. The life that had been Anna had been transferred to this baby, and he would never see her again. He was sure of it. How would he explain to Mandy and Tom? What if the news media learned of it? What would happen? Would someone try to take away the baby? How could he raise a baby by himself? Tears spilled, wetting the top of Jon Thomas's little brown head.

Twenty-Five

The stewardess had borrowed a diaper from another mother on the plane and given it to Michael. He had changed Jon Thomas in the tiny bathroom, nearly dropping him in the toilet, his eyes wide with wonder, flinching when Michael flushed.

With the time change, it was around five p.m. when the jet landed. The stewardess had said that a missing person's report had been filed and that he would be interviewed once inside. He brushed that aside, worrying only about his encounter with Mandy and Tom. He gripped Jon Thomas. He was whimpering, snuffling Michael's chest. He would need to stop somewhere and buy formula and a baby bottle.

Indeed there was a policeman waiting there as he entered the cool terminal, but he kept his head down and marched forward, headed to the baggage area. It worked, and he had to pee and entered the men's room. It was best to use a stall, and he did that, balancing his backpack, Anna's carry-on bag, and the baby. He had to hang the bags on a hook and then unzip, holding the baby who was being remarkably tame. Michael reloaded and turned the corner quickly headed for the escalator down. The airport was fairly quiet, people moving at a leisurely pace. He passed the rental cars and squinted to see which belt would be his flight's and then little Jon Thomas had had enough and began belting out a tune.

"Oh Lord," said Michael. He maneuvered next to the belt waiting for it to clank along. "Jon Thomas. Jon Thomas. It's okay. Daddy's here, gonna go buy some food for you." He bobbed him as best he could. A porter tapped him on the shoulder and asked if he needed help, which he did. "I'm fine." He scouted the area for the policeman. The alarm sounded and soon the luggage was making its rounds. It took a few minutes, but soon he had the two bags. He decided to get outside quickly and struggled to hold both bags with his right hand and then manage the two carry-ons. He couldn't do it and looked around for the porter, but he had found another passenger in need.

"Fuck."

He left the bags sitting in the middle of things and hurried to get a cart, but it was two dollars. He fished out his wallet, nearly dropping Jon Thomas, who was screaming like a boiled lobster. With his stuff on the cart, he saw the cop coming down the hall, and he turned and exited through a large revolving glass door. He fought to remember where he had parked and just headed into the parking garage as fast as he could. He stopped to shift arms. He was sweating, his back and forehead.

"Come on," and the elevator opened.

He exited on three and on a hunch just started walking. He wasn't sure where the car keys were. Finally, he stopped and dug around, finding them. He pressed the button and heard the beep and saw the flashing taillights of his silver Corolla. He didn't have a car seat and just lay Jon Thomas on the front passenger seat, his face a knot of red and mucous.

Sweat pouring down his face, he finally was locked in and safe, he hoped. He half expected a patrol car at the exit, but he passed through, paying thirty bucks. On the road, he puzzled his next move. What store to go to? He wasn't sure. Maybe a Walmart and he headed to the nearest one, the AC blasting, his hand on Jon Thomas who looked terrified.

"It's okay Buddy, gonna be okay."

With screaming baby in the crook of his arm, he headed into Walmart and took a buggy. First, he located the car seats. Then the diapers. Then the baby food.

Finally, he was at Mandy's house, completely frazzled, his hair a mess, the combover not looking so hot. He hopped out, scooped up Jon Thomas and stepped onto the familiar cement porch. He knocked, holding his breath.

The door opened.

"The baby!" said Mandy. Tom was right behind her, smiling.

Michael pushed his way inside, hoping against all hope that maybe Anna would appear from her bedroom. Jon Thomas seemed stunned, as if holding his breath.

"Anna? Where's Anna?" said Mandy. She put her hands on her hips. "Did she take another flight?"

"No. She . . . disappeared. On the flight." He sat on the couch with Jon Thomas. "She's not here, but Jon Thomas is."

Mandy's body trembled. "Disappeared? How? Why? That's her baby." She moved closer but was stunned.

"Are you sure?" said Tom.

"Yep. She was on the plane. I fell asleep. I woke up and the baby was in the seat by himself. We searched the whole plane. Maybe she'll come back. I don't know what else to say."

Mandy looked through the curtains at the car. "Is this a joke? I mean. I want to love on that baby . . ."

"Not a joke. It's real. I was stunned." He lay Jon Thomas on his lap, exhausted.

"She'll come around," said Tom. "Maybe she just needed a break."

Mandy sat beside Michael, her eyes on the baby. "He's so tiny, and he has Anna's eyes. Tom, look." Tom came closer, his arms folded.

"I'm sorry," said Michael. "Maybe it's my fault, focusing too much on the baby."

"Let me hold him," said Mandy. She took him and held him to her chest. "He's so warm." Jon Thomas began to search with his mouth and make bleating sounds like an injured lamb.

"He needs his mom," said Michael. "But, he needs you too. I bought food." He stood. "I'll be right back."

"Precious baby," said Mandy, cradling him, rocking him.

Tom came closer, scratching his head.

"What do we do?" said Mandy. "Tom, what do we do?"

"Well . . . we wait. See if she comes back. But meanwhile we have to take care of this baby. What's his name again?"

"Jon Thomas." She smoothed back his dark brown hair.

Michael returned with diapers, formula, and bottles. He'd bought a bottle warmer as well. "I have this stuff. Do you know how to make a bottle?"

"Yeah, sure," said Mandy. She was in her jeans and a red t-shirt. "Here, I'll be right back."

Michael took the baby. "Want to hold him?"

"You hold him for now," said Tom. He took a seat in an armchair and adjusted his ballcap. "This is just all so unexpected. Maybe she shouldn't have gone on the trip? Did the travel do it?"

"I don't know. I don't know," said Michael. He stretched out his legs and sighed. Jon Thomas continued to cry, almost seeming to give up.

"This is going to be very hard on Mandy."

"Yeah, I know."

"What can we do?" said Tom.

"Just hope is all. Meanwhile, there's the baby, her baby, my baby." He moved his shoulders back and forth trying to soothe him.

Mandy returned with the bottle, the kind with the plastic bag. "It's not warm." She handed the bottle to Michael.

Michael cradled Jon Thomas, his baby, her baby, and let him explore the nipple, a drop of formula there. He made one loud cry and then began to suck, his eyes open, looking for Anna.

About the Author

Pushcart Prize and *Best American Short Stories* nominee Russell Helms has had stories in *Whitefish Review, Driftwood Press, Bewildering Stories, Drunken Boat, Sand,* antiTHESIS, and other journals. He holds a lectureship in English at the University of Tennessee at Chattanooga with degrees from Auburn, Yale, and Eastern Kentucky University.

About the Press

Unsolicited Press is a small publishing house in Portland, Oregon. Operated by volunteers, the team works to produce stellar fiction, poetry, and creative nonfiction.

Learn more at www.unsolicitedpress.com.

www.ingramcontent.com/pod-product-compliance
Lightning Source LLC
Chambersburg PA
CBHW051636180726
48284CB00006B/1756